# This
# Is Not
# an Accident

# This
# Is Not
# an Accident

stories

and

a novella

## April Wilder

VIKING

VIKING

Published by the Penguin Group
Penguin Group (USA) LLC
375 Hudson Street
New York, New York 10014

USA | Canada | UK | Ireland | Australia | New Zealand | India | South Africa | China
penguin.com
A Penguin Random House Company

First published by Viking Penguin, a member of Penguin Group (USA) LLC, 2014

"The Butcher Shop" first appeared in *McSweeney's*; "We Were Champions" in *Zoetrope All-Story*; "It's A Long Dang Life" in *PRISM International*; "Me Me Me" in *The Sun*; "Christiania" in *Guernica*; and "Three Men" in *Southwest Review*.

LIBRARY OF CONGRESS CATALOGING-IN-PUBLICATION DATA
Wilder, April.
[Works. Selections]
This Is Not an Accident : Stories and a novella / April Wilder.
pages cm.
ISBN 978-0-670-02604-3
I. Title.
PS3623.I5375T45 2014
813'.6—dc23      2013018401

Printed in the United States of America
1  3  5  7  9  10  8  6  4  2

For my father and mother, and Timothy,

without whom not

*We eat the color of a cake, and the taste of this cake is the instrument which reveals its shape and its color [. . ] Conversely if I poke my finger into a jar of jam, the sticky coldness of that jam is the revelation to my fingers of its sugary taste.*

—Jean Paul Sartre, *Being and Nothingness*

# Contents

# This

# Is Not

# an Accident

# This Is Not an Accident

Each week the driver who'd made the least amount of progress took home the Decelerator Award. The thing itself was an actual gas pedal removed from the instructor's late-model Tacoma, a pedal she believed to be not only faulty but the true cause of her multiple citations for unnecessary acceleration. "As it happened," she told the class, "Toyota recalled these pedals for that very reason, among others."

Kat raised her hand. "Among other reasons or among other pedals?"

Everyone laughed, though Kat wasn't sure why. She wondered, too, why an accelerator was being used to denote deceleration, but the one question was enough to let everyone know she was awake.

The instructor backed up, half-sitting on the lip of the desk and crossing her short sturdy legs. She was an all-business blonde who worked for a bail bondsman and claimed to be related to Houdini (a fact the class wise guy, Roger, had pounced on: "Yeah? I'll bet he coulda got himself out of those acceleration tickets"). Behind her on the whiteboard was this week's Thinking Point:

**passenger ≠ hostage**

"So how did it go for everyone this week?" she asked.

A girl in braces raised her hand and said it hadn't gone well. She'd forgotten to close the door of the car before backing out of the driveway and an elm ripped it clean off. Yes, she whispered, the driver's side. People said *Aw* supportively as the girl sat blinking like someone in front of a cake who can't think of a wish.

Next the guy with the multiple ripped-apart-heart tattoos said he'd caught himself driving too fast four times.

"All right," the instructor said, "OK. Who can help us with that?"

A shy kid raised his hand, his skull cap pulled down level with the eyelids. "Should he try and leave earlier?"

"Good! Yes!"

Encouraged, he added, "That way he wouldn't have to speed because he'd have more time to get where he was going."

"Excellent. Thank you."

The offender said, "But I wasn't really going anywhere so I don't see how it'd help to leave earlier. So I mean, leave earlier for what?"

The instructor looked puzzled. "I guess we're wondering why you would need the use of your vehicle in that instance."

"Just cruising, trying to cool down when everyone's done pissing me off." He looked around for allies, flipping an obvious hand over.

"OK," the instructor said. "This raises a good point—let's all pull out our workbooks and turn to page ninety-seven."

There was the pulling out of the workbooks and the locating of page 97, which had a self-evaluation form that began: *I drive best when* _____. Kat couldn't think of a time she drove best or even better so she wrote "N/A" in the blank, and then, over in the margin, drew a picture of herself driving. Kat was not all there today. She'd slept in her car three nights in a row and could honestly say the only thing she wanted in the world was to make it home after class instead of driving the two-hundred-plus miles to Iowa, sleeping in her car again, driving home, then possibly, if it happened again (whatever it was that happened between the times Kat wasn't-then-was driving to Iowa yet again) turning around and repeating the whole horrible awful awfulness. It didn't seem like much to ask, to know where she was going when she got in her car. To have some basic say in the matter of her whereabouts.

Across the table, Roger said, "Your face looks better this week." He was smoothing down the legs of his mustache, while their third tablemate, a man with a recent-looking brain-surgery scar, nodded along. It didn't help to ignore Roger, on whose constantly sunburned face was the smug, slightly obscene expression of a man who's dodged every major responsibility in life. Halfway through the first class, he'd yawned and asked when the movies were going to begin. "*Red Asphalt*, anyone? That's a classic."

In front of the room now, the instructor was clapping and hollering: "Everyone! In front, please! I'm seeing a lot of erasing and I'm wondering why that's happening. This is a *self-evaluation*, people. Your self is supposed to evaluate itself, OK?" She looked from face to face, settling on the Spanish couple who huddled over their *Safer U Safer Me* workbook like they were picking out patio furniture. "*Comprehen-day-vous?*"

The couple nodded.

In forty-six minutes class would end. Half an hour before that, Kat would start to panic. In the GOALS box she sketched a map of streets between the Technical Institute and her apartment a mile and a half away, darkening in the quickest route home, mouthing the mantra she'd adopted from (the entirety of) page 7:

**ALWAYS BE COGNIZANT:**
YOU
ALONE
CONTROL
YOUR
VEHICLE!

It was set in boldface, in some maniacal font—36? 48?—and though it looked true, even axiomatic, controlling your vehicle was really just the goal, the hope.

Kat was not an obsessive person. Which was what made it so disheartening to run out for coffee only to find herself—just this morning this was, and yesterday morning, too—shooting past the corner café, past two Starbucks and a Pete's and the Octopus Car Wash, then seeing signs for the Beltline and thinking she should turn around; noting a few miles later, *I did not turn around*. It was hard to say when she fully understood she was headed back to Iowa City. Maybe at the Wisconsin–Iowa border. Definitely by Verona she knew. Absolutely by Dodgeville.

Copies of that week's *News Clipping* were passed around the room while her tablemates complained about how difficult it was to get to class—Roger because he had "people to take care of," while the other guy just sort of vaguely didn't like the time class started. They made Kat think of her sister's stream of boyfriends. *It's not enough to just walk around not drooling,* Angel would tell the men, *reach for more*—a line she and Kat laughed uproariously at because Angel was a forty-two-year-old mermaid who considered overdraft protection a source of income.

BEAUTY QUEENS DIE IN HEAD-ON CRASH.

The assignment was to read the article and fill in a "Could This Incident Have Been Prevented?" form, but they never got that far when there was a photograph with the article.

A girl at the next table said, "If that's her jaw there, then what's that supposed to be?"

"Her elbow?" Kat was trying to figure out which paper would even print a picture so graphic and ghoulish. Roger made a game-show-buzzer sound. "That would be the steering wheel, ladies."

Both drivers had been local beauty queens, a fact that made the accident seem less than accidental to Kat, or at least not random. Kat had no opinion on beauty but trusted that things of seemingly infinite complexity would be the worse for any substitution on any level: the cashier in the joke who threatens to staple the duck's feet to the floor *must* be driven to do so by refusing the duck *grapes*, grapes exactly. The idea of the duck wanting instead a doughnut or a roll of film disorients Kat profoundly. She ekes a living out of a syndicated gag cartoon called *The End Times*, so she thinks a lot about what's funny and not funny. Probably a third of her own cartoons, the most popular ones, she doesn't entirely get herself.

"One lesson to gleam here," the instructor said, "if you think it's just idiots and drunks getting killed, stop and ask yourself whose vehicles those idiots and drunks are running into. Yours and my's vehicles, that's whose."

"Another lesson to gleam," said Roger, "is that even hot people die."

*Could this incident have been prevented?* Kat often asked herself this question. Months back, before all of this started—and despite her status as the worst driver anyone she knew knew—Kat's record had been clean. Mysteriously clean. The kind of clean that made her wonder if the cops were really paying attention, if they cared the way they used to. Then her answer came in the form of two speeding tickets in one night.

She was racing to meet a man from a dating site whose username was ONE&ONLY99; he seemed relaxed and educated enough for her to ignore his constant referencing of the ex-wife, or the many pictures he'd posted of himself standing beside or seated in the cockpit of a helicopter he apparently couldn't fly. (*Helicopter?* ONE&ONLY99 replied, *Oh that, yeah, there was a story there but I forgot.*) Kat's free trial on the site was ending and this was going to be her well-intentioned honest last stab before she quit men forever (then waited a day and quietly joined a new site). "Maybe if he was local," Angel had said, scrolling through the guy's profile on Kat's laptop. "But you can't drive to Iowa for this hairline."

Kat swiveled the screen on the bar so she could see. "We're not young. Men lose their hair."

"I give him two years before he goes clown top," Angel said. She tipped her head, looking deeply into Kat's life. "Did you not date a thirty-year-old albino with, as I recall, full dentures? What is your attraction, do you think, to people who are missing things? Appropriate pigmentation, couth?"

Kat frowned. "At this point I'm more interested in, you know, is he sober and does he have a job."

"Yeah?" Angel said. "Owns his own business, does he? That's probably what his helicopter is for." She glanced down the bar, eyeballing the regulars' glasses, then came forward on her palms, her gray-spoked green eyes intent, her chlorine-fried hair bristling. "It's all guys like that have left—the power to stand up people like you."

"And what is 'people like me'?" Kat asked.

Angel sighed to indicate the summoning of her limited patience. "People willing to drive three hours to meet a total doofus. Listen, if you don't want doofuses standing you up, then you have to be a person doofuses wouldn't stand up. And that's not me talking, that's science."

Kat said, "Fix your clams." Angel retracted and glanced down at her clam-shell bustier, which was more cute than denigrating when it was on straight, but when one or both clams were tilted it was like watching someone grope her right in front of you.

It'd been a rough week for Angel too. She and the Castaway's other career-term mermaid, V, had been pressing Stan for new equipment for a year or years, then V comes waltzing in with a top-of-the-line Atlantis monofin. "This thing's got fucking scales," one of the bartenders, Mitch, had said.

Now they all watched V in the tank, and there was something legitimately fishier in her locomotion. Covetously, Angel said, "You know the price tag on an Atlantis?"

Down on his permanent stool Jerry said, "So blow Stan and get an Atlantis for yourself."

"Do it for the nutritional value," the disbarred attorney said.

Angel said, "The only way I'm blowing Stan is if I need gas and he's got some in his"—here shifting into a don't-wake-the-kids whisper—"penis."

Angel was always right about Kat and men. She did herself no favors, but if Angel was right, wouldn't ONE&ONLY99 have to be waiting at the bar to know Kat had shown up so he could stand her up as a punishment for showing up? And if ONE&ONLY99 were there waiting, then (it seemed to Kat) he hadn't stood her up. But maybe only the kind of person Angel was talking about—the kind who got stood up for being a person who got stood up—would try and think this through. The other kind would just know not to go. She went home and shaved her legs and tried to decide which kind of person she was. It was a long drive to Iowa, after all, one she didn't want to make if she were the kind of person she suspected, the kind who got stood up more or less because her much cooler sister predicted she would. By the time she Googled directions it was too late to drive to Iowa City safely, anyway.

So she drove there the other way.

The first cop pulled her over in Blue Mounds, Wisconsin. He fingered a hearing aid made of beige rubber and said, "Didn't you see me? I thought you saw me but then you sped *up*." Kat apologized and said she had to go to the bathroom. He said she'd just sped past five gas stations, all with bathrooms. Kat said yeah but that she had to go too bad to stop. He chewed on that, then removed his hearing aid and wrote her up for twelve over. She'd need a police escort to make the date now, but she figured she'd try since no one got two speeding tickets in one night.

The second cop nabbed her forty miles outside Iowa City. He shook his head and said he couldn't see risking lives for an online date. "You hear those things work out with the younger crowd, but I don't know that that technology suits people of a certain age." He glanced up from her license, clipped to his mini-clipboard. "I'm not sure we can handle the power."

"But we invented the power."

He reached his hand forward into Kat's space, and said, "I accept all major credit cards."

By the time she made it to the Hayseed ONE&ONLY99 was gone. Or had never come. Gone, Kat decided. Come and gone. She couldn't think Angel was right and he'd stood her up. She couldn't think it. She drank as much as she needed until every guy in the bar looked like the one she'd come to meet, then she bought cheap champagne in the Conoco next to the Motel motel, which was all she could afford after $300 in speeding fines. In a not-hot bath she drank the stuff warm then, drunk, dripping, and out of towels, she dried her face on the bathmat.

Then she was in her car alive and in daylight, tearing home. She needed Gatorade and water and coffee and more water and orange juice and french fries, immediately, all of it, but she kept her eyes fixed on the hood of the car and she drove. The main thing was that she'd made it through a night that was over now and could never happen again, unless the doctrine of eternal return was right, which was unthinkable when the aim was to somehow trust that the worst thing you could think of wasn't always about to happen just as a matter of course. She had to learn to make room for an average day.

An hour outside Iowa City the itching started. Mildly at first, the itch from a too-light caress. On her temple. One on her cheek. Then it spread. She scratched harder and deeper, stopping in the middle of scratching one itch to jump and emergency-scratch another, then back to the first rekindling itch. By the time she reached Wisconsin her face was an anthill-craze of sensation. The worse the itch, the faster she drove. She pulled into the Walk-In Center in a skid.

The doctor said, "Seems to me we're dealing with athlete's foot here."

"But on my face?"

"Let's not worry about what it's called. Let's be glad it's not the kind that stinks."

"I'll definitely tell people that," Kat said.

He took a scraping and left her on the butcher paper with orders to sit on her hands and not scratch. She looked back on the rush of images—the men in the Hayseed, the one who hadn't come, the warm beery champagne—and with a long hollowing inside like hunger, she realized she couldn't remember the actual drive home. She remembered staring down the creased hood of her car, feeling miserable and thinking about feeling miserable, but she couldn't picture the road or a single landmark—not the scenery or billboards or pulling off.

*Had she pulled off?*

When the doctor returned she was sad and anxious and sick. "Apply this sparingly," he said, handing her a prescription. "Maybe it would help to think of itching as your skin laughing."

At home she applied the cream sparingly but several times, figuring the only risk in overdoing a topical would be in healing faster than the recommended pace. *Whatever you do*, the doctor had said, *don't scratch*. So she lay in bed with oven mitts on, her cheeks itching on the outside and the inside and whatever was between the inside and outside, itching. In the mad physical buzz she couldn't think anything through: she thought the phone rang, but maybe it hadn't. She called her doctor but while she was on hold she forgot who she'd called and hung up.

A week later Kat started traffic school. During introductions, one guy claimed to have racked up nineteen tickets with no license. Someone asked how these tickets were even processed; he shrugged and said, "They don't tell me and I don't ask. I don't use blinkers neither, because it's nobody's business where I'm going."

The immigrant couple introduced themselves elaborately, with great joy, and possibly some confusion between the DMV and INS. "Citizenship can be wonderful," the instructor had said, "but probably the greatest thing about America is the American interstate highway systems and even those plain vanilla back roads that get us to the drugstore."

"Aren't those the roads that got us to traffic school?" This from Roger.

"You go to another country," the instructor continued, "you'll see what I mean. I honeymooned in Tijuana so I can tell you first-hand: you're safer driving through napalm than you are on foreign roadways."

Roger found a seat across from Kat with the air of a man checking to secure an escape route. When he got good and comfortable, he took a long look at Kat and asked, "What happened to your face?"

Everyone turned to look at Kat's face while Kat sat and had her face looked at. Her rash (as she was calling it) had calmed down, but the healing was ugly. Makeup made it worse: scales, she saw, when she looked in the mirror.

The instructor asked Roger to introduce himself and tell them why he was there.

"Depends how you look at it—my attorney and I don't quite agree." He shrugged, and said nonchalantly, "I guess he knows the law, I know women." He winked at Kat and again she felt the hollowing, followed now by a supernatural sense, before Roger was two sentences deep, where his story was going. "The facts are these," he began. He was driving an RV on a two-lane road. A woman he somehow didn't see was driving toward him, then passing him, and in passing nicked the tail end of his RV, sending her blue compact spinning off the road, where it rolled down an embankment into a tree. She died instantly. "But you don't know," Roger told the class, "that's just what they tell you to not be dicks."

He said it had been windy out, so his back end would jag from time to time and that was normal and why he didn't feel her car hit him. He didn't even see her approaching. The first and last he saw of her was in his rearview mirror, when he glanced up and saw the blue car tipping off the road "like off the side of a ship." He wasn't even sure he saw what he saw until he pulled over to check.

During break Roger edged up to Kat at the vending machine he had just been banging around and held out an open bag of pretzels. "I was hoping to score those Combos, but free's free, right?"

She wasn't at all sure, but it seemed possible he thought he was flirting. She asked, "So she drove right past you and you didn't see her? Or feel *anything*? Not a noise or anything? Even later now when you think back? If you don't mind my asking?"

Spitting pretzel bits, Roger said, "Nope." Kat saw that that was going to be all he said, then he softened. "You know, I'm driving much higher up, like yay-high and there's that rumbling nothingness in the middle of the day, and this flat-ass road that goes for-fucking-ever, and you just fall into it. My attorney says *Do anything that looks good before trial*, like I'm the bad guy. *She* should be the one in there with those boneheads—" he motioned at their classmates, who were gathered around studying the microwave like archeologists who'd just pulled it out of the ground. He shook his head. "You know why it's me here instead of her?"

Kat stood blinking.

"Because she's dead, that's why."

"I was afraid you were going to say that."

"Yeah? Well there you go, Little Miss Face." He made explosive sounds in his cheeks, accompanied by crazy titillating fingers going over his supposedly exploding head. *"Ka-blam,"* he said, or *"Ka-blowie."* Kat felt like she had known him all her life.

The Woman in the Blue Compact.

Reaching for a dial middle of the day and sunny and no one around but Roger, who doesn't even notice hitting you, killing you.

It could be so loud inside a car. The inside of your head could get so loud, stupifying.

Of her drive home from Iowa that morning, Kat remembered nothing. It had been like a full-blast waterfall in the far recesses of her head's interior. And Kat's car made a lot of noise. It was a hand-me-down from her uncle, an old FBI-style car you'd win in a poker game but never buy yourself.

How could you know you hadn't hit someone, was the question—know like you knew it was Tuesday?

The grinding brake pads.

The never-checked fluids in her car.

And it had been so loud in her car that morning, with the itching and the pressure, and were there cornfields or was that something she'd imported from Roger's story into her own? Because beneath it all, all the time she was thinking deeply about Roger and why she seemed to think he could unknowingly hit someone but she couldn't—as though there were things that could happen to a Roger that couldn't happen to her. Finally she couldn't think about Roger without thinking about her car.

It was still dark the first night of class—four a.m.? five a.m.?—when she kicked off the sheets. Out under the carport she ate an apple and circled her car looking for dents, for scratches, for . . . she hoped she would know when she saw it. She turned the engine over and checked the instrument panel for warning lights, but it'd been over a week since the drive to Iowa and there was a light or two on before, for a few years now.

She didn't make an active, conscious decision as far as she could recall. One minute she was looking, deciding which warning light to worry about, then she was steering herself past the corner market and the Starbucks and the Pete's and a while later she was crossing into Iowa, scanning the roadside for crosses, a single upside-down shoe. She didn't know. She thought of Roger sitting up high in his machine, of the champagne in the Motel motel, of ONE&ONLY99. She had the sensation of not being able to see what she was looking at, like an eyeball trying to see itself. It seemed like she could turn around any time she wanted, which made it hard to explain why she wasn't turning around and didn't until she reached the Hayseed three-plus hours later, parked, stretched, then drove all the way home; or why, instead of going immediately to bed when she did at last reach home, she sat in the idling car seemingly trying to access a photographically complete and accurate mental picture of the entire two-hundred-plus miles of roadway she'd driven that night; and finally why, when she couldn't do that, she let herself decide she might have hit someone *this time*, while she was distracted looking for the body she might have hit last time, and she watched in resigned horror as the car was shifted into reverse by herself and steered out of the parking lot, past the corner market, and on its predetermined path to Iowa again.

In the next four days she drove at least three thousand miles. She wasn't ready to see a pattern until she'd made the trip enough times, and knew the road well enough, to consider it from the perspective of laps, with everything repeating as regularly as wallpaper: the fruit stand and burned-out barn, the tractor with the upside-down rake at the wheel. She drove and drove, scanning the roadside for glass, for torn-up gravel and grass. She ran over the same rubber strip again and again, twice while eating the same microwavable hamburger bought at the same Shell station. A waitress in an IHOP in Dubuque began filling her coffee on her westbound drive, setting the cup aside, then refilling it on her return east. She called everybody sweetheart in a way that made you feel like Kat imagined people coming out of confession felt. She was beginning to lose herself, trawling the roadside for a detached hand or arm. In place of thinking there was the sound of the road in her head, with every now and then a dull pang reminding her of the deadlines she was missing and had to miss because there was no way to work when she was driving to Iowa, which she usually was. Last time she checked her e-mail, an editor at the *Chippewa Herald* had written, *We wonder if the line between funny and terrifying is as thin as you would make it out to be?* This in response to a cartoon where, in a therapist's waiting room, Princess Di shares a loveseat with an emaciated beggar, his head orbited by flies. *At the very least,* the editor had written, *remove the flies.*

Kat wrote back: *Remove them how? They're not real flies. They're made of INK.* Then, crying, she'd gotten back in her car and driven to Iowa again.

In the IHOP toward the end of the week, Kat sat next to a kissy-face couple who tried to drive her away with whispering and canoodling and hostile looks. There were open seats all up and down the counter and Kat guessed she could've moved. Instead she flipped her paper over and said, "Just pretend I'm not here. That's what I do."

The woman picked her head off her man's neck, looked at Kat, and barked a loud surprised laugh. Then she tried to start a conversation, but Kat was bothered by the exchange, a feeling it had all happened before—which, she soon realized, it had: in one of her first cartoons. That cartoon had come from a whole shit-show she'd choreographed for herself where this man Ralph acted wild about her while standing her up time and again, at restaurants and bars, at the Cineplex and the man's own house—yes, his own home— and even at the green Octopus Car Wash, through which they'd planned to race (passively, seated in their cars). To complicate matters, string her along, Ralph did make every third date or so, but Kat would just spend the whole time preoccupied he wouldn't come back from the bathroom. When she tried to break it off six weeks and countless stand-ups later, Ralph yelled, "That's bullshit! I'm coming over right now! *Do. Not. Move.*" She waited three hours, then got in bed and cried and sobbed and called everyone she knew and no one was ever home and that was her fault for never answering her phone or calling anyone back and she cried more and decided she would start calling everyone regularly, and she thought about how much time it would take making all those calls, and when that got depressing she looked at the work she'd brought home (she illustrated greeting cards then), romantic scenes with, for instance, a couple riding bikes through a park and only the apples in color in the woman's bike basket. She normally didn't bother with the copy, but on this day she wrote inside:

*Apparently you're the best I can do right now.*

She loved that. It wasn't even that funny but she laughed her head off and tore into the other cards she'd brought home, filling them with lukewarm and passive-aggressive sentiments in flowing flowery fonts. She didn't leave her apartment for days. The cards were taped to her windows and fridge, lined on the mantel and sills, knowing this new work—wherever it came from—was finer than anything she'd done before.

No one liked the mean greeting cards except Angel, but Kat kept at it, come what may, and in a manner so obvious as to seem predetermined, the mean cards turned into cartoons, and Kat found her calling. Her cartoons were picked up first by the *Green Bay Gazette*, then a slew of tribunes and registers and so on. A couple of years later she quit her day job and Angel took her to celebrate in Chicago, where they ate like drug lords and danced in a club they were much too old for, and in the cab at the end of the night Angel said, "You know you've always done this. Cartoons, I mean." She elaborated, "You make some horrible thing happen to you, then right before you go insane you find some way to amuse yourself with it."

"You're saying I do this?"

"I'm saying it's the only thing you do, and the only thing you have ever done."

"Why didn't you tell me before?"

"I assumed you would notice the only thing you've ever done. Also, it's kind of amazing to watch, when it's not too scary." Angel wanted to know if and how it could possibly be worth it, the cartoons and generally how Kat processed the world, if it meant living the way Kat lived to do it. It was an uncanny question, really, because Kat didn't think anyone (even, frequently, herself) could trace one of her cartoons back to its real-world elements—which would be like hearing a doorbell in a dream and knowing, even as you went on dreaming, that that doorbell was actually a honk out in the street you'd imported into your dream so as to continue dreaming—then in Angel's case, hearing that doorbell in another person's dream. "I mean," said Angel, "There must be a better way."

Kat thought hard, then let out a diabolical laugh. "I don't think there is!"

Angel said, "Holy ant balls, Batman."

Kat was unable now to access the feelings she must've felt that night that had made it possible for her to have answered like this, but she had; she had come out and said it was worth it, the horrible awfulness that seemingly had to happen for a cartoon to take root and grow, which is how she knew that if no one stopped her, she could be driving to Iowa and back for the rest of her life. She needed someone else in the car. Period. And another set of eyes.

"So that's not ever going to happen," Angel said. "When I think of all the things that would happen before that would happen"— she raised her eyebrows for effect—"wow. That is a long list." Around Angel's eyes the skin gathered, a look similar to the one she got when Kat explained how someone had wronged her, and Angel would cut her off and say, "OK, wait a minute: so you seem to be proceeding under the assumption that other people are telling the truth. Is that right? Is that your plan for getting through life?" And Kat would be left making minnowy gaping motions with her mouth.

Now Kat said, "I've got, like, car bedsores."

Angel pumped a martini shaker over her shoulder. "Explain this to me again: you did or did not hit someone?"

Kat said, "No, that's not the problem."

"So you *didn't* hit anyone?"

"My rational mind says there's no way."

Angel looked at Kat appraisingly. "Why do you look disappointed when you say that? Why is that your look?"

Kat tried to explain she didn't really "believe-believe" she'd hit anyone; it was more like how you don't need a locked door to sleep, you only need to have checked the lock.

"All right, then," Angel said, "if this has nothing to do with your actual car or an actual dead body, then drive to Iowa on that stool there."

"I don't even know I'm going to do it," Kat said. "I'm just suddenly on the other side of town, then I'm in Iowa, then everything goes to hell."

Angel lined up three shot glasses on the rubber and free-poured Jägermeister for three drunk Canadians at the end of the bar. They'd been making noise about the empty tank and the missing mermaid and now one of them climbed on the rungs of his stool, threw back his shot, and yelled, "We drove three hours to see the she-fish!"

"Seriously, if you know it's not real," Angel said, returning, "then I don't see why you need me." She speared a mug on the cleaning brush, and for a second Kat thought Angel might be privately reassessing some aspect of her sister, which Kat forgot could even happen between them.

A second Canadian stood now, ripping his pearl-snapped shirt apart with his pals clapping and egging him on. People jumped in the tank all the time when a mermaid called in sick, which Stan's insurance man didn't like one bit (though when he was there to see it, he understood how hard it was to stop). One happy hour a woman in her fifties, a divorced secretary, swam head-on into the glass and knocked herself unconscious. Stan had to scramble upstairs and fish her out with the hook, with everyone on the floor hooting and cheering like they were watching an animal-rescue show, the woman's skin-colored bra and panties all bagged out.

Angel started for the stairs. Kat listened to her footsteps on the catwalk, Angel's lifting sort of walk. One thing Angel somewhat weirdly didn't remember was this show they'd watched as kids called *Man from Atlantis* about a guy with webbed feet powering himself around the ocean with this same motion of Angel's—which was the only way you could swim with a full-zip fin on, pumping from the hips, your legs joined and beating as one. Kat could very clearly see Angel as they watched the show, balancing herself seesaw-wise over a bamboo ottoman, her stomach acting as fulcrum while she mimicked the man from Atlantis's smooth, continuous kick. Kat thought the show's premise might've been that this man was the last surviving member of his species.

The Canadian who'd started to strip was seated again with his shirt tied on his head, and the three of them watched the wall of aquarium glass while Mitch distributed another round.

"To mermaids!" the lead Canadian shouted.

They threw back the shots just as Angel dropped through the water in her signature pike, bubbles streaming from her nose.

"And one for the lady," a Canadian said. They were staring down the bar at Kat now. She caught Mitch's eye and shook her head no, and the Canadians got uglier then.

"Just a sip," the one said.

"Wet your whistler."

Behind Mitch, Angel pulled up to the glass, heaving her fin around and sitting back in the water, her hands scooping out tiny circles, as her hair levitated in all directions. Angel was one of the only people Kat knew who could do a thing ironically and straight-forwardly at the same time, which is what made her actually inter-esting to watch, in costume, in motion. One man used to fly up from Georgia a couple of times a year to watch her swim. Kat tried to remember when he'd stopped coming.

Angel corkscrewed by as the Canadians persisted. "Don't have us driving home disappointed."

Kat turned on them then. "You're not even watching." She was off her stool and vaguely off balance, swatting at the air. "You made her get in there and now you're not even watching."

She was outside before she could think, stepping into her car and sliding over the bumpy powder-blue leather. She watched her hand come up with the car key, then her vehicle was backing up and moving forward, rushing out of the parking lot and through the streets, past every avenue home.

In the parking garage the last night of traffic school, Kat nearly rammed Roger's lima-bean-green Impala as it came squirreling around a column aiming for the exit ramp. She braked hard to avoid him and he, overcorrecting, skid into the circular cement wall.

"Listen," he said, inspecting his bumper, their hazards clicking, out of their cars, "this isn't exactly my car, so let's call it a draw."

Kat said, "But I didn't hit you. You did that yourself."

He was, Kat realized, actually cleaning his ear with his car key. "Don't wet your maxi pad," he said. "I said I'd take care of it."

"But why wouldn't you take care of it? I didn't do anything."

"Whatever you need to tell yourself," he said.

She looked at him. She listened to what he'd said again. She swallowed. *All she had to do was actually hit someone.* Not hit to kill. She only needed to make contact, feel the impact. Once she knew what it felt like to hit someone, she'd know what it felt like *not* to hit someone, and she would be cured. If she wasn't cured, she would at least have a new and probably bigger problem, which was a form of being cured. And if there was a man to hit and a car to hit that man in, this was the man, the car, and the hour to do it. It was all laid out, how things were going to need to go.

Roger's machine burped into gear, its tail end tipping up as he coasted down the spiraling exit ramp. Kat followed him out of the parking lot into rainy vacant streets. They headed west, winding around the capital and through the bushy, run-down part of town where people looked like they'd be slow to notice or report an accident. Before Kat could think how to hit him—logistically, how this was done—they were veering onto I-90. Roger veering, Kat veering in kind. It was loud in the car. Her wipers yo-yoed back and forth while two car lengths ahead, Roger drove with his arm slung over the seat like God had given him a promotion. Just very loud conditions for driving. She began to realize how awkward it would be to ram a car moving in the same direction, at the same speed, from behind. Briefly she considered gunning up and around him, then slamming on the brakes, but that would cause *him* to hit *her*, which was a different scenario entirely.

They drove out of the rain and back into it.

They drove to Albion.

To judge from her gas gauge, Kat had to make her move before

Janesville. If she pulled off for gas, Roger would keep going and she'd lose him and her adrenaline and before she knew it she'd be on the road—to—

She eased down on the accelerator. The engine still seemed to have plenty of give, but she couldn't tell if she'd be able to reach collision speed. She'd never sharply accelerated in these conditions, topping seventy with rain spitting from their tires, rain striking the headlight-lit pavement like jacks beneath Roger's tires. She changed lanes on faith. They were shooting along, their wide beachy cars half lifting off so it almost seemed like it'd be safer to hit him, have the impact to organize their velocities around—she got within a yard and yelled *You alone control your vehicle!* and she opened the thing up.

Roger was at her window shouting to see if she was OK. She had hydroplaned across both lanes and into a soft rainy field, where she halted facing the opposite direction and the car sank in the mud, the left tire, then the right, like something taking its first steps.

"Help me out of here!" she yelled.

"I'm trying, you ape," Roger yelled back. He managed to heave the door eight or ten inches open before it foundered in the mud, then he was maneuvering her head (Kat actually had to say, "Please be careful, that's my head") through the opening like one might a bowl of potato salad. Over the rain Roger shouted, "You almost hit me again. And what're you following me for? You freaky chicks."

What Kat discovered mid-180 was a stillness so perfect, there in the hands of physics, where whatever was going to happen had, in a sense, happened, and she understood that everything that had ever happened was always still happening, and she felt an over-whelming peace spread through her.

They were arguing on the shoulder when the cop pulled up—his siren chirping, then his high beams lighting the side of Roger's face, who said, "Showtime. How do you want to play this?"

"Play what?" Kat said.

The cop stepped out of the cruiser and started toward them, his poncho snapping with rain. Roger said, "Can you see if he's got dogs in there?"

"Why would they send dogs for an accident?"

He turned to her and said, "Read my lips. This is not an accident."

The cop, crouching and moving his flashlight's beam over the Impala, said, "I don't see anything to indicate contact. The way you were driving, I'd guess you just lost traction, which can feel jarring."

Roger said, "I apologize, officer. We're both currently enrolled in traffic school and we should have recognized the roads were slick."

The cop rose, leveled his flashlight on Kat's face, then swiveled it back around onto Roger's, light-saber style. He said, "You two know each other?"

"Just from school, officer. We're pupils at the Technical Institute. Or I guess co-pupils, I should say."

"OK. Everybody in the car," the cop said, "Let's move."

In the cruiser they waited on backup and a tow truck while the cop ate a soggy sandwich off the dashboard and Roger appeared to be trying to name-drop people he knew in local law enforcement. "Not even Ed Crowley? I thought everyone knew the Crow. Great guy." When he couldn't interest the cop in mutual acquaintances, or in racing or real estate, Roger told him, "Our friend back there is a famous artist, did you know?"

Between bites the cop said, "Yeah? My kid likes to draw."

"I'm a cartoonist," Kat said, "and I'm not famous."

The cop said he had one for her, free of charge. She got this a lot, when they found out what she did, people donating material. She no longer nodded or acted entertained; she just waited for the punch line and then, later, asked Angel if it was funny.

"So then after the *ambulance* wrecks," the cop said, "the cop says, 'Now step on it!'" He dropped his sandwich-holding hand in his lap and shook his head, amused to the point of disgust.

Kat waited until Roger's accompanying but much longer-lasting laughter died down and said, "That's really more of a joke."

"Thanks," the cop said.

"I mean, a cartoon shouldn't just be a joke with pictures. They should work together."

He appeared to think about that in the rearview mirror, then told another joke, this time describing pictures to go along with it—a couple, a flat tire, the husband in a full-body cast. "So you make the guy say, 'At least now it can't get worse,' then you make the lady say, 'Would you quit saying that?'"

Roger turned his whole torso to face the laughing officer, clapping and egging him on: "You have some bold material there, you know that?"

Kat rolled her eyes and addressed the back of the cop's head. "Is there some way you can not give me the driving-too-fast-for-conditions ticket *and* the speeding ticket? Because those seem like the same thing."

In the rearview the cop, looking suddenly drawn, said, "Would you quit saying that?" His transposed face again broke into laughter.

Beside him Roger said, "Touché. Touché indeed."

"It seems like the reckless driving ticket's implied in those as well," Kat continued. "What if you just gave me the failing-to-signal-a-lane-change one, or the—" she tried but failed to read the fifth infraction. "The thing is, I've already got two tickets pending, and I'm already in traffic school."

The cop dabbed his eyes and said he wished he could help, he really did, but the tickets were already in the system. "Maybe you could get some of them dropped." He unhitched his CB, spiraled it in front of the rearview mirror. She wasn't sure she understood the caste system there in the cruiser; how Roger ended up in the front or why the cop would only address Kat's reflection. "Maybe the judge is in a good mood," his single transposed eye said to hers, "maybe he likes your looks."

The courthouse in Blue Mounds, Wisconsin, was a double-wide trailer with four parking spots and a wooden plank you had to walk to get to the front door, which was suctioned shut like a thermos. Outside on a stepladder was the cop with the hearing aid—the first cop who'd pulled her over during that first abject night she drove to Iowa against everyone's (including even her own for the most part) better judgment—cleaning the windows with a squeegee, which was apparently part of his job. Inside were rows of unfolded metal chairs and a standard Costco-bought banquet table serving as the judge's bench, with three flags intended for a larger and grander building, looking in this trailer exotic in the manner of those hypothetical living rooms they set up in furniture stores, with plastic ice cubes in the cocktail glasses. Kat took her seat among the ten or twelve defendants. A handful seemed to know one another from the court circuit in the way scalpers and bookies do, with equal parts intimacy and indifference. "I mean it," Angel had said, "Blue Mounds and back. Do not cross state lines in my car." With Kat's own car still in the shop she hadn't driven in a week, and talking Angel out of hers had been touch and go. Honestly, though, she felt accomplished just being there, having made her turnoff instead of bearing down, whizzing past the exit for Blue Mounds, and continuing on her hellish circuit. It did seem anticlimactic coming here now with all the new tickets piled on top of the first one, but she had to start somewhere. The lawyer she'd called said point-blank that what she needed was a bus pass, not legal advice.

Just after five a tall, listing woman pushed through the door with the air of someone coming downstairs for their first cup of morning joe. She slipped into what looked like a supply closet and slipped out ninety seconds later in a judge's robe, calling the court to order three minutes after she'd parked her car.

They were given a few minutes to remember or decide whether they were guilty, then each in turn was called to face the judge, solemnly intense with the Dr. Seuss–tall flags behind her, and the bailiff (window-cleaner from moments ago) standing bow-backed as a queen's guard—all of it was starting to work on Kat's mood, folding into and building on the events of the last six weeks.

When she was called Kat pled no contest, which seemed to mean something like *no comment*, which is what the others were doing. It seemed like the judge, if she had to take all of Kat's offenses in front of her into account, would be forced to revoke her license, even impound her car and make her volunteer at a trauma unit somewhere. Her mind, absorbing the revoked-license idea, took to it like it was a microphone she could sing into if she wanted.

The judge moved some papers around in a file. "How can you help me here?" You could practically hear through her skull the sound of the onions she was thinking about dicing when she got home.

Kat repeated what everyone else had said (*First I'd like to say . . . and this is my first . . .*) but she was having trouble with the conundrum of fighting for her license with that road out there waiting for her—that rubber strip—the counter at that IHOP (*Hi, Sweetheart*)—and why wasn't the smart thing to take what she had coming and donate her car to charity, or the FBI?

"Are you OK?" the judge asked. "Do you need a glass of water?"

At which point Kat more stated than asked, "You're not going to take my license, are you."

The judge again glanced down at the file, "For twelve over? A first offense . . . ?" As she spoke, the sun dropped suddenly, illuminating the window behind the judge's bent head, a light so intense it was as if the sun inched up right next to the window.

The judge said, "You look disappointed."

Kat could feel that she looked disappointed but in fact her face was stuck, enraptured by the blazing glass.

The judge asked, with a nudge of a nod toward the others, "Would you like to ask your colleagues what they're doing?"

Behind Kat's ear a voice came in low and fast, like an auctioneer's. "First you'll appeal to have the charges lessened—say you'll pay the fee but you don't want the points because of your insurance." When Kat closed her eyes now she could see the window in her mind, its afterimage, only inverted—a dark rectangle with light ballooning out all around it. The voice continued, "She'll say she's not comfortable doing that, then she'll change her mind and do it for you anyway."

Kat felt herself nod while inside the blazing rectangle in her mind, the judge appeared and said, *What can I do? Every time I throw the book at you, I miss.* Or no, that was dumb but it could be someone standing there saying, *What do I have to do for you to remove me from the road?*—that was awful, too, but for a few days it would all be stupid, until Kat got to the good stuff. She was looking around for something to write with because if she lost any of it now she could lose all of it, and the only utensil in sight was a pencil sitting by the judge's hand, or perhaps technically the judge was semi-holding the pencil in her hand, so that Kat had to both apologize and, she felt, bow to Her Honor as she stepped forward and very gently removed the pencil from Her Honor's hand, apologizing and explaining she needed to take a note down for her attor—

"Are you—are you drawing there?" the judge said, raising a robed arm. "With the pencil that you removed from my hand, are you drawing a picture?"

Kat drew a stick-woman judge sitting in a high-backed chair, the picture plane aslant to the window and the bailiff, chest out, in earplugs; and the table angled so you could see the judge's tailfin protruding from under the table (there were never mermaids in Kat's final cartoons but she often started with one).

It could be Roger, brought before a mermaid court.

A repeat offender of some kind.

Roger as the man from Atlantis.

Roger: the last surviving merman.

With Roger in the frame now, the good feeling was starting and Kat knew things were going to be good and would stay good because right at that moment Kat had months of material if she could get out of there and get to it in time, because this is how it came to her:

all at once, only once.

"Thank you," Kat said. "I'm very sorry." She stepped humbly forward with the pencil outstretched and a firm intention to return it to the judge in the now-stupefied silence when she heard in a chamber of her mind the voice of the last cop saying *Now step on it!* and she stopped and drew back, quickly taking that down, then attempting to step forward humbly a second time and return the pencil.

Into the silence the judge said, "No, please, take your time. I'm enjoying this."

"Incredible," said a woman in back somewhere.

Kat bowed like an old-fashioned Chinese man, apologized again, delivered the pencil to Her Honor, returned to her place, and delivered her lines about the fine, the points, the insurance. She was back on top and she was going to stay on top this time. The new Kat: *on top and in control*—that actually made her (in the process of trying not to laugh) sort of snort, a snort that was perhaps closer to an oink.

The judge sat back, resting her cheek on her propped-up fist. "I'm not sure I'm comfortable charging you with something you didn't do."

"I understand," Kat said.

She would never let this happen again. Angel was right that she didn't have to live like this, that surely there was a better way.

The judge was flipping through a code book reading off lesser offenses that she seemed to be offering Kat instead of the speeding— throwing a banana peel out of the window; something about the bike lane.

"Could you read that last one again?" Kat asked. "What would I have to have done to get that?"

The judge looked over to her bailiff for an answer.

The bailiff said, "It'd be like growing a lilac bush so it covers a stop sign."

Kat considered the lilac. She considered the bus, and the only problem with the bus, the only place she couldn't get to was the Castaway, to see Angel. She could manage fine otherwise, but there was just that one thing, that one place. She could take cabs, she guessed, but that would get expensive given how often she was there—days she passed, at times, sitting at the bar doodling and running lines by Angel, who would off-the-cuff shout out the line Kat needed in order to think of the right line. When Kat explained the night of the ordeal with Roger, that the cop said she hadn't hit him, Angel (pre echoing the judge) had said, "So why do you look disappointed? Why is that your look?" Before Kat could answer, Angel had ducked under the hinged flap on the bar, moving through to the customer side and lifting Kat off her stool by the armpits—*No no no*, Kat resisted, *I hate swimming. You know that.* "That's because you don't swim," Angel fired back, "All you do is try to not drown." A few times a year Kat would give in, and they would swim together after closing in what seemed like, with all the lights in the place out but the pool's, moonlit water. At first Kat wouldn't be able to stop giggling, a laugh like from aggressive tickling, when you look like you're enjoying it but actually you're trying to say *stop*. Normally what Kat didn't like about swimming was the feeling, when she was submerged, of being the place in the water that wasn't water, of being, herself, the negative space in the element, which is how the man from Atlantis had to feel out there, pumping his sad solitary conjoined legs, waiting for the sight of any other being at all like himself. That was the one place the bus wouldn't go.

"Let's do that with the lilacs. I like lilacs."

The judge laughed, Kat didn't know why.

# The Butcher Shop

Jack circled the block looking for Ann's junker Saab and tonguing his lower left canine, which was loose and clicked in his gum like a light switch. He thought of calling to see if she was running late, but then he remembered they were rethinking their boundaries. Whatever that meant in the middle of a divorce. In the alley he parked in a tow-away zone because he didn't want some smart-ass valet having sex in his car (Jack had been a valet in college), and because fuck it. He liked the idea of taking another trip to the impoundment yard, where everyone looks like they're in line for a lobotomy.

Inside the restaurant, he found Monahan sitting alone at a table for four. His hair was parted and groomed the way it had been since second grade. It looked like a piece from a Lego set, a cap he snapped on in the morning and off at night. By way of greeting, Monahan half-stood, then sat. "You're in for a treat," he said. "This guy cuts a forty-ounce porterhouse."

Jack said, "I heard that."

Monahan checked around behind Jack but didn't ask about Ann. He was the only one of their friends who didn't become uncomfortable when they showed up places together. People didn't like divorced couples remaining friends. It was in bad taste somehow.

Monahan said, "Turtle's in the head."

Turtle was Monahan's first girlfriend in twelve years. Jack would

be the last of their pack to meet her, though the reports were coming in from all sides—more about how Monahan treated her (calling her Little Turtle) than about the girl herself. After they'd been
dating less than a month, Monahan's condom broke. He told Jack
at a Padre's game, top of the third. Of course the condom broke,
Jack said, it was probably twenty years old. "Scared the shit out of
me," Monahan said, "but then when it turned out she wasn't pregnant, I was really in the dumps. Weird, right?" Monahan drank too
much and got weepy about fatherhood. He started hugging children he didn't know and security helped him find the exit. Jack
stayed four more innings because he wasn't ready to go home.

At home Jack sits in his empty living room in the red club chair
whose mate sat in Ann's new apartment across town. He sits in the
dark and stares at Walt's house across the street, recently painted
the color of a blueberry snow cone—which was fine for the barrios
east of the 5, though (according to the real estate agent Jack called)
they were coastal. (They didn't feel all that coastal, but the agent
said they'd get a lot more that way.) Jack mixes drinks he doesn't
drink and pictures himself reacting when he finds out Ann has a
new lover, or a lover from before they split, when the house across
the street was beige. He wonders how they're going to sell their
house to pay for the divorce with a ten-ton block of marzipan across
the street.

Jack's first impression when Turtle walked up was: too much
time in the sun, but cute. She had a dent in the tip of her nose and
hair the color of bleached pine. Her bangs wisped into half-penny
eyes that Jack imagined could be seductive in the right light. Everyone agreed she would've been out of Monahan's league, except she
grew up in a Christian cult, which skunked her with a strange
perfume for life.

The first thing Turtle said was, "Were you able to find Kitty a
home?"

It took Jack a minute. Then he realized she was referring to a gag
e-mail one of their friends sent around earlier that week—a picture

of Jack's face and a cat's face morphed together in Photoshop. *Kitty Sad, Needs Home* the caption read. Jack saved the picture on his hard drive and looked at it several times a day, with his office door closed. Now he said, "That wasn't a real cat. Those were my eyes and mouth, but the ears and whiskers were, um—" He couldn't believe he was explaining this joke, then he saw in Turtle's face that she'd gotten it, and was making a joke of her own.

She said, "It fit you."

Jack took a swig from Monahan's longneck.

Turtle said, "What I mean is, in my drawing class we learned everyone has an animal spirit and if the portrait doesn't resemble the animal it can't resemble the person."

The waiter brought flatbread. It came in a steel basket as from some futuristic dishwasher, in keeping with the unisex waiters, the light from unidentifiable sources. Jack caught the waiter eyeing Monahan's mini bottle of Worcestershire, an idea Monahan got from Ann, who carried a pepper grinder in her purse. The waiter started disassembling the fourth place setting, but Jack stopped him and said they were waiting on one more. The clock behind the bar said ten past. This meant Ann was stuck on the 405 in the slow lane with her blinker on to switch into an even slower lane, or she'd pulled off to watch the sunset, something she claimed to do routinely now—compensating for all the sunsets she and Jack had supposedly missed over the years, one of the reasons she gave for leaving ("We live a mile from the beach and haven't seen it in over a year"). If there was another woman after Ann, Jack would be upfront: he didn't like the ocean, it smelt like death, which is why he liked to keep it close but not invite it in.

Turtle said her art class decided her animal was a warrior horse.

Jack looked at her, squinted, then said, "I guess I assumed your animal was a turtle."

She looked puzzled, then laughed. "No no no. That's not why he calls me that."

Monahan mouthed very slowly, "It's because she's *s-l-o-w*."

"I'm definitely a horse. See this jawbone?"

Monahan made a whinnying sound and Turtle elbowed him. Jack guessed he could see horse, but not warrior horse. That was some hippie art teacher blowing smoke up her ass, or something Turtle decided and the rest of the class agreed to because they could see she needed it. He pictured Monahan eating corn on the cob and decided his animal-double was a rat. Turtle agreed and Monahan took playful offense. Jack wasn't sure if Turtle knew that Monahan was taking actual offense as well until she leaned against him and said, "Rats are survivors," and Jack wondered how Monahan planned on keeping her.

Already Jack couldn't remember how people got together, how you walked up and imposed yourself on someone so completely.

The menu came on a birch clipboard—one page of food, then twenty pages of wine. Jack pushed his loose tooth as far as it would go in one, then the other side of the socket. He tried to think when he last got a full meal down. "Where's the rest of it?" he said, flipping the clipboard around. "There's nothing but steak."

Monahan leaned into Turtle and said, for Jack's benefit, "You see what I mean? He marries into a higher tax bracket, he forgets his roots." After almost aborting this remark, he went with it. "I'm talking about dead animals. I'm talking about clubbing and groaning and blood, and I'm talking about a little thing called protein."

Turtle said, "You know, loincloths actually have an interesting history."

The waiter stopped by to see if Monahan was ready for another beer. There was a ventriloquist type of numbness in the waiter's face so it didn't look like he was talking when he was talking.

Turtle asked, as though the waiter were a nurse, "Is that his second already?"

Monahan said, "You want I slow down, Lady Monahan?"

After some silence, the waiter said, "To clarify. I will or will *not* fetch the silver bullet?"

The night before Jack bought a $30 bottle of scotch with red wax on the cap and sat in his chair picturing himself getting good and lit the way he would if a young Jack Nicholson were starring in a movie about him, but he could hardly get a glass down. In the morning the bottle and glass were still there on the table by the chair, nearly full. This was more depressing than a hangover, so he went outside and mowed the shit out of the lawn. It was six a.m. and his tooth had kept him up half the night. Every time he took a turn and saw that clown house across the street, he threw himself into the mowing with extra oomph. He mowed over a dead bird, and then he mowed under his orange tree, with mutilated rinds and pulp strafing his bare legs, his yard smelling like an Orange Julius.

Turtle suggested that they order for Ann; she could eat when she got there. Something about the way she said Ann's name, with such ease and ownership, made Jack feel like she'd plucked it from him. He could feel it in his tooth. His dentist told him the tooth was secure and to leave it alone, which was the only thing Jack was sure not to do. He asked if the Caesar salad tasted like anchovies then said never mind and ordered Ann a Cobb with no bacon and extra avocado, and a filet for himself.

While they were waiting on dinner Turtle told Jack about the day Monahan came into her shop looking for a calendar with teddy bears on it—for his niece, he'd said. She'd known he was lying, that the bears were for him, and thought it was sweet. Now Turtle wanted Monahan to admit he knew right away she was the One. Nodding, Monahan said he was thinking about having a Super Bowl party. Jack wondered if he should walk over to ask Walt to repaint his house, as common courtesy. He was pretty sure Walt would resist since Jack had never done anything remotely neighborly—and in fact, against Walt's wishes, routinely left his trash cans at the curb for days on end.

The front door hadn't opened in so long Jack wanted someone to leave just to see it move. He considered the possibility Ann wasn't coming. The first night they spent in the house, Ann stopped in the middle of kissing good night and said how strange it was to say good-bye to someone you'd be lying next to all night, but as empty pods. Jack said, *Yeah, we're going to sleep*, and Ann said, *I know we're going to sleep, I'm just saying how strange it is—our bodies are here all night but we're really not in the same room*. Jack said, *You're just defining sleep, is all*. And she said, *Right*. He thought that's how he lost her, saying things like that.

Now he sorted through last night's phone call, one of those maddening conversations in which Ann wanted to know how he was, how he *really was, deep down*, and Jack—who just wanted to keep her on the phone, talk like in the old days—said, *You really want to know?* and e-mailed her the picture of the man-kitty. Which she found troubling. With Walt's house in full bloom across the street, Jack had said, "You wouldn't believe what he's done with the place. We'll get twenty grand less with that thing over there."

Ann said, "I worry you're not talking to anyone about this."

"I'm serious—we'd be better off with police tape and a chalk outline on the lawn."

Ann said, "Maybe he always wanted to paint it that color, and after Marta died he finally did it."

Jack couldn't believe how painful it was to hear that. He said, "So who are *you* talking to about this?"

She was silent awhile. He thought maybe she'd fallen asleep, which she did sometimes while she was driving or waiting for a prescription. Then she said, "I'm trying really hard to handle this right, and I don't know how that is, and if you do I wish you'd tell me." She paused. "Should I not come to dinner?"

"Come or don't come," Jack said, knowing nothing pissed Ann off more than answers like *sure* or *whatever*. But could she really not come? How could she miss seeing Monahan with a live, living woman? For years the community joke was that Monahan was gay. (Someone had a newspaper printed with the headline MONAHAN COMES OUT! above the picture of dancing multitudes on V-day. Monahan thought that was great and tacked the clipping over his bed.) On top of this, Ann had been talking about trying out the Butcher Shop for months. In the last week alone the chef was written up in both the *Reader* and *Tribune,* one commending his respect for vegetables, the other investigating rumors that he chased his staff around with knives.

Now Monahan got up to go to the bathroom, only instead of going down the hall with the restroom arrows he walked out the front door into the street.

Turtle said, "Where's he going?"

"There's probably a line," Jack said.

She looked at him. "For the men's room there's a line?"

Next door was a dive bar where Monahan was going to slam a beer. He did this. He did this even when he was out with the guys. Probably a potential Mrs. Monahan should know about this but Jack figured he was the last person to butt in on another relationship, plus he'd known Monahan too long, driven too many miles with the guy on impulse (once they drove for three hours to buy swords at a truck stop in Barstow) in cars that broke down as often as not. So he took a bite of flatbread, poppy seeds flying.

"So how are you holding up?" she asked.

He stopped chewing. He wasn't expecting this, and, off guard, he heard himself say, "It's not what I want." All of his friends thought the breakup was mutual.

"Does *she* know that?" Turtle asked.

He wanted to take back what he said, start over, but it was out there now. "She knows."

"But have you told her?" There was a hint of frustration in her voice that surprised Jack.

"Trust me," he said, "she knows."

"Trust," Turtle repeated, like she was checking to see if he pronounced the word right. "I always seem to find people don't know as much as you assume they do."

Jack had the feeling the conversation was going somewhere darker and smarter without him. He wondered with a fluttering in his chest if Turtle somehow knew Ann, and Ann had confided in her that she'd changed her mind. But no, he reminded himself, he was a man in the middle of a divorce talking to a woman in love. He picked a piece of flatbread and, experimenting, saw how little pressure he could exert before it snapped. He said, "I hope I don't have an agenda telling you this, I don't think I do, but he's borderline with the drinking. He can't just slow down. He has to stop." He looked up. "You know, not that I'm an expert."

She said, "Thanks for that."

He tried to think what it was about Turtle that brought these things out of him, and wondered if she might agree to go and talk to Walt. Walt was at a time in life when he should be thinking about salvation. So maybe Turtle could turn up on his doorstep with a Bible. "Is ostentation a sin, do you know?" he asked.

"Vanity is."

"Would a bright blue house qualify?"

She didn't get a chance to answer. The waiter and another waiter came up carrying their entrées, service napkins protecting their hands from the dishes. "These are hot," the waiter said. He came around to each place setting's left side and rotated each plate like he was setting a compass. "Don't touch these."

In the corner of his eye Jack saw the Cobb and Ann's silverware and napkin. He sunk his knife into the center of his filet, a silky two-inch cut on the medium side of rare, but rare. He pressed the loose tooth, hard, until it hurt. Ann could be forty minutes late, easy. Jack should've put off ordering but the food was here now and the best he could do was stall.

He said, "This isn't rare."

The waiter said, "No?"

Jack said, "I ordered rare."

The waiter sort of bowed and took the plate from the right-hand side. As he turned to go, Jack said, "And a glass of Zinfandel to go with the Cobb."

The waiter looked at Jack as though he were ordering this in shackles, from inside a jail cell. He said, "We're pouring Storybook by the glass."

"Perfect," Jack said.

Monahan was back splashing Worcestershire all over his meat almost before he sat down. Jack told Turtle go ahead and eat, not to wait for him, but she just smiled, letting her silverware lie, brightly chatting away. At the far end of the room the waiter pivoted and backed into the kitchen with Jack's entrée. Through the portal on the kitchen door Jack saw him hand off the plate, then curl his hand in the air near his throat and waggle it, like he was hanging himself.

Turtle had her purse in her lap and for some reason Jack thought she was going to present him with a house key. Instead she handed over a laminated card with a picture of an empty canoe floating on a misted-over lake at dawn. Over the canoe it said *Happiness is not a state to arrive at, but a manner of traveling.* All Jack could think was that the guy riding in the canoe fell out and drowned. He turned the card over, then back. He imagined the man-kitty sitting in the canoe and at the same time realized he'd been holding the card so Ann could see it, too.

Then he saw the salad. Jack was on a date with a Cobb salad.

He felt warm, feverish, and he was picking up a dirty-penny taste in his mouth.

Without thinking, he pulled a $5 bill out of his wallet and handed it to Turtle.

She stared at it. "What's that for?"

"It's for the this—" Jack held the card between two fingers like the ace from a magic deck.

A little light went out of Turtle's eyes and he saw she thought it was a joke, a cruel one. Without taking the bill she said, "It's for you to keep. I have a lot of them."

Monahan nodded at this, still not talking, while Turtle took a minute to collect herself. She did this, Jack saw, because she felt sorry for him. Ann wasn't coming—it was there in Turtle's face, which meant it was in his face, too. He could feel it. He pressed his palms on the underside of the table and waited, and waited. He should've explained about the card—she managed a stationery store, he thought she sold these, was selling this one—but he didn't. He was tired of trying to make things bearable while at the same time suspecting they weren't unbearable at all, only unsafe and un-known. He wanted to tell Turtle he wasn't himself, that alone at home he felt like a man trapped in an elevator with a distant cousin. He talked to himself in clichés. *No rest for the weary,* he'd say. *A man's got to eat.* When he was in an especially gory mood, he would make a point of laughing out loud while watching TV, tossing his head back, really making a scene.

Monahan was cutting his meat into dice-size cubes like his mother did when he went home. Not looking up he said, "I'm just gonna go ahead here."

The thought of eating made Jack's stomach twist. Outside the sun had gone down, muddying up the windows so the reflection of the restaurant stretched out into the street, into nothingness. Tucked into the vanishing point was the reflection of the kitchen door. Jack turned and looked at the actual kitchen door on the op-posite end of the restaurant. He saw a ponytail pass, then the white shoulders of someone giant. The chef, maybe. He wanted to think it was the chef, the one with the temper, a big bully banging around his cage like Walt in his blueberry palace. Then it hit him. An idea so elegant, so smooth, Jack felt like he'd thought it up with a bor-rowed brain. His idea was this: Walt came out of his house once a week, on Saturday, to go for groceries. The rest of the time he was on lockdown, watching game shows. Walt didn't know what color his house was. That's what was so infuriating to begin with—it was the neighbors who suffered. So. Late Sunday night Jack will sneak over in camouflage and paint the place with a spray gun. Just the front, just what you can see from the curb. Jack's place will sell in a week, two weeks tops. If it doesn't sell by the weekend, he'll sneak

over Friday night and paint it blue again for Walt's weekly run to
the market. This was revelatory. Jack decided that as long as he
could sit there sending meat back to the kitchen, he could figure
his entire life out. Just then the waiter set a new filet before Jack
and handed him a clean knife.

This time he barely opened the filet, just made a little wound in
it. "I want it to look like beef," he said, "not beef jerky."

The couple at the next table stopped talking. The waiter shifted
in his shoes, not sure what to do. Then he did the only thing he
could, prices being what they were, and took the plate.

Monahan waved his knife up and down in front of Jack.
"What's this?" he said. *This* meaning Jack. It was a pet peeve of
Jack's since forever, sending food back, harassing waitstaff, as Monahan well knew. Turtle looked back and forth between them, un-
comfortably not in on the joke, and Jack thought how if Ann were
here, it'd be Monahan and Ann ganging up on him, Monahan
with his little crush on Ann, and Ann one of the guys.

There were fewer and fewer servers on the floor. Each time one
of them flapped into the kitchen, Jack got a look at the waiter, in
the center of the gathering circle. He looked like he'd just let go of
a bowling ball and he was watching to see what it did. Jack had
never been good at thinking things through, but the fact was, people like a scene and the waiter would probably get a filet out of the
deal. Then pots started banging. The servers came dodging out of
the kitchen, syllables and spurts of shouting spilling out after them.

A guy, possibly on tiptoe, pressed his face to the portal and scanned
the restaurant. The kitchen door bucked open again and he strode
out in one of those straitjacket-looking chef shirts and checkered
pants. On the end of a serving fork, in midair, he held a raw steak.
He was short, his hair pulled back and his eyes too round, too close
together, and riveted on Jack. He looked like one of those guys you
think is athletic, then you toss a ball at him and it bounces off his
face. The bartender shifted the blender to a higher gear and then

turned it off. He poured pink slush into a row of glasses, but the bar patrons had all turned on their stools to watch. People stopped pretending not to stare.

Monahan's eyes were watery, weepy. This was where he would normally excuse himself and slip next door again, but he didn't. For the first time in their lives Jack realized their positions had flip-flopped, and he hoped but couldn't be sure that their friendship didn't depend on Monahan's being the comic loser. It was a terrible thought, and worse, he suspected only Monahan knew if it were true.

The chef reached the table, the raw filet drooping on the fork. It looked like a kidney or heart, and it made a suction sound as he slabbed it onto Ann's bread plate. He dabbed his forehead on the sleeve of his nut suit and said, "Rare as I can get it, brother."

In the entire place, the only person smiling was Turtle.

Jack looked down at the steak, the strings of blood on the white plate. When he pictured himself painting Walt's house in the middle of the night, he saw it from their bedroom window, from Ann's side of the bed. He picked up his fork and Monahan's knife. Under the blade, the raw meat bulged like a fat lip, purple red with gossamer seams. The plate pulled on the tablecloth; ice tinkled in their glasses and Ann's Cobb wobbled. At the bar, a guy slapped a bill down and said, "One bite and he yaks."

A woman two tables down in cat's-eye glasses moaned when Jack forked the first bite in. He had never eaten raw meat. It was like bloody chewing gum. He chewed and chewed and the food seemed to be chewing back. He heard his jaw pop in his ears. When he swallowed, the sweaty blob clogged his throat and for a minute he thought it wouldn't go down or up: he would die this way, win a Darwin Award. The next bite he cut half that size, like a wet little cat kiss. The still and staring restaurant faded and Jack was overcome with an underwater consciousness of himself in which he wasn't anything but the pure animal exertion of chewing, eating for real, to survive.

On the fourth bite Jack felt a *suck-pop* in his jawbone. He froze.

There was a warm streaming sensation in his gum, but if it was blood, he couldn't taste it through the raw meat. He was pretty sure there went the tooth, but he was afraid to move his tongue and find out.

The chef said, "What the hell am I looking at?"

What he was looking at was Monahan's bottle of Worcestershire sauce. He was looking at Monahan's Worcestershire-drenched cubes of porterhouse, lined up in a perfect crazy row.

"You," he said, pointing at Monahan. "Out."

Monahan said, "Why me? What'd *I* do?"

The chef pointed at the door.

Monahan looked at basically everyone, then asked, "Can I take my meat?"

Jack thought how exciting it was to lose a tooth as a kid—how your parents were for some reason proud, and paid you for it—but as an adult, at this moment, he couldn't imagine anything lonelier. In another way it was perfect, a tiny secret uncorking, which was why, instead of doing the smart thing and spitting the tooth out in his hand, he washed it down with a slug of Zinfandel. This felt strangely *right* and he imagined himself swigging Zinfandel and swallowing teeth, eyes, nose, arms, until he was nothing but a stomach digesting itself.

When Ann calls, Jack's standing in the alley waiting for his cab, examining the tracks from the tow truck.

"So? How was *Meet the Monahans*?"

He can hear through the phone what she's wearing—Catholic-school skirt, clogs, that oversize jersey that says LIBERTY. He clears his throat, afraid of all the things he could say, and all the things he won't. He wants to tell her how he waited and waited, how he ordered dinner for her, but he hates feeling like she's leaving him all over again, so instead he says, "You could've come."

"I thought you told me not to." She coughs, and the cough sounds so *her* it makes him momentarily woozy. "Indulge me," she says. "I'm too sad to read and today I watched the neighbors make their dogs fornicate through the fence."

"How would they do that?"

She laughs. "I *watched* through the fence, they didn't—"

"I get it," Jack says, "OK." He backs against the brick wall, an awning of shade formed by the streetlight and building. "There was a lot of baby talk. Possibly I insulted her."

"Oh, goody. Let's hear."

Jack feels himself smile. "I'm thinking about seeing about keeping the house."

She makes a little noise of regret.

A door opens farther down the wall and someone pushes a milk carton into the alley to keep it propped.

Ann says, "You don't sound so hot."

"I don't feel so hot." He dips his tongue in and around the naked gum. He wants to tell her about his tooth and how he's going in Monday to give his dentist hell, he wants to tell her about the card and the $5 bill and mowing down that pile of oranges, but he knows he has to start not telling her things or he'll never make it out of this. He'll start small, is what he'll do, and work his way up.

# We Were Champions

A few days after Stephanie called and told me Bob had shot himself in the foot, then in the gut, Sammy Sosa got caught corking his bat. My feeling on that was I didn't care if his bat was made of cotton candy; he had the sweetest skip-hop in baseball, and he couldn't stay in his shoes at the plate. As for Bob, that was more complicated. I guess I was surprised he'd used a shotgun, and that he took his foot off first, because I didn't see the need for that, unless he was trying to keep himself from getting away.

Bob was our high school softball coach, an ex-marine who stood on the foul line with his arms crossed and his legs spread, sucking on an old bullet, rolling the slug on his tongue. He rocketed around town on a Ninja 650r at any speed that suited him. The cops rarely pinched him because he was the kind of driver who terrorized everyone else into slowing down, so letting him go served the greater good. That was Bob's theory, anyway. He was full of these theories. He said our lives would ease up infinitely once we were willing to be taken for morons, which was an interesting but difficult idea to work into a cheer. His batting signals were equally cryptic. If he spit, then tugged on his ear, that meant to finesse it, and none of us knew what *finesse* meant, so we hit away.

I hadn't seen Bob in fifteen years, and then only in news clippings Stephanie had sent my way. COACH SUSPENDED FOR SUPPLYING MINORS. COACH ACCUSED OF SEXUAL MISCONDUCT. COACH

FACES FELONY CHARGES FOR SEXUAL ASSAULT. The charges had revolved around a team he'd coached in Guerneville after we were all graduated and gone. I remember the *Register* quoted his pitcher as saying, "I didn't say anything at first because no one else was saying anything and I thought, you know, *We're OK*, or something." I liked the way she phrased that—reminding me of that time in life when you waited for other people to tell you whether or not you were OK, and you trusted them, as if there were no other way to find out. When they hauled Bob off, his team was 0–12, which the Guerneville mob took as proof Bob had messed the girls up, but that was sloppy thinking. I'm no cop, but 5–7 would have seemed more suspicious to me, depending on how the wins and losses sorted out, because any season has a rhythm—any obsession, too. They should have looked for the girl batting .500 then striking out five games in a row.

When the Guerneville story broke our parents wised up, wanting to know if Bob had tried anything on us. The only girl who stepped forward was our right fielder, and I guarantee he never laid a hand on her. This girl had an extra pinky, or part of one, and she still couldn't get her batting average over .200. I'm speculating there, but the numbers talked to Bob. Dead players talked to and through Bob, and I believed everything he told me. I believed Jim Thorpe could hit a ball anywhere on the field plus or minus a yard. I believed Ty Cobb filed the metal spikes on his cleats so he could gouge the second baseman's shins. Maybe Bob was the last man I believed, and the sooner that man comes along in a life, the sooner you can relax and quit worrying whether you're OK.

I held off telling my boyfriend, Mack, about Bob because I wanted to work it out myself first, and because I wanted the right *Simpsons* episode to come on, which was the best time to drop disagreeable news on Mack. He knew every episode and every scene he was going to laugh at, but still we had to sit quiet and wait for his cues, which was true about guys and that show. Mack was six-four, 180, and no fat, but he was a passive and pent-up man, always on the lookout for that one future unforgivable wrong. He had tiny, eyelashy eyes and a laugh with actual *ho*s in it; and some days that made the whole damn mess worth it, that laugh. The episode with Homer conducting the monorail was starting, and I didn't see any improving on that, so when the teacher wrote on the board *mono=one, rail=rail*, I told Mack about Bob's suicide, about the day Bob took me shooting in the woods. When Homer stopped the careening monorail with a doughnut, I told Mack about the other girls.

He stared at the screen, asked why Bob wasn't in jail. I said he was, or had been, that he'd done three years in Vacaville, which didn't improve Mack's mood any.

He said, "Stephanie, too?"

I said, "Yeah, Stephanie, too."

Stephanie was Mack's favorite friend of mine. When she brought a man around or we saw him on TV—she coached basketball for UConn then and so finally met guys her own size—Mack picked him to pieces. I told myself he wasn't more disturbed to learn about Stephanie than about me, only more surprised.

He sat on the couch for a long time, nodding then not nodding, then nodding again. Then he picked up his keys and didn't come home until three the next morning.

Mack's second reaction was to buy a dead pig. Some background on that: We lived half a block from Wrigley Field, and on game days we sat in the street drinking Killian's Red out of baseball mitts. The gang we sat out with had been talking for two seasons about roasting a pig. Everyone knew we'd never do it, until one of the wives started talking side dishes, and the guys got defensive and turned to logistics. We settled on Saturday's game because Roger Clemens was pitching for New York that day and he was chasing three hundred wins, and we wanted to see Sammy put a hold on his plans. But now that Sammy was on the bench, Saturday wasn't making any promises, and the talk about the pig fell off. However, the business with Bob put Mack in a nasty way, and suddenly all he cared about was laying claim on this pig. When the lowest quote landed at $300—money we'd slotted for camping gear—I wanted particulars on how he planned to roast this thing. He said the guy up in 2D had gone to Ohio State, so he knew all about roasting pigs. I told him 2D wore an Ohio State sweatshirt, and a diploma and a sweatshirt weren't the same thing. I told him you couldn't just throw a pig in the trash.

"So we'll eat it either way," Mack said.

"You're prepared to eat a raw pig?"

Mack said, "Isn't that what ham is?"

"They have hair, you know," I told him. "Pigs are hairy."

Mack thought about that. "So we'll shave it, then eat it."

That was the most we'd spoken in a week, and there were smiles in our voices even if our eyes didn't match, so I shook hands with the idea and walked away from the camping gear.

What you have to understand about our softball team that year: If it hadn't been for Bob, we never would've stepped onto the field. We played volleyball—that was our game. Two years running we'd flown down to L.A. and swept state. The problem with that team was the same problem with every team Stephanie was on, which was figuring out how to get her involved in every play. On the one hand, she had the softest set in the state—the ball floated off her hands as still as a knuckleball. But she also had the most consistent kill shot, even if you set her at the ten-foot line; and she had the kind of hang time where her legs relaxed in the air, and you'd see her up there looking like she had to decide to come down. She didn't like the attention sports drew, but her father had been in a coma for five years, so she played to give her mother something to do. Later that year you'd see her out at shortstop toeing the dirt between plays like she was the last girl waiting on the last bus anywhere, and if it never came, that was fine, too.

But that was Stephanie. The rest of us walked around school in our warm-ups thinking everyone else was a biohazard of uncool.

We got Bs and Cs, and we said things like *I am mightily vexed*, and we ate baby food to be coy. That year women on the circuit switched from wearing shorts to those ass-huggers, and so did we, taking the court in what were basically panties with our numbers on them, and we were sixteen and we were champions and we knew exactly what we looked like out there. Which is where I get confused about Bob, and who did what to whom, and what did people think would happen when he rolled up to our exhibition game on his Ninja and asked how we planned on staying out of trouble now that the season was over, then said, "I'll tell you how, you're going to play ball for me."

We said, *All right*. We said, *Nice bike*.

The guy from 2D, clown that he was, knew another guy in Bucktown with a barbecue mounted on off-road tires. This thing had an actual license plate on it, and we figured if the DMV could get behind this machinery, so could we. While 2D went to pick up the grill, we set up our chairs in the street—camping and beach chairs, those cheap aluminum deals that leave a weave pattern on your ass, some asses more than others. Through traffic honked and hooted "Go Cubbies," the kids waving those lame foam hands out the window.

Mack and his oldest friend, Spivy, had picked up the pig that morning and stored it in the basement, then Spivy headed down to Murphy's to interview tailgaters on the Sosa affair—to get their views on Sammy's story that he grabbed the corked bat by mistake. Spivy said everyone just repeated what they'd heard on the news, so he bailed to help with the pig.

Spivy wrote a column for the *Sun*, and you never knew when something you said would wind up in the paper, so we all had opinions. One guy who was temping at an engineering firm said his bosses said corking didn't help, that if anything, it hurt. Spivy said it depended who you were, that you could get a corked bat around quicker, so if you needed the extra time, like Sammy, it helped, whereas for a Barry Bonds, all it did was take some distance off.

The temp's brother said, "You're saying Sosa's got a slow bat?"

Mack said, "He's saying he's no Barry Bonds."

"He doesn't need to be Bonds," the temp said. "Why would he want to be Bonds if he's already Sosa?"

A guy I'd never seen and who hadn't spoken said, "I'm just saying what I'm saying."

I said everyone knew you practiced with a heavier bat, not a lighter one. Spivy popped his beach chair back a notch and said, "Not in pregame. In pregame you've got to please the crowd. Who you've got to feel for is Dusty—a few million witnesses, and he has to back Sammy's crackpot story."

The temp's brother said, "But what did they see?"

"Cork," Mack said. "They saw cork." For some reason he was glaring at me. Wherever he was headed with this, I had to let him. There were too many people around, and when he drank like he was drinking, his mood could go anywhere.

"But the question is," the temp said, "did he grab the wrong bat?"

Spivy said, "No homers since the beginning of May, and he was two for fifteen taking the field. That's a special time to grab the wrong bat."

Mack paced to the end of the block, watching for the grill to show up. The fidgeting wasn't like him, but that week I wasn't sure what was like him. In the guy-ways he was impossible to know— kinky in bed until he knew me well, for instance, then old-fashioned and quiet until, toward the end, sex became more like jogging—something we did at all the same places and times but not strictly together.

At the corner Mack yelled over his shoulder, "No getting in another man's head. Only Sammy knows." I thought of that line years later, after the scandals that followed and guys like Bonds and Clemens came through on top, where Sosa and Mark McGwire tanked with the fans. I thought that's because they'd put on a face—Sammy with his fist-on-heart thing and all that—whereas Bonds and Clemens didn't try to be liked. They let their games talk.

Someone's girlfriend said, "I read Sammy sleeps with his bat and cares for it like a baby."

The crude guy whose wife was always sick said, "Check that baby's diaper; what you'll find is cork."

Mack stomped back and pulled a fresh Killian's out of the cooler. "Did you know, sitting right here"—he waved the Killian's over my head—"is the champion of California?"

While I sat looking like an idiot, the building manager's second wife asked how long I'd been champion; then the sensible tuba player from the broken home asked, sensibly, "Champion of what?" His mother shushed him like it wasn't polite to ask.

Spivy leaned in and asked only me, "The hell's up with him?" He knew us well enough to recognize that Mack had a rotten taste in his mouth and wanted me to taste it, too, but before we could get into specifics 2D wheeled around the corner with the barbecue hitched to the back of his Jeep. Mack clapped a few times and said, "We in business, boys."

It worked like this: Bob would stop you after practice and say, "Stay and bang the erasers," which meant help with the equipment, which you would. Then when all your rides were gone, he'd say, "Let's get you home," and you'd wind up in Bob's dumpy hatchback nowhere near home, the bats and balls clattering in back and Bob talking baseball. I don't know where he took the other girls—I like to think we all had our own personally tailored routes—but me he sped into the hills and parked on this tiny stone bridge. All but one or two of these rides were harmless. Sometimes he never even turned off the car.

The first time we went up there, Bob handed me a collage of yellowed news clippings in a beat-up frame. He wiped the glass with the fat of his fist and asked if I'd heard of Ty Cobb. I hadn't but said I had, and looked at the pictures. Three were action shots of Cobb spearing basemen with those infamous cleats. There was a close-up of the cleats, spike-side up, and a face-shot of Cobb, with his crazy see-through eyes and mouth of a killer. Down in the corner, in a DID YOU KNOW? box, I learned that Cobb's father had married his mother when she was twelve, and years later—mistaking him for an intruder—she shot and killed him.

With the stick shift and a phone book between us, Bob said, "You're going to break the stolen base record this season. You're on target to do it."

I didn't know how that could be, since we hadn't played any games yet. I said, "I'm not that fast. I just look fast."

"No, you don't look fast, but you know how to read people."

I'd always felt like I looked fast, so that was a blow, maybe calculated. Then Bob worked around to the real object of our talk, which was getting me behind the plate, catching. He talked about me gunning down runners, fucking with their minds. He said catcher was the most important player on the field. Even I knew that was stupid, but as I said, I didn't much care about baseball or softball—boring to watch, boring to play—and if I was going to spend my spring on the diamond instead of getting high with my brother's friends, I'd just as soon have my hands on the ball. Besides which, I liked the clamor of the catching gear, everyone lashing around and tearing the pads off when I was on deck. I liked the horror-movie mask and the ump hunched flush against my back.

That was the first time, in the trickle of the car's interior light, I saw Bob up close—how rough he was, his sexy bad skin, his lipless mouth set in parenthetical grooves that made everything he said seem incidental to what he was leaving out. I don't know if he had one pair of 501s or twenty, but they all fit the same—the bulbed-out knees, the tucks and folds that marked his thigh-heavy stride. On the sideline, in those jeans, he had the air of a guy pissing in the shallow end of the pool while kids snorkeled by and dove for pennies. I have tried to explain Bob's appeal over the years, but in the end we wanted him because he was a ballplayer, and after one of those rides you understood that was the sexiest thing a person could be. It was silly, really, we were teenage girls and baseball wasn't even open to us, but he talked like that's what we were playing, even teaching us how to slide headfirst—a play that wasn't legal in softball. I don't even know now, and didn't think to ask then, if Bob had played the sport himself with any distinction, but his skin was the color of that deep orange infield dirt and he was the first man I wanted until it made me tired looking at him. So I looked at the pictures of Cobb instead, I read and reread a quote of his I remember to this day: "My whole plan on base was to upset batteries and infields. How? By dividing their minds."

Bob said no team of his was handing out bases for free, so one Saturday he took me and Stephanie out for a special practice, just the two of us, looking to perfect my throw to second. He blew out the bottom of a moving box and set it on its side between the mound and second base. I was supposed to skip the ball through the box, make it bounce once and rise low into Stephanie's mitt right at tag level. "You see this box?" Bob said. "I don't want to see this box move." My arm was powerful but wild, and that box danced all over the dirt. I missed the box, I beaned the box; what I didn't do—as the drunk on the swing set tirelessly pointed out—was make it through the box. After an hour of this, Bob revised his command. "We're not leaving until you get this down or destroy the box." I was more a destroyer of boxes than a getter of things, so that's where we ended up—with Bob dragging the mutilated box off the field and Stephanie and I snorting-laughing. None of this mattered anyway, because Stephanie could catch anything and get anywhere before the runner wised up and headed back to first.

I guess Bob couldn't figure out which one of us he wanted to drive home that day, or maybe Stephanie and I cared enough for ourselves or each other not to let him stand there and decide, so we walked off together, said we'd see him Monday. We'd always respected each other on the court, but we'd never quite been friends.

I was intimidated by her comatose father and the isolated life that went with it. I'd known a kid who drowned, but that girl was a twin, so it sort of seemed like the family had a spare to work with, the tragedy incomplete.

Most of the walk, we laughed about Bob and the box. She said it was an impossible target, which was sweet and untrue. I could've done all right, I thought, without Bob in my line of sight, in his 501s. Who knows what I was trying to hit.

We entered the brambly alley by her house, and Stephanie said, "So what record are *you* going to break?" I told her stolen bases. "Let me guess," she said. "Because you can read people." She laughed, then her arm flew out and snatched at a branch, ripping off a bigger sprig than I think she'd intended. The tree shook behind her.

I asked what she and Bob talked about. "What does anyone talk about with Bob?" she said. "Ted Williams." She took a strange pigeon-toed step and said she thought he'd been driving our pitcher, Tracy, around lately, which made sense when I thought how her pitching had improved, how he had her switch-hitting now.

We came out of the alley onto Stephanie's street, a dead end with a barn and three known lunatics living in the ten or twelve houses. Stephanie nodded at a long ranch house snarled over in bushes and scrub. You couldn't even see the front door. She said, "That's me."

The barbecue was a mean piece of hardware—a steel barrel sawed in half, with posts and prongs and a crank welded to the sides. It was the work of a country boy consigned to a cubicle, the kind of guy who gets fired for clogging up the network with right-wing chain e-mail.

In gardening gloves and plastic butcher aprons—and where did a sportswriter and an options trader come by those?—Spivy and Mack carried the pig across the street pallbearer-style, hooves-up. I'd assumed the pig—Lola, Mack called her—would come groomed or flayed or prepped in some manner, but all they'd done was peel back the skin around her eyes, which bulged in the naked sockets. Maybe this is just how a pig's face is built, but Lola looked like she was smiling, a sort of *fuck all y'all* grin like the joke was on us. She looked less like an entrée than the heroine of a children's book. You live so intimately with the idea of pigs in the world, you assume you've seen one, but I realized I never had, not in person, and this one was full of funky features—ears like those horns on old-time record players; short, sparse, grassy hair; and bulldog folds on her neck. But it was the dishpan-hand skin that got me: I knew I could either watch them cook Lola, or eat her—but not both.

Originally I opted for the eating, but mounting Lola on the grill became such a slapstick of horrors that I decided to forgo the pork, gorge on junk food, and watch Mack and his crew botch the job. Expensive fuckups were valuable currency in a relationship like ours.

Mack drove the spit in; a cheer went up at Wrigley. We got this a lot, the random cheers and boos. Try having sex or fighting when you have detractors and fans. Sometimes I think living that close to a ballpark candies your mind, the way living near Disneyland would.

When the time came to insert the prongs into Lola's fore and aft, not even Mack could stomach noodling them in. We stood around drinking and stalling until the lady gym teacher stepped up and said, "For Christ's sake." After she stuck Lola in the haunches, she paused for a long time, then stood. "I hit bone," she said. "I felt it." We were all looking down, peeling at the labels on our beers. You can do anything you want to the dead, and what people don't like about that is the reminder that you can do anything to the living as well. Finally she said, "Well, you're on your own with the face," and went and sat in her chair.

Mack stepped forward then, as he had to, sucked down his Killian's, and took the second set of prongs in hand. The guy from 2D warned, "Don't go in through the eyes. When it gets hot enough they're supposed to, like, melt or something. We should probably see that."

Mack said, "I thought you'd done this before."

Spivy and I passed a glance, seeing Mack was on his way. At least it wasn't his whiskey drunk—that meant someone was going to jail. I cocked my head toward the chairs and, with most of the others in tow, sat with the sulking gym teacher.

Back in our circle, the tuba player's mother said, "Why don't we try it? Cork a bat ourselves and see if the ball goes farther?" This was after she noticed Mack and his guys stringing orange extension cords together. "What do we need to do it?" she asked.

Spivy said he thought it worked pretty much like you'd guess: that a drill and Krazy Glue should do it. And the cork.

I heard the grind of a power tool, saw in my periphery Lola shimmying and shaking and Mack at the helm, wearing ski goggles and looking crazier than on his passport photo.

Bob came for me the Saturday before our play-off game. I'd never ridden with him on a weekend, but he was in town running errands that morning, or so he said. Personally, I couldn't see him buying milk or mailing anything, but I got in the car.

We headed off on our normal course, but when we got to our turnoff he kept driving. It had rained all through the night—sideways, leaf-slapping rain that sounds like applause, then when you listen again, like boots marching in formation. The deeper and higher we swerved into the hills, the darker and damper the road became, with a high hiss in the air. When Bob finally pulled off, we were miles from anything recognizable to me. He worked the lock on the gate to a private driveway, jogged the fence open, drove us through, and jogged the fence closed, jumping and tagging the NO TRESPASSING sign on his way to the car.

We drove jerking and bobbing along a dirt road with a strip of grass down the center. Maybe half a mile in, Bob cut the engine and we rumbled to a stop in a clearing. The first sun of the day lit the field into a fire of green, ballpark green, which was the one poetic thing baseball had on its side. Bob had run around, popped the hatch, and was fiddling in the trunk. Then he walked past my window and crossed the field, the wet, wild grass slapping at his pant legs. At the far end of the field, he kicked over a fallen log and set up a row of cans.

The gun was a .38 Special, what cops use. In Bob's outstretched palm it looked fake, like spray-painted wood. When I told him that, he half-smiled, like it was a cute thing to say. But he didn't pull the gun back.

I said, "You're not thinking *I'm* going to shoot? I don't like guns."

"You don't need to like them. You need to know how to use them."

I looked at him, at the cans. I had no intention of shooting, but then the gun was in my hand and Bob had come around, fit himself against my back. He wedged his knee in between my knees, nudging them apart. "You want your feet about like this."

Still I didn't intend to fire, but I liked Bob there behind me arranging my arm like a mannequin's. It was that same sensual feeling you get at the salon when they wash your hair and really dig in, and you don't care if your hair's clean or falling out, you're thinking, *Jesus, hair lady, just keep going.*

"Remember," he said, testing the resistance at my elbow, "it's going to kick. Be ready for the kick." I felt the stubble on his cheek but not the skin. Then he stepped off to the side, crossing his arms, copping his stance.

I don't remember much in the way of operating instructions, and though I didn't know guns I knew I'd just as likely shoot the man as not. He was well within my firing range. All around us the trees were dripping with the previous night's rain.

"Let's go," he said.

I told him I was trying, which I was. I think. Then the thing went off. My arm tore up and back and the gun flew out of my hand, *thunk*ing down somewhere behind the car. For some time I stood with my hand over my head, fluttering like I was waving at someone on the other side of the field.

Bob laughed and said, "Do it again." In those deaf after-seconds, I more lip-read than heard this, and for that span of time he looked different to me, happier and like cardboard.

He said, "Fire one more shot."

I couldn't pull the trigger that second time, nor was I convinced I needed to. Sometimes defying Bob was the strongest kind of obedience. I told him I was done and to please come and take the gun. He paused, then started over. He was the only thing moving in the field. He came in behind me as if to take the gun, but it was back in the grass somewhere, which I'd forgotten. "Please take it," I said. Then his hand was moving up the small of my back, his fingers scrabbling at my belt loop, the other hand digging under my shirt. I lost track of how many hands were at work and where. I was looking all around. He smelled of BO, but there was the smell of the wet grass to counter it. One of his hands moved up my inner thigh and stuck, and then Bob picked me up a little off the ground and I tried to think if there were any way to stop this, and did I want to, but he was doing so exactly what I wanted done I might as well have been doing it myself. I remember: the orange Afro hair on Bob's stomach, the hard pimples on his back. How I fumbled and snapped the elastic on his briefs, and he tumbled into my hands like a bunch of rotting fruit. Then the switch from fast-sexy-hot to interminable hard labor, like two people struggling to fit through a turnstile. And then the disaster afterward, watching Bob feel around for a personality—and me, of all things, *helping him*—until he reverted to a boyish flirtation that embarrasses me even now. But that, the part at the end there, was what I'd looked forward to most, meeting the man behind the bullet sucking and statistic spouting, but there was no one there. Or no one with any language for the afterward. He's not the last man I could say that about, but he was and remains the saddest to me. It's strange how much you miss and overlook, how little you know about the one you want most.

While the gym teacher made a run to school for mitts and balls, some neighborhood kids measured out the 60.6 feet from the mound to home plate (there wasn't room for a full diamond), where we slapped down a HOME SWEET HOME mat. I heard the guys at the grill talking about a beer run, which was the last thing we needed, which was usually when someone went for beer.

Alone in the circle of chairs, Spivy sat corking the bat. Once, late at night, he'd talked to me about pitching in college, about quitting when he realized playing the game didn't make him happy. When he pitched poorly, he said, he didn't sleep for days, but when he pitched well he felt only relief, "like I'd dodged a bullet." And at that moment, as I watched him handle the bat—blowing off the sawdust, sifting in the cork with autistic precision—his past became real to me. I sometimes thought if it weren't for Mack, Spivy and I would've given it a go. But probably our attraction depended on having Mack there between us—without him we wouldn't have known each other at all.

Each batter got five swings with the corked bat, five with the solid one. You weren't allowed to know which was which. I'd taken practice swings with both and they felt the same to me, but to detect a difference of ounces I think you'd have to know bats the way chefs know knives. Grounders didn't count.

One of the girlfriends led off. The kids scattered with mitts and hopscotch chalk to mark where balls struck the pavement. Spivy tossed in a hittable yet not patronizing pitch, which she swung at, in heels, after the ball was in the catcher's mitt. Mack yelled from wherever he was, "That's one, mama." She was up a long time and whiffed on every pitch.

The gym teacher was up next. She managed to pop a few in the air, which pleased the kids. Then the fourth or fifth pitch struck her in the shoulder. She took it personally and dropped the bat, returning to her chair with a limp, like she needed her shoulder to walk right.

Down at Wrigley some of the fans were letting out early, including a pack of soused options traders who worked with Mack at the Mercantile Exchange. They'd come to see the pig but ended up more interested in our experiment with the bats. The married moms asked them to tone down their language. The rest of us were glad to have them swinging. Certainly Spivy was. One guy had played a season in Triple-A and sent a pitch clear down onto Addison. The kids went nuts over that, and soon we had chalk marks all over the street.

Mack being Mack, he took the plate with a longneck in one hand and the bat in the other, swinging one-handed, missing the first two pitches. The third grazed the tip of his bat; the ball changed course only slightly and headed full steam into the lounge area, causing the gym teacher to topple backward in her chair, flashing a red thong none of us had time not to look at. The ball bounced once, then smashed into the front of the grill. A tire came loose and the grill dropped to the ground, embers and coals spilling out in a steaming mound. Then there was a creaking sound and Lola slid snout-first down the spit like she wanted to see what was for dinner.

The guys from the Merc hopped to it, maneuvering Lola off the spit, fitting her into one of the chairs. She was hot, smoking from both ends. One guy lit a cigarette on her hoof, took a drag, then inserted the lit cigarette into the side of Lola's mouth, gangster-style. Another bowed and made the sign of the cross over her head. Mack watched from home plate, not joining in, which surprised me—these were his guys, his kind of thing. For a second I thought he might even stop them. Instead he turned and held the bat out to me. "Let's see the slugger take a whack."

To advance in the play-offs we had to beat the unbeaten Pioneers, and we had to drive four hours to do it. Bob drove the infield in Tracy's parents' Suburban; and since your parents' things count as yours in high school, it was her duty to suggest we stop for beer. We figured: why not. We were batting practice for the Pioneers, and all of us knew it.

Bob said, "You're dreaming." He said, "If you girls don't think you can win this game, pipe up and I'll turn around right now." That wasn't believable in the least, if only because he had nothing better to do. "There's no reason you girls don't go out there and blow beans today."

Pug said, "Blow *wha*?"

Some miles on, we pulled into a Shell station to fuel up. While Bob went in to pay, we started flirting with the guys at the next pump, in the middle of which Pug bumped me and said, "Well lookie here. The man do have his moments."

Bob was pumping across the lot with four plastic bags full of wine coolers. He'd never bought us alcohol before, and if we lost this game, we were done. Not that we thought much about it at the time. Except for Stephanie, who pressed her hand to the window and said, "Why would he do that?"

Bob swung the bags in back and we took off. While we drove, the bottles made a huge unhide-able racket, but we knew to keep our mouths shut, that nothing was ours until Bob gave it to us. We turned up the music. We waited. When he was ready Bob said, "You can have one, ladies. One means one." But there were sixteen bottles, Bob didn't drink, and four of us weighing a hundred pounds apiece who would drink whatever we were handed. He said he was only doing this to get our heads out of our asses and our mind on the game.

I said, "*Minds*, Bob. *Minds* plural." He slit his eyes in the rear-view mirror—our first eye contact since that day in the field. Whatever was in his look, I couldn't read it. We were as separate then as hands on a stopped clock, and his bad skin wasn't sexy; he needed Clearasil, was all. I saw the day nearing when he'd pull up to the gym on his bike—whatever gym, whatever bike—and the girls would pass on by, murmuring, *What a dork*. Because maybe in life you like what you like, but the hitch to liking girls—at least the kind Bob got anywhere with—is that they don't care if you're a criminal but they care if you're a dork, and no one can sniff that out like a teenage girl.

Not until we pulled into Fort Bragg and the car and the music stopped did we take stock of ourselves. Pug was lacing her cleats on the wrong feet. Tracy said she didn't know if she could walk, let alone pitch. When she opened the door a bottle cap spun to the ground, and we listened to its tinny whirl the way you watch a top until it stops. During the ride we were in it together, but no one could sober another person up, or help her see a speeding ball.

Twice during the game I tipped backward onto the umpire's shoes, but when he helped me up I smelled beer on his breath and figured we were square.

The Pioneers' pitcher smoked in strike after strike, looking like she was dislocating and relocating her shoulder with every pitch. Stephanie took a couple of hits off her. The rest of us more or less stood in the batter's box waiting for the ump to tell us when our turns were up.

Bob paced the dugout, dragging the score book along the fence. "OK. She's faster than we're used to, but we can hit that."

Pug asked how we could hit a ball we couldn't see.

"Watch her hips," he said, "her point of release. You have to decide sooner, that's all."

"Pretty much, like, now," I said.

Fifth inning the hangovers hit. A mousy thing stepped to the plate and launched one deep into left-center. Pug took the cutoff. The ball crashed into the backstop fifteen feet behind me. I didn't have time to scramble for it and make it back to the plate, so I hunkered down. The girl was rounding fast. With no ball in my mitt, I can't guess what I was thinking. It's not something I would do today, but maybe that's because I've already done it.

I dove. I took her out at the knees.

No one knew how to react, including the ump, who came bumbling forward, hoisting his pants, making this chewing motion with his mouth. Then he pointed at me and said, "You—you can't do that!" Which we'd all suspected but I guess needed to hear.

The off-duty postman who came to all our games yelled, "Atta girl!" And just like that, the game flipped from blowout to farce. I was sorry for that. I saw what a delicate and fragile thing a game is, and games have mattered in my life. I never would've stepped onto a volleyball court drunk or half-drunk, or even tired.

The ump gave them the run and we finished out the game, but not before this: a mean line drive up the center with no one and nothing to stop it. Stephanie in a dive you wouldn't dare in the absence of a pool. Her mitt, with teeth, snapping up the ball. Stephanie *whoomf*ing down, hobbling to second on her knees, scorching the ball to first for the double. Then, still on her knees, Stephanie spinning, puking in the grass. Sure, you see this in the majors any day, minus the puke. But this was high school softball, and when you see a play like that, you start feeling around for your keys and purse, suddenly unsure that you are where you thought you were.

No one in the stands seemed to notice Stephanie get sick. I noticed. Pug noticed. Because the thing was, Stephanie didn't care about winning—she certainly didn't sweat a loss. She gave the minimum and still outplayed us all. So why pick that laughable, unwinnable game to turn on the juice? Because—and maybe only I knew enough to know—she wanted to win, single-handedly if she had to, for Bob. For the rest of us Bob was experience. Bob was practice. But he'd gotten to Stephanie, and I'd played a part in that. We all had.

After the season ended, I didn't talk to Bob again. Not for any particular reason—because I'm lazy keeping up with people. But Stephanie visited him in prison, which I think embarrassed her, so I didn't ask about it. Then one year I was in town and we were driving around. Bob was due to be released from prison, I knew, and Stephanie said, "I keep wondering how he'll be when he comes out."

I wasn't sure what she meant. I said, "He has that thing in him. I don't think that ever goes away."

We pulled to a stoplight and Stephanie said, "You know what never made sense to me?"

"The drive to Fort Bragg."

She tipped her head back, smiling wide so that I immediately knew the answer. Then she laughed and said, "You tackled that girl. You just—tackled her." She gave a tiny honk of the horn. She turned to me. "That was the best thing I've ever seen."

I said, "That was the best thing I've ever done."

Two teenage boys passed in front of the car—one a devastating dirty-blond who glanced our way, squinting into the sun. Stephanie sighed. "I'll be thirty-two next month, and I still think about that game."

I told her I didn't think the drinking mattered, that only she could've hit off that pitcher.

"Sometimes I think he wanted us to lose," I said.

"That," she said, "was the scariest part."

The light turned green, so it was chance more than sense that stopped me from asking, *Part of what?*

Spivy asked if I was ready for the heat.

I said, "Let's see what you got."

He sunk his cap low on his eyes, did a slow, jokey windup, then I heard the ball crack in Mack's mitt behind me. I more felt it go by than saw it.

I puffed up. "If that's what you call *heat*, bring it."

This pitch I fully intended to hit, but the bat didn't move. It was then I got what Bob had tried to tell us all those years before, which was: guess. When you see the pitcher's arm come around and you've got no bat time, *guess*.

Mack said, "Strike two."

We were flirting, the three of us, in a way that had to do with girls and guys and sports and whether they could ever take you seriously as a competitor or simply as a physical person, so when I saw Spivy's knuckles, I swung.

It was nothing I could've done twice—just one of those dumb, fluky things you'll always have when you're commuting or doing dishes years down the road. A good hit could fix anything for a time, and I'd forgotten that.

Someone whistled. One of the guys yelled, "Booyah!"

I was about to do a victory lap, but something made me turn to Mack. He'd turned, too, and was facing everyone but Spivy and me. "You see that?" he yelled. "That's what happens when your softball coach molests you."

The guys from the Merc busted up as though they were in on the joke. The girls looked at me for a reaction. We stared at each other, Mack and I. What could I say? I knew the man's face. I knew he would've taken it back if he could, but he'd been building to some ugliness all week. I have thought that even relationships of any substance or length are vulnerable to that one dumb slip that sours the thing forever—that last lie, the one jealous outburst too many. And maybe you'll go on for months or even years, but when it does finally end, that will be the moment you point to—*That*, you'll think, *that was the end.* At the same time, it all felt like a horrible accident, but starting when? A week before? A year? When I took that first ride with Bob?

I picked a ball from the bucket and beaned it at Mack. I threw to hit him, to hurt him. As I let go, I remember thinking how soft the tops of his feet were. He didn't try to dodge it, but I missed him anyway. The ball bounced once and slapped into Lola's side, leaving a dent that disappeared while we watched. One of the guys picked up the rolling ball, jogged over, and shoved it in her mouth like an apple. Her fattened, half-cooked lips sunk around it like a mitt, and I stared. I stared and wished Mack hadn't named her. The name made her look used, and victorious, and sick.

Mack looked down, thinking to himself. Then he walked over, got to his knees, and pried the ball out of her mouth. I thought he was going to hurl it back at me, and I was ready. Spivy must've thought the same because he hurried over, but Mack leaned in skew and—he kissed her. Right on the lips. His guys made a lot of noise, but Mack wasn't with them then. He was with me. I'm not so dumb as to think kissing that pig was the same as kissing me—me he hadn't touched all week—but I knew everything we did right then was important, and I tried to think how I'd want to remember acting. I knew Mack didn't completely understand what he'd said, or why—or how he'd acted that week or why—and I felt obligated to comfort him for that. Which is something guys do to you. I set the bat down and walked over and kissed his greasy, pig-tasting face. Which was gross, and OK. We kissed a long time, an old-people kiss, where your mouths meet and that's it. I would've given more if I could. Which is something else guys do to you.

We lasted another eight months and kept in touch for a while after that, but other people came into play. I last saw him in a line at a Bears game. That was five or six years ago now. He looked fleshier, but when we got to talking, like himself. It was snowing, and we talked leaning against a cold cement wall. We both had people waiting. I was surprised how much I loved his ready laugh, and I felt achy the rest of the day—the ache that comes with the helplessness of endings, any ending. I realized the pig roast alone carried as much weight in my mind as our thousands of shared hours before and—how awful—the way memory recrops everyone for the better or worse. So before we parted ways, I tried to put Mack right in my mind. I tried to envision one man finding a little of another man in himself, and hating what he saw, and deciding to hate the girl who was the link, only to find loathing and self-loathing aren't that different in the end. I got close on that, but walking away my thoughts returned to Sammy, and never could I see—if you cared about the game, cared the way Spivy did and even Bob—grabbing the wrong bat.

# It's a Long Dang Life

Laney leans on the butcher block and listens for the front door. In her other ear, her daughter-in-law, Julia, lectures her about an eighty-year-old woman who was assaulted on top of her dryer. "You need a real dog, Mom," Julia says. "No place is safe." Laney wonders if she's supposed to be that age already—saying a rosary and pulling on clean underwear every time a repairman comes to the house.

Julia taps a hard-boiled egg against the bowl, deviling eggs no one will eat, because even the children sense that slighting their mother in this way gives her a dark satisfaction.

The front door *whumps* open. Odd ducks in, sets a Miller Genuine Draft fridge pack against the wall and, overcompensating for the bad hip, strikes his Wild West stance: his torso squaring off, hands hovering quick-draw over his front pockets.

"I'm here to shoot some kids!"

A delighted squeal from under the wing chair.

Odd's eyes dart after the sound. He's got those thick froggy eyelids that take so long to close, and the bulge of the eyeballs moving underneath. He says, "I'll give you Commie slime buckets two seconds to turn yourselves in."

Laney's grandson Oscar dashes out from behind the TV. He drops and worms his way under the couch, one of his brothers laid out on the springs with the cushions arranged on top of him in funhouse tips and tilts. Laney thinks these guys are out of their minds, if they were in them at all yet. She loves everything they do.

"Lousy pinko bastards!" Odd pulls a cap gun from each pocket and fires off two rounds, twirls the guns on his trigger fingers. "I'll tear your eyeballs out, shoot your brains into brain stew!"

The door of the coat closet bumps twice from inside.

"This is your last chance, suckers!"

Odd waits a fiendish beat, then starts shooting, firing the guns in alternation. Pink strips scroll out of the barrels as cottony puffs open all around him. Burned sulfur wafts through the room.

Julia keeps right on talking over the commotion and Laney keeps on ignoring her. Odd's been around long enough now that people tune him out as you would a jackhammer when there's work being done in the basement. Thirteen years ago he was, Laney knew, the talk of the family: Was Laney dating this man? Was Paul Odd her *boyfriend*? Laney overheard her youngest, Herbert, say that what made it hard to tell was the way Laney entered places some feet in advance of Odd, as though he were a homeless man who'd followed her in off the street.

"Man, I *cannot* wait to pop that first head off! You dug your graves, boys."

The closet door springs open and ejects five-year-old Tucker full throttle. Tucker on those hormone-deficient stick legs high-steps up and over the couch—his brother *ouch*ing and *ooch*ing under the cushions—then lashes himself around Laney's calves. She feels tears soaking her pant leg.

Odd says, "Gutless, Charles. You think that cracker's gonna save you with her good looks? Do you?"

Laney scrabbles her fingers through Tucker's hair and hands down her Diet Coke. "Have a sip of this, honey." Then she mouths across the room, *"Cool it, Odd."*

"You hear that! The FO tells me cool it. I wonder what she'll think when this place is . . . *splattered with kid guts*!"

Triplet number two guns it out of the coat closet, abandoning his brother, who has spilled out tangled in a vacuum cleaner hose. Odd spots easy prey and starts monster walking over, pacing it out, giving the kid a chance to free himself.

The triplets had to be injected into Julia's womb. They're nearly three now and don't speak, as if they're uneasy about being man-made and about their pumpkin-colored hair that grows like grass and even emits a vegetable odor when it's freshly cut. When Herbert called to announce the injection's success, Laney told him straight he was going to wind up with one too many kids. She advised rescinding one triplet before they came due but Herbert wouldn't hear her. Now there seem to be eight grandbabies rather than five, and that's what the fifth kid will do.

Laney urges Odd, a bit louder, "I said, 'Cool It.'"

Oscar wriggles out from under the couch as all three triplets scramble for the sliding glass door, one screaming with panic, one screaming with joy, one just plain screaming.

Odd noses his cap guns into his pockets and flicks his peppery hair out of his eyes. Still all that hair. Laney can picture Odd in college pumping down the basketball court—his sweaty black ringlets and white satin shorts. Daddy Long Legs they called him, or Daddy-O. He is still a looker, long-limbed and sexily slanted to one side, watching you as he did from behind the wheel of his 1957 Thunderbird. He'd drive two hundred miles in those days to pick up rims or a door handle for that car. Laney'd go along for the ride, dealing blackjack between them on the seat. Odd would accuse her of palming cards so he could pull over and frisk her, and she'd make sure there was a card to find. *Never trust a woman who doubles down on a suicide king*, he'd say.

Now the sixty-five-year-old Odd stoops for his fridge pack, comes and circles around behind Laney. He leans down and whispers, "Marry me."

Laney turns her head a little, nudges into his voice. "You've already got a wife. Her name's Miller Genuine Draft."

"Why can't I marry you both?"

"We are jealous gods," Laney says. She doesn't like to refuse Odd and can only do so with what spunk or color she can muster.

He drops his head in behind her ear, takes a schoolboy's toke on her perfume. "You'll marry me, Laney Jane. You wait."

He slips out the screen door soundlessly. Next Laney sees of him is on a goose chase across the backyard—Tucker with the black hood to the barbecue pulled over his head, Odd yelling, "I'm gonna rip your arms and legs off!" and Oscar last in the chain, clubbing Odd in the back with a Whiffle bat.

This marriage talk is new. Two weeks earlier Laney awoke in the middle of the night, feeling watched, and there was Odd propped on a pillow with Laney's reading glasses on. "We should get married," he said. "Probably tonight." She looked at the clock and rolled back to sleep, but Odd's been proposing ten times a day ever since. When Laney pulls back the shower curtain, Odd's standing in the tub, fully clothed. "OK. I'll cut back. I need a few for the protein, but no more blacking out." When Laney goes to adjust her rearview mirror, there's Odd in the backseat like a spy. "Swear me in, LBJ. Let the Oddman *do for you*."

Just that week Odd recounted their whole history to the checkout girl in Safeway, who regarded Odd the way you might a talking ape. "Now you tell me that's not a true Hollywood romance, and yet here she is *turning the Oddman down*." The girl scanned through a twelve-pack and a box of bran. "Do you think it's the Oddman's shoes?"

The girl said, "Can the Oddman please take his foot off the conveyor belt?"

But he left it up there, his scuffed tasseled loafer, sockless. "These shoes weren't cheap, I can tell you that."

Those feet were flatter than ground round, but when Odd padded down to the draft board to cash them in, the army took him anyway. Odd's curls in a pile on the military barbershop floor. That strange erotic terror when you know something irreversible is happening but you can't see it yet.

Seven months into his tour of duty, Odd stopped writing. His letters had gotten more impersonal and piecemeal until the last one (which appeared to be missing the first page) spiraled into a tailspin about a Vietnamese boy from a nearby village.

> . . . *this guys goddamn gorgeous with brown eyes that see to the pit & this guyd come and trade for C-Rats but last time he took my boots. that doesnt make sense bec. the boots were on & so how did he get them off my feet? It makes no sense but I have to laugh too bec. how did he get them off my feet? thats what I cant get is . . .*

On it went, round and round. Two months after the letters stopped, Laney's mother came in and sat at the foot of her bed— Laney thinks now for no reason, just to rest her bunions a minute. But Laney braced herself for word of Odd's death. While dicing onions or clipping her toenails, she'd imagined Odd in every posture of gore and mutilation and asked her mother simply, *Just tell me how.* And her mother, who hated Odd and wanted Laney to marry a carpet salesman who worked for Laney's father, seized the moment in a Godzillian stroke: *Landmine.*

It never occurred to Laney that anyone, even her mother, would lie about a man dying in combat. Not even when her father's protégé, Edmond Edmondson, started showing up soon and often for dinner, then for parlor games after dinner. Edmonson was a noisy eater whose sense of humor should've predicted future meanness, but to Laney there was only Odd and not-Odd. She played Monopoly for fourteen months then married the guy. Two kids into the deal Edmondson started pushing her around. Pushing her into the fridge when he was horny. Pushing her down the stairs when he was hungry. One night Lancy took a pretty hairy spill, broke her leg in three places, and with her boys looking on. When the painkillers ran out, she hired the area lawn man slash rental goon to break Edmond's leg in *four* places. Instead of cash, she agreed to do the man's laundry for a year.

"What if instead I broke each leg in two pieces, six pieces total?"

The guy was half albino, which Laney had heard was unlucky, but he was affordable.

"That's fine, too," she said. "Whatever's easiest."

"Easiest is just to kill him. You get him on the run and *splat*, without having to get Methodist about it all. Now that's if we do this in my car. 'Cause if you want me on foot, we'll need to resettle on the fee."

Here Laney did consider backing out, but then she got an itch deep in her cast. "I need to know if you're able to do what we said and not kill him."

"I can try."

"I need your guarantee. He's a father," Laney said.

He picked something out of his teeth, examined it, and put it back in his mouth. "For the pups' sake, then."

This conversation made more sense when, five days later, instead of harming Edmondson—in fact, *swerving around* Edmondson— the man ran over their beagle, Dunce-1.

In his tasseled loafers and cutoff jean shorts, Odd huddles in on Herb at the barbecue. From clear across the patio, Laney can hear Herb say, "I think Mom just doesn't want to get married again. Period. To anyone."

Herb pulls back the barbecue lid and lowers in his baster. As boys Laney's sons were darling, toothy and alert, but their features had aged strangely. They looked like child actors grown up: Herb with his huge pink face and dragon nostrils, Ron with that hole-punch mouth. Also, their arms had stopped growing at some point. The sight of them struggling on the monkey bars was a lot to take. Odd said once, *Those boys didn't have to look like that. If you'd just waited on me.*

Odd opens a fresh beer and studies the playhouse in the corner of the yard. At one time, Herbert had ventured into the custom playhouse business, but he was too much of a perfectionist and too little of a salesman to make a go of it. Each house took him a month or more to build, and with no time to solicit work, the bills piling up, Julia taking on triplets, Herb gave in and joined his dad at Carpet Jungle! This one playhouse remains: a two-story Victorian with fish-scale shingles on the façade, a brass knocker and rolltop garage door. It's the size of a minivan, only taller; all of Herbert's children can stand up inside.

"That right there is something fine," Odd says, waving his beer toward the playhouse. "What that says to me is *You got to do that thing right there or die.*" Herb shakes his head, doesn't want to talk about it. "Forget the god-dang money. Whatever you got to do *to do it*, do it." Odd crumples his beer. "It's a long life when it's the wrong life, man."

Oscar whizzes across the patio and starts circling Odd. Each lap, he pokes Odd in the gut with an action figure he's gripping like a hunting knife. Odd plays it cool—see nothing, feel nothing—then swoops down and slings Oscar upside down over his shoulder. Oscar shrieks and kicks and starts slipping out of his swim trunks, oozing headfirst down Odd's back and Laney has asked Odd not to pick up these kids when he's drinking, which means *don't pick up the kids ever*, but before there's time to splt Odd contorts himself forward and sets the boy on his feet.

"That's G.I. Joe!" Oscar says.

Odd takes the doll in his hand, eyes the hypnotized doll eyes. "I'll tell you, man, he doesn't look like any GI I've ever seen. They did it right, your guy here'd come with a little bag of weed. A coupla boom-boom girls—a couple of prostitutes, you understand?" He pulls the tiny camouflage pants down, points at the doll's smooth-surface privates. "He'd have a dose of the clap, maybe a little Saigon Rose."

Laney reaches Odd and cups her hand over his mouth. "Slow it down, Odd. Slow it down." She glances around for Julia, who tolerates Odd only conditionally and kept the boys away for two months the previous spring after Oscar raised his hand in class and asked if they could play hide the salami (turned out an older kid put him up to it). When Julia does come out of the kitchen, Oscar's doing a little dance, hula-hooping his hips and chanting, "Boom-boom girl, boom boom boom." Julia thinks this is cute and joins in the dance. She sings, "Boom boom boom." Herb gets one look at this and starts laughing so hard he squeezes the baster out on his shoes. He has always been a good son, but Laney's not sure about the man as a husband or father. What puts Laney's mind at ease is that while she can take or leave Julia personally, she knows the girl would've had an answer for Edmonson. She would've left him when the boys were in diapers.

It's five o'clock and the turkey's still pink inside. In the kitchen, Laney and Julia and Herb covertly debate a Domino's pizza bailout when Julia says, "Hold on a minute, Mom." Laney hates the girl calling her Mom. Nothing personal. "Does it sound too quiet to anyone?"

They listen, wake up to this.

"Where are the children?" Julia says.

Next there's the metallic chirping sound of Dunce-2 trundling down the hall. This once-speedy dog was a length behind that neighbor's cat when the old coot clipped him with a .22. A double amputee now, he gets around with Oscar's roller skates fastened onto his hind stumps. He seems to know something they don't, so they follow him outside and file in along the edge of the patio. Dunce-2 raises one ear and barks a question toward the playhouse.

Laney says, "Well, would you look at that?"

The playhouse is all eyes. Tucker and Oscar lie on their bellies looking out the living room windows. The triplets are stationed across the bedroom windows upstairs. Then—it takes Laney a moment to understand what she is seeing—there's Odd, somehow packed like a jack-in-the-box into the east wing, his eyes and nose framed in the master bedroom window upstairs, with each hairy knee in a dining room window below.

Laney turns to Herbert. "How'd he get in there like that?"

"I'm not sure," he says. "Oscar must've taken the floor out. The real question is, how's he gonna get out?"

The garage door rolls back and Tucker charges into the sun with a red wagon in tow. He high-steps across the lawn, his sherbet tongue lolling, and curls the wagon to a stop some feet from the patio. "OK," he pants. "We got that house hostage. For our demands, we want a banana split for each person"—Tucker pronouncing person *poison*—"and Grammy has a say she'll marry Mr. Odd. If Mr. Odd don't get her demands, we zap somebody ten minutes from now."

Julia asks, "You'll what?"

"Zap him."

Laney says, "Oh, for crying out loud. Sweetie, you go and tell Odd that he and I will discuss this *in private*." Odd glares through the tiny master bedroom window as if he can hear. "And while you're at it, remind him about our friend Miller."

Tucker scratches his head. "What his friend name is?"

"Miller."

Truth be told, Laney could live with the material ugliness of drink—the sour breath and bloat, Odd pissing on the neighbor's cat. But he blows half a paycheck on tasseled loafers when his teeth are dropping out of his head. He takes every phone call like there's some big shot on the line; sometimes Laney thinks he's still talking after the caller's hung up. When he's drinking he's not *there*, is the problem, and she has waited for him long enough.

Tucker parks his wagon next to the ice chest and, with a wild look at Julia, crashes his hand into the icy slush. He drops a black and gold can in the wagon and reaches in for the next.

Julia starts over. "Tucker, if that man wants a soft drink, you tell him—*put those*—Tucker, *put those back*—" Tucker arches his back to dodge the swipe of Julia's hand. "So help me, Tuck, if you don't—" Tucker U-turns and takes off for the playhouse again, beer cans wheeling in the wagon bed.

Julia glowers at Herb. "I've warned you about this."

Herb says, "Come sit down."

"He's inappropriate around children. I'm sorry. He is."

"Come sit down."

Julia hangs a hand on her hip. "Now we have a situation."

"We don't have a situation."

Julia smiles. "No?"

"I see you trying to make a situation by calling it a situation."

Julia pulls her strawberry-blond hair back, holds it in a ponytail. She has shampoo-commercial features and should be pretty, but she wasn't born in any mood to energize her looks. "Our five-year-old just made a beer run, Herb. Our children are demanding ice cream for dinner."

Laney sees Odd's hand poke out through one second-story window and reach a beer across to the next window, which he un-hitches with a pinky, angling the can in.

When Laney was a girl, she had an uncle like Odd and knows the exhilaration of being dropped, then caught before impact. It is a sensation she has known only once as an adult, when in a café in San Francisco she looked up from her coffee and saw sitting at the bar—not fifteen feet away—the dead love of her life, Paul Odd, not dead. Not anything like dead, but eating shrimp cocktail. Under the table Herbert and Ron, then six and eight years old, were driving Matchbox cars up and down Laney's shins. Odd looked right at her. She poured cream all over the table. It'd been ten years since the landmine, only there had been no landmine because here Odd was, his black curls grown back bushy and lusterless, like a wig on him now. He was stoned. He held up a shrimp and made it wave with its tail, and just then Herbie climbed up on a chair and held his Matchbox Le Car up in answer to Odd's shrimp. And they waved like this. Shrimp and Le Car. Le Car and shrimp.

Herb is saying now, "I don't care about my children's safety?"

"I didn't say that," Julia says. "I said you don't think ahead."

Laney says, "Those children are safe with Paul."

"Mom, we don't know that. He's had too much to drink."

Herb says, "Who's cooking that turkey if I don't think ahead? It's not cooking itself!"

Laney looks over at the turkey, which, snug on the grill, does in fact appear to be cooking itself. Herb must notice this, too, because he kicks his chair out and squirts the bird with lighter fluid. Ribbons of flame curl off the bird's rear and Herb's face eases into an expression of awe. He squirts the bird again, then fastens the stream on its igniting body.

Julia says, "Real mature, Herb. We have mouths to feed."

Herb says calmly, "There's something wrong with the bird. We'll order pizza."

A series of cracks issues from the playhouse. Laney jumps, touches her hand to her heart. "When I get my hands on those cap guns—"

This time Oscar bursts from the garage door. "We warned you!" he yells, tripping and hauling the red wagon across the lawn. "This is what happens when you don't listen!" A limp freckled arm springs out sideways from the wagon bed. What looks like blood on the hand. Then Oscar wheels over a sprinkler head and the wagon topples, dumping one of the triplets onto the lawn, his body gelatinous, not moving, more a heap of parts than a whole.

Julia gasps.

Herb's beating the turkey with a broom, one drumstick madly ablaze. "What?" he says, "What?"

Dunce-2 reaches the body first. He noses the boy's crotch, takes a drag on his armpit, then nudges the boy's head up and over. It takes Laney a minute to find her grandson's face, which looks like it's been dragged a few miles on hot asphalt, his forehead and one cheek smattered in maroon-purple brain-looking matter, a chunk of which Dunce-2 snaps up in his jaws.

"Get him off of him!" Julia screams. "Get that dog off—" She takes hold of Dunce's collar and yanks him clear off his front legs.

Herb runs out with the broom and kneels beside his son. "Baby," he says, "Can you hear me?" He bends in closer and sniffs his son's face. Then he fingers the wound and he . . . *tastes it*. He pauses, lets Julia suffer a second longer than she has to, says, "It's hamburger meat. And ketchup."

Julia catches her breath in her hand. "That's terrifying."

The corpse giggles and rolls out from under Herb.

Back in the playhouse, Oscar belts out, "That's what happens when you don't listen! People die!"

The windows are drawn now in the east wing, but Laney knows Odd's watching, because Odd never stops watching, and everything he sees is real. Even his hallucinations happen the way dreams really happen in your heart and your head, as anyone who's ever woken up unaccountably heartbroken knows.

Julia picks a clump of hamburger off the grass, squeezes it in a way that seems lonely. "Am I the only one who thinks there's something sick going on here?"

After Laney ran into Odd in San Francisco, she bided her time, knowing he would call, say, *Come with me, Laney Jane.* He called twenty-one years later. Laney was sitting at her kitchen table with a cup of tea and a Magic Marker, blacking in the pages of her plaid *Betty Crocker Cookbook (2 tablespoons butter or margarine* becoming ▮▮▮▮▮▮▮▮▮▮▮▮▮▮▮▮▮). She'd done more or less the same thing to portions of her memory, a kind of willed amnesia. You sometimes saw infomercials for memory-enhancing supplements, and Laney always shook her head. Halfway through the "Sauces" chapter, the phone rang. Instead of a voice, there was someone munching nuts on the other end of the line, and the uncanny thing was, Laney knew it was Odd, recognized the timbre of his munch.

"So I thought I'd call and apologize about the other day," he said.

Laney heard herself laugh. "The other day as in nineteen seventy-one?"

"Yeah, yeah, that's it." The sound of a smile in his voice. "That was a great suit you had on you. What color do you call that?"

"Coral."

He ate another nut. She could tell he was nodding.

"Hey, does your boy still have that little car?"

"He's twenty-seven years old; he drives a regular-size car now." She knew the smart thing to do was hang up, but he already had her. And when he asked where in California he was calling, Laney didn't even blush. "The same place, Odd. I never moved."

Julia announces she's getting the boys herself and going home. She's halfway to the playhouse when a whistle blows and the playhouse roof cracks up and over like a lid on a tank. Laney's five grandbabies stand a minute in the open air, crew cuts bristling, eyes adjusting to the light.

Oscar points at Julia and yells, "Open fire!"

In unison, the boys let fly a raft of bright white soaring—what? Eggs, is Laney's first guess, but they're too cushiony for eggs— pelting Julia *fwap fwap* on the thighs, *thoop* in the breast, *ptahh* on the forehead. One flies astray. Marshmallows. They're throwing marshmallows. They duck to reload and, panicking they won't throw their share, fire off two, three, a handful at once. Julia twists and turns in the blitz, a figure in strobe lights. Julia pelted high and low but soldiering on.

Then someone throws a rock. It glances off Julia's knee in mid-bend, her leg snaps straight and she jerks, genuflects, and goes down, lying on her back. She slings both hands around her knee and starts rocking back and forth in the grass.

Tucker yells, "Mommy hurt is—"

Laney can still see Herbie's face the night Edmondson bumped her down the basement stairs. She can see the pointed tips of Ed's boots jutting over the top stair, his fork in his hand and a stab of butt steak on the tines. He ordered the boys back to the table and watched five innings of a Giants game before he checked and found Laney had not gotten up. But before that, Herbie snuck back to the landing, stood where his father had stood. Through clenched teeth, Laney told him go back and eat before his father heard. He obeyed, but not immediately: first he hesitated, ogling Laney's leg while she lay doing rag-doll splits at the bottom of the stairs. Her heart went out to him, her little Herbie, thinking he wanted to race down and help but feared crossing his father. Then she wasn't sure. He wasn't crying or screaming. He was sort of teetering there, looking the way he looked at air shows. And though Laney would always love her son, she would never forgive that second of Otherness, of brute curiosity, Herbie looking down from the top of the stairs, though he was as innocent as she had been in shipping Odd to war.

Julia wants to call the police. Herb's helped her into a chair and plumped a cushion for her, now he's positioning an ice bag on her knee. "This is bad," he says, "I'm not saying it's not. But let's not get carried away." The turkey's burned Herb's eyebrows off and large patches of arm hair. "If Tucker says it was an accident, that's what it was."

"Throwing rocks? How is throwing rocks an accident?"

"There was one rock," Laney says.

"Herb, please just bring me the phone. At this point, no, I'm calling the police." Dunce-2 paddles up Julia's leg. He positions his forepaws on her thigh and starts pumping his hips, metal wheels squeaking in and out of a small arc.

"Call them on who, Jules? Our own kids? We'll look like idiots."

Julia comes forward in her chair, points at the playhouse with her entire arm. "On him! *He's* doing this."

Herb considers. "He looks like he's just sitting out there to me. Mom?"

In the chinked curtain, Odd's stare is cold. It's getting to be that time of day, Odd's eyes sink in rings of melting like ice cubes sitting out, and you have to let him be until tomorrow, when he'll wake up and try his best for as long as he can.

Laney tells Herb, "I've told you I won't do this with you."

It's then that Julia looks down and notices Dunce-2 grinding away. "And this dog is disgusting. How old is he to be doing that?"

Herb snaps his fingers, "Dunce, come on boy. Dunce Cap, *come*."

Laney says, "Those children are safe."

"You know what I just realized?" Julia looks from Laney to Herb. "You two think exactly the same thing I do. Bottom line, you won't go out there because you don't want to excite him, because you think he's dangerous."

Herb says, "Maybe if you went and talked to him, Mom."

Laney says, "Those kids aren't under control."

Julia says, "It's Odd who's not under control. He's got my kids hostage out there."

Laney says to Herb, "Maybe first things first, you get your wife under control."

Not even the pizza, when it comes forty minutes later, smokes the kids out of the playhouse, though Herb makes a show of it, popping the steaming pizza-box lid and peeling off the cheesiest piece. He strolls around the yard in front of the playhouse eating off his hand, slurping strings of mozzarella off his block chin. "*Mmm-mmm, is this ever good!*"

Two minutes of this and Oscar cranks a window open. "We're not stupid! Pizza's not what we want, and we're still in command!" He draws back and launches a paper airplane into the dusk.

Julia says to Herb, "Don't you dare go and pick that up."

Herb looks out at the airplane in the grass. "But I want to."

"So help me God," Julia says.

"Just to see what he's thinking," Herb says.

"What he's *what*?"

Herb kicks the G.I. Joe—the doll's pants spin off and land by the dog dish—then he walks out and picks the airplane off the lawn. "He wants us to call a priest," he says, reading while he walks. As if in some larger spirit of offering, he holds the note out to Laney long before she's in range to take it.

*LBJ,*

*1. the pizzas bullshit. the grands want splitz—*
*2. call father B and marry me laney jane, happily ever as*
*long as we got—*

*PZO*

Herb pulls a chair up next to Laney, unloads himself with a sigh. She feels him study her profile then look away. "Have you thought of marrying Odd? Independent of all this?"

Laney blinks the playhouse in and out of sight. All the shades of green in the yard have merged into a wilted-sandwich-lettuce green. *Independent of all this*—as if a mother ever has even a minute without her children in it.

"It's getting late. What about calling Father B.? Just to talk."

"Trick Odd, you mean?"

"Not trick him, Ma."

Laney folds the note back into an airplane, pricks her finger on its nose. "You did a beautiful job on that house, Herb. You did superbly."

Herb crosses his arms, holds a finger to his lip. "You think?"

"I've always said so."

Julia talks around her leg like it's in traction. "For me," she says, "it's the priest or it's the police, and I don't particularly care which."

Herb says, "I couldn't make a living at it." He smoothes the hair over his ear, like he's always done when he feels momentarily understood. "I'd be stone broke. That's what I'm saying."

The neighbors on the other side of the fence switch a light on. Laney loves the creep of evening, how someone comes along and insists on turning a light on, and because of their itch to do it you let them, and they're right and the room lighting up makes you happy, so you thank them, and she bets there's a word for this in German, a word like *schadenfreude* only darker. "You need a certain amount of disappointment in life. It's something you can rely on later on."

Herb stares, his eyelashes minuscule curls of ash. "I'm a disappointment to you?"

"Don't be dramatic, sweetie, I'm talking about people." Laney glances at the uneaten pizza. "Listen, I won't trick him. If you think calling a priest is the answer, then call him."

"Meaning?"

Laney meets his eye. "You think he's a danger to your boys? Out in that house right now? You think that?"

Julia says across the porch, "It's more like how can we be sure, Mom?"

Laney tightens her grip on the airplane.

Herb says, "It's getting late. That's all I know."

While they're waiting on Father B., Tucker sprints across the lawn from the playhouse, tripping the motion-sensor floodlights and not breaking stride until he's balled in Julia's lap. No questions asked, Julia molds down around him so they are like a fist within a fist and they breathe like this awhile. Then Tucker flies up to give his report. "I have a wait to escape until Oscar goes to sleep. And Mr. Odd is stuck out there, too. Oscar made him get in there, but him is too big to get out."

Herb says, "Tuck, you're saying Odd's trapped?"

"He's not Lassie, Herb. Let him talk."

Herb pushes Julia's shoulder, not hard, but her hair moves.

"Oh," Tucker's face broadens, "Mr. Odd is stuck bad. He really is. I think the house is have to come apart to get him out. And it's Oscar put him in there because he doesn't want chicken and then Mommy gets hit with a grenade and Oscar said it could probably tore her legs off."

The doorbell rings. Julia picks Tucker up, shifts him onto the saddle of her hip. "See," she says, kissing foreheads, "Mommy's legs are fine. Good as new."

Father B. steps out onto the patio, his smiling cheeks the size of a baby's bottom with one dimple so deep Laney thinks it's a stab wound. His foot turns funny and it almost sends him over. He bends down and picks up the naked G.I. Joe. "What do we have here?" He inspects the small plastic buttocks.

Herb jogs out with his drill and a crowbar. He jimmies molding off the corners and starts working his way clockwise unscrewing screws—his arm recoiling and the drill engine fluttering as each comes loose.

Father B. says joyfully, "Seems a funny time of day to run a drill."

Tucker says, "How'd you get out of the church?"

Father chuckles and scratches his neck with G.I. Joe's feet. "Oh, they let me go now and again."

Just then Herb yells, "Here we go!" and scampers out away from the playhouse. For a moment, nothing. Then the playhouse sort of looms forward. The façade peels apart from the building, creaks, then accelerates into its fall, landing in the grass with a *thunk*.

Father says, "Well, isn't that a picture."

Herb moves his flashlight beam over the rooms, open now to the night like a sitcom set. Oscar's curled up in a miniature wing chair with the triplets upstairs in a snoring, litterlike mound. On the other side of the wall, two-story Odd slumps forward in a lawn chair, his hands and knees and feet nuzzled in pairs. Herb says, "It looks like a suicide cult."

The felled particleboard thunders beneath Laney's feet and she steps on a beer can in such a way it cleaves to her shoe. She sets her palm on Odd's forehead. His chest takes in air in quick punches and he's sweating, feverish. Laney lets go. Something so personal in that heat. The inside-out look he gets when he's sleeping.

He wakes squinting into the floodlights, glancing left and down to place himself. Then, grumpy, adorable, he finds Laney. "I'm tired, LBJ. I wanna go home."

"We will."

"Lousy pinkos trapped me."

"I know."

"Lord love 'em." He smiles himself back to sleep and an entire dream plays on his face all in a span of seconds.

"Father's B.'s here," Laney says, "like you asked."

He pulls Laney into his lap and belts his arms around her waist, locking his punch-flat knuckles and shifting her against him. Over her shoulder he says, "Father B., good to see you. How's God?" He says this every time he sees Father B.

Every time Father B. responds, "God is good."

Oscar crawls out and shuffles over, his shoulders in a penitent hang. He climbs onto Laney's lap, who's in Odd's lap, and she belts him in, too, holds a kiss to his cheek so long she has to breathe through her nose. His skin smells like when you open an empty glass jar. "You hurt your mother," she says. "And you hurt her feelings."

He picks at her sleeve, watches his own fingers. "I don't know why I do it."

Julia's on her way out now with Tucker riding piggyback, his arms cranking like a symphony conductor over the podium of her head.

Odd's telling Father that Laney's going to marry him, but not tonight, not until she knows herself it's right.

"Of course not, Paul, but I guess I'm confused as to—"

"I'm saying it is a long dang life, Father, and look at these boys. A guy like me can only take them so far. You understand what I'm saying?"

A few feet off, Herb sits in the grass reorganizing his drill bits.

Father B. rests his chin on G.I. Joe. "You want me to bless them?"

"Give 'em all you got. Your full horsepower."

Laney is trying to remember how they go, the vows. It's hard to believe now she said them once. This close to it, she thinks it's not marriage she resists as much as the words, the vow-taking itself.

What she has now is her life, how things happened, in what order, and it would hurt too much to pretend all that had been taken could be restored, or that Odd was a man without habits or demons or secrets, a man she could trust with her babies and her babies' babies. But he will drink too much again and he will play too hard, he will pick them up, *the grands*, hold them screaming in midair, and some day he'll play until he's not playing anymore. And Laney won't stop him. She never will. If he asked her, if it's what he needed to make it through the night, she would deliver them to him in her own arms.

# Me Me Me

When my younger sister, Fawn, told me she'd decided to adopt a little girl, I was skeptical. The girl's name was Sam, and she lived in a group home run by—according to Fawn— gang members, illiterates, and pervs. Fawn had a master's in social work and had been working with lost youth for years. She felt it was time she took one into her home, gave her a shot at a normal life. Plus, Fawn had been bent on having a kid by the time she was thirty; she was thirty-four now so (by Fawn's math) adopting a five-year-old would still get her there. Fawn was single and three years sober, but she had a past, and the only kid they'll remand to someone with a past is a kid with a past—the one with bizarre scars and nightmares, the one no one else wants. Both of Sam's folks were in the slammer.

"The mom might be out on parole," Fawn said. "No one's heard from her. It'd be just my luck: I paint her room then the mom shows up and wants her back."

When Fawn called, I was in the middle of playing the board game Sorry! with Stuart, my on-again off-again of seven years. Stuart and Fawn didn't get along, but he knew to watch what he said about her to me, limiting himself to eye rolling and sound effects.

I suggested she get a dog instead, one of those big, lazy hounds you can use as an ottoman. "Maybe a St. Bernard with a terminal disease?"

"You're not listening to me. I'm doing this. The paperwork's under way."

"So what'd they do to this kid?" I asked.

"God, you name it."

I named some things.

"Come on, this is a real little girl you're talking about."

"I'm serious," I said, and I was. I wanted to know what she would have on her hands.

"Listen, I put you down as a reference. If they call, your last name's Bennigan. Just tell them I'm fabulous." She exhaled into the receiver. There was no point in nagging her to stop smoking, because she quit almost as often as she lit up, and wound up more addicted to quitting aids than to the cigarettes themselves. Even this, guys found cute. Fawn was a dead ringer for a movie star from the '70s, an America's-sweetheart type who played the sexy ditz in half the romantic comedies of her day. No one watched those films anymore, but Fawn knew them by heart.

After we hung up, Stuart said he thought you had to be married, financially sound, and not on antipsychotic meds in order to adopt. He shook his head wearing that same hopeless look he got whenever the Green Party lost an election it had zero chance of winning. "It's a free-for-all out there," he said. Stuart felt Fawn was blindingly self-absorbed—a trait he disliked above all others—and she accused him of being a "lookist," of hating her for her looks. *And you*, he'd counter, *act like there should be a support group for beautiful people.*

What Fawn didn't know was that Stuart had kept her out of jail some years earlier: she and a married restaurateur had gone on a weeklong coke binge during which Fawn withdrew most of my mother's savings ($8,000) from a series of ATMs. It wasn't until Stuart spoke to my mother that she decided not to involve the law. My mother respected Stuart, and he was the last man any of us expected to speak in Fawn's defense. I alone knew about his brother, who'd once signed for a UPS package with a heroin needle sticking out of his arm.

A few weeks later Fawn brought Sam home to live with her as a foster child while the adoption people reviewed her file. I drove up from San Diego to talk sense to Fawn. She—or, I guess, *they*—lived in one of those smog banks east of L.A. where guys grow television-detective mustaches and moms push shopping carts across the parking lots like they don't care if they ever make it to their cars. Fawn had moved out there after a bid at acting and modeling. She'd gotten bit parts, enough to string her along, but in the end her agent told her that her torso was too long: "I can only get work for half of you at a time."

Through the screen door Fawn asked if I'd brought a toy.

I hadn't. I asked the girl, who was nuzzling under Fawn's arm, if she'd accept a check.

She nuzzled in closer. "Cash is better."

They were both wearing bandanna halter tops and skorts. Fawn had warned me of the freaky resemblance, but holy nuts if they couldn't have passed for mother and daughter, with their slitty blue eyes and overlong torsos, curls like pencil shavings framing their foreheads. Fawn had had their auras analyzed by a specialist who felt that in a prior life they had worked together, Fawn and Sam, to saw lawless invaders in half.

We slid a batch of brownies in the oven and went out back so they could show me their garden—a modest square of churned earth. They giggled as they tried to remember what seeds they'd planted. If I knew Fawn, it would all die before they found out, but I acted interested. Already Sam was calling Fawn Mom, which made me feel like we were on a movie set. Why didn't *I* call her Mom while we were at it? Why didn't we take turns hiding in the pantry, playing Anne Frank and the Gestapo? (Which we did end up doing later, so perhaps that's not the best example.)

A guy called through the fence, "Hey, Fawn." He was sitting in a baby pool in the next yard making a face like he was receiving a massage. He looked twenty, tops, though judging by Fawn's expression, there'd been foul play between the two.

"Hey, Joe," Fawn said.

Little Sam, mimicking Fawn, jutted out a hip and said, "Hey, Joe."

Joe said, "Hey, Sneaks."

That night, after their baths, Fawn and Sam came into the living room in lab coats with their hair wound in pink towels. Fawn undid the clasps on a portmanteau, which converted into a display for the skin-care products she sold on the side. Sam pasted a strip of transparent tape across my nose, walking it down with her fingertips. When Fawn gave her the go-ahead, Sam tore the strip off my face.

"Hey," I said, "that really hurt."

They examined the strip under a powerful cosmetic lamp. Fawn asked, "When's the last time you exfoliated? Your pores are totally third world." I could see Sam, too, found cause for concern. She gazed at the sullied adhesive as though it were a window into my past, the years Fawn and I had roomed together in Westwood. Guys would dart across three lanes of traffic to chat up Fawn, pretending to have seen her in a magazine or a movie, glancing at me as if I were the maidservant. I'd dealt with this all my life, though I was no hunchback; when I didn't think about the lisp, it went away altogether. Fawn shrugged off their advances. "What am I going to do," she'd say to get a rise out of me, "fuck everybody?"

After she got Sam tucked in and off the phone (who does a five-year-old call at midnight?), we made daiquiris and sat down to talk. "At your age you can't just throw in the towel," she said, continuing her pitch. "You've got to be on top of this shit. I have a C-booster serum that will make you look ten years younger. . . . Well, five."

I asked if she was sure she was ready for this. *This* meaning Sam.

"Thanks for the vote of confidence," she said.

"I'm just saying, better you didn't take her in at all than wait a year or two and give her back. Then she's really screwed."

"I understand that, thanks."

When we were young and Fawn would, after a beating, cry and run to tattle on me, I'd catch her and pull her onto my lap—Fawn the darling towhead, all ringlets and bobby socks; I the tomboy, big boned and elbow kneed—hugging and loving on her, and I'd tell her, *That was Bad Gilda. But Bad Gilda's gone now. Good Gilda is here. Good Gilda won't let anything bad happen to you!* Fawn would hug me tight and say, "Oh, Good Gilda. I'm so glad it's you! I hate Bad Gilda! I wish we could kill her." I'd tell her I hated Bad Gilda, too, but she was hard to find when you were looking. Eventually Fawn figured it out, of course, that I was both Gildas, and I don't believe, from that day forward, she was ever again able to trust me as a single organized entity. I sometimes wonder now if part of taking Sam in was Fawn's wanting to revisit and improve upon her girlhood relationship with me, the way we are said to search for our fathers in our husbands.

Fawn said now she was tired of thinking about herself all the time. "It gets so boring: me me me me me. It's a disease; it really is." She combed her hair forward, automatically checking the condition of her ends. "I mean, don't you ever think there's something else?"

"Something besides . . . you?"

She pushed her hair aside and stared at me. "You think I'm using her."

"Isn't that motherhood? I don't remember anyone asking me if I wanted to be born."

She told me she'd never felt this way before. "It feels so *right*. I love that feeling when she's at school."

When I looked up, I thought I saw a small hand pull the bedroom door closed, but I'd been drinking, and it was late, and Fawn never lived anywhere where the doors worked right.

———

My therapists (I like second opinions and I like to talk) agreed I was a textbook compartmentalizer: I coped with people and problems in my life by keeping each in a separate box. This strategy (once explained) struck me as clever. I didn't grasp right away that they were describing a *disorder*. I was skeptical of mental health professionals in general, having worked for years in human resources, attending retreats where my colleagues and I debated the most efficient way to gather pine cones. But OK. I paid these people (except for the one appointed by the court), and they seldom agreed on anything. So I thought, *This one I should look at.* I decided to start writing to myself, get the compartments talking to one another.

> *Dear Gilda [I'm named after my grandmother, a name and person hated by me],*
>
> *I hope you don't find it presumptuous, my writing to you. In the time I have known you, you have made some difficult choices, and though you often choose poorly, you do so with gusto. You have your moments. Only last week a salesgirl failed to ring up a hat you wished to purchase. The hat was yours for the taking. Instead you pointed out the error, and only when the smug whore got smugger did you stroll with the item. This hat, by the way, does not look good on you. Stop wearing it. Who even wears hats?—are you a mime? As Grams used to say, "All things are not available to all people." True, she often said this after having cut a pie into too few pieces, but I wish today to re-impart this knowledge to you, from you. Your sister suffers, as we all do. Remember this. Be decent when you can.*

The trouble with Sam started with an ear infection. The doctor prescribed medicated drops, but when Fawn got Sam into the bathroom with the dropper, she would have none of it. I don't know any children myself to compare her with, but Sam seemed to me inordinately large for a five-year-old. So when the two of them went at it—wrestling over the sink—my sister went down, toppling into the tub on her behind, elbow jogging the faucet as she went. Water drummed her face while Sam hovered over her, demonic. "And stay the fuck off me, you slut-fuck," she said.

"That's just the part I'll repeat," Fawn whispered. "You've never heard the language comes out of that kid's mouth."

I couldn't tell if she was furious or crying. "Where are you?"

"I'm under the kitchen table till I can figure where she went to."

I suggested she locate and sedate the girl, but Fawn refused. "Don't think I haven't thought about crushing valium in her fish sticks, but she's not mine yet. They can still take her away, you know, whether this stuff's my fault or not, because no one cares whose fault it is."

"Whose fault *what* is?"

"Shit just happens, OK? You're not a mom; you don't know. But if you're the one holding the bag when the shit comes down, you're standing in the rain with a fistful of flowers."

I didn't like the way she sounded. That weekend I drove up. As I got out of my car, a little girl stopped me and asked if Sam could come out and play. The girl had frizzy red hair and a rash of orange freckles that made her look filthy instead of cute. She was holding a tennis ball frothed over with dog slobber. She said, "Sam wanted to French-kiss me. Then she put her tongue in my ear and tried to hump me."

When I went inside, Sam came out of the dining room holding a brush dripping bright green paint. It dashed down her knee onto the new beige carpet. "Hi, Aunt Gilda. Mom's nursing a hangover, and I'm painting."

Fawn came up behind her holding a ceramic cupid with bright green lips.

"There's a girl out there looking for Sam," I said.

The two exchanged a look. My sister said, "Red hair? Freckles?" Then to Sam, "Hon, get me the phone. I'll call her mom."

While Sam was out of the room, Fawn explained that the girl was a lesbian and unable to keep her hands to herself. "She's not supposed to come around here. She got caught making out with Dougie down the street."

"I thought you said she was gay."

"So she's bi."

"Isn't everyone bi when they're five?"

"Whatever. She's bad news. Let me clean up and we'll talk." She shifted her eyes toward the bedroom. I went, though it was always pain and agony, what went on in there—Fawn, telling me about the new guy, whichever one. "Stop me if this gets too graphic," she'd say.

I stood looking at the poster over her bed, a blown-up photo of Fawn in the backseat of a taxi, playing Jodie Foster's character in *Taxi Driver*. A USC film student cast her in the scene and wouldn't stop groping her between takes. I want to say I was unaffected by Fawn's parade of men. But I looked at that poster, the way Fawn lived, the way Fawn loved, and I wondered whether without her I would have seen things differently. Seen men differently. Fawn pretended I could pick any guy I liked, treating Stuart like a placeholder I would one day spurn for a fancier man. I should've straightened her out, but I was too proud to admit she thought so little of a man I thought so much of. I remember one night after Stuart and I started dating, he flew to Vegas for a bachelor party. It was our first night apart, and he arranged to get away at midnight to talk. I knew he would call at twelve on the dot. It was a sweet time for us, when even a phone call was delicious. At ten till twelve, Fawn called. "Pick up," she said, "Pick up pick up. You won't *believe* what happened." A midnight call from Fawn meant she was in jail or in love, and I could smell the candles burning through the line. I knew if I picked up the phone, I'd walk away thinking Stuart should be more like the guy filling Fawn's car with balloons, or tattooing her name on his neck, though her infatuations never lasted or ended well.

How easy it seems to me now: let her go, call her back in the morning. But I picked up the phone. She played me an entire mix tape made by her new soul mate, a guy she met auditioning for a UPS commercial. I listened for an hour—why?—and missed Stuart's call. He left several messages, each longer than the last, until he said he guessed I'd turned in early. He wished me sweet dreams. The tiny betrayals are worst, the ones that don't cross any official line. Those you live with alone.

Now Fawn reached for a novelty glass case that said, IN CASE OF EMERGENCY BREAK GLASS, which she attempted with strokes of the miniature ax. "So you remember the hottie from next door?"

"The guy from the baby pool?"

She smiled and off she went, sprawling out, pressing a frilly pillow to her brow. He thought she was a "golden goddess." He had to wear looser pants now because the ones he had got tight just thinking about her. He was open to the idea of their raising Sam together.

"And this would be after you get out of jail for statutory rape?" I said.

"Firstly, he's twenty-one. Secondly, I'm a mother now, and I don't intend to jeopardize that. Which reminds me. Don't get too close to Sam while you're here. They sent her home with body lice last week."

"American children get body lice?"

"We washed her in special soap, so all the little guys should be dead or dying by now. But I'd keep my distance if I were you. I don't fully know what we're up against here."

The next morning I opened my eyes to find Sam snuggled up on the futon beside me, her forehead pressed against mine. We were so close I could see in her eye the reflection of my eye reflecting her eye. I said, "What are you doing?"

She said, "What are you doing?"

I scooted back. She scooted, too. I watched for any unseemly scurrying on her skin, lice preparing to jump. I said, "Where's your mom?"

She said, "Where's your mom?"

"Please don't do that."

"Please don't do that."

"Really, stop it."

"Really, stop it."

On the drive home I kept hearing Sam, her tormenting little echo and the fury it roused in me. I thought of Fawn as a girl, curled in my lap—in Good Gilda's lap—and the welling of love as I calmed and coddled her. *Bad Gilda's gone now, Good Gilda's going to take care of you.* The mountain air was close and ashy as I drove; a small town had burned to the ground and it was taking days to blow off. Farther south, closing in on Camp Pendleton, a big-bellied plane flew in low over the ocean at such an angle that it appeared to be stuck, suspended in midair. I drove and drove and it just hung there like a moon.

*Bad Gilda's gone. Good Gilda will protect you now.*

When I got home there was a letter waiting from "An Admirer." Only when I reached the end and saw the signature did I recognize the letter as mine. Not even the handwriting clued me in. The eerie thing was, as I read, the voice in my head was not my own but Sam's; I smelled her synthetic skin, even as my own itched with imagined lice.

Also waiting for me was a message from Mavis at the adoption service. She sounded perturbed I hadn't returned her previous calls, and stressed the importance of my doing so. I wasn't trying to dodge Mavis; I had every intention of calling as soon as I knew what I wanted to say. But something in Mavis's voice threw me. She sounded like someone you'd want to tell the truth to, and a large and growing part of me wanted to *stop this thing.* My biggest fear when Fawn took Sam in was that she'd give up on the girl like everyone else, be one more disappointment in the girl's life. I didn't want to believe enough could happen to a kid to squash her for good, but I was starting to think Fawn was outmanned here, and maybe in bigger trouble than Sam.

I sat down with a glass of wine and wrote myself back.

> *Dear Gilda,*
>    *Thanks for writing. Your letter came as quite a surprise. I have just come back from seeing your sister and the youth she's taken on. While you were gone you found you missed Stuart, as always, more than you expected to. Sometimes you miss him when you're with him. What does that mean? The night before he left, you watched him sleeping. He was on his back, his hands behind his head and one leg propped up, a smile on his sleeping face, and you thought, as you had umpteen times before, that beside you was a man complete in himself, ultimately inaccessible to you. And to love a man who's whole, this is the loneliest thing.*

My therapists were split on the letter writing, in part because I wouldn't show them the letters. In my opinion, you've got to keep some kernel of privacy in this world, and if that means lying to your therapist, then it's probably the healthiest thing you can do. My regular Friday guy worried that the letters, handled improperly, could trigger a split personality. He suggested, as an alternate exercise, that I transfer Fawn's sexuality onto a large blue pillow in the corner of his office and share my feelings with the pillow, tell it honestly how it affected my world and relationships.

I told him I didn't want to talk to the pillow.

He steepled his hands in front of his mouth. "What about this: What if you were to transfer your *passivity* to the pillow and talk to the pillow about that? Or you could hug it."

The pillow looked unclean to me. I told him I didn't want to hug it.

"Sometimes that's exactly the time to hug it."

"I'm not going to hug it," I said.

"Hug it."

Before long I was writing myself once or twice a day. I wrote at my kitchen table on plain lined paper. Once I got going, I gushed. This was no diary, let me be clear on that. There was a sender and a receiver, and only in body were we/they/me one and the same. I didn't realize how much I'd come to depend on my correspondence until one Saturday, when Stuart came to pick me up for a barbecue at his boss's house. The mailman hadn't come yet (dress a grown man in culottes and knee-highs, of course he's going to dawdle), and the idea of heading out and missing my letter put me on edge. I almost told Stuart to go on without me, but he was up for a raise, and had recently read a study that correlated higher salaries with males who appeared to be regularly copulating. He needed to show up with a date.

For the life of him Stuart couldn't drive at a constant speed. We surged and dipped in his rattling Ford Element while he explained how the toilets of the future would analyze our urine and suggest changes to our diet. He could be a dazzling conversationalist, especially when it came to topics like computers taking over the world. He looked like he might've punched a guy once for saying it was OK to freeze eggs.

At the party the boss's wife cornered me. She'd heard from Stuart about Fawn's recent trouble with Sam and strongly urged me to intervene. Helping kids with special needs sounded romantic and all, she said, but unless you were a saint you'd wind up special needs yourself.

"Sam's not exactly special needs," I said, explaining somewhat.

Slurring, sloshing wine on her shoes, the wife said, "Trashy? You want trashy?" She spoke then about her autistic daughter, whom she wanted to put in a home. "You try and do something nice? The answer is screaming. You can call her whatever you like, as far as I'm concerned, she's retarded." All I could think was that the mailman was at my door *now*. Or *now*. Or *now*. After an hour I feigned illness, and Stuart drove me home, tucked me in, and left. I listened for his bumper to scrape backing out of the drive. Then I hopped out of bed and ran for the mail. One of my shorter and shallower letters had arrived that day, but it was no less enlightening for all that. I got out all the old ones to reread them. Halfway through one of my favorites, I got a ticklish feeling and looked up to find Stuart standing in the doorway, holding a brown bag. He set the bag on the table. "Soup," he said. "For your cold."

He looked at the table scattered with letters. Perhaps recognizing the handwriting, he picked one up and read it. I let him. He read another. "These letters are from you," he said.

I lowered my gaze.

"How long has this been going on?" he asked.

"Awhile now."

He nodded, like he'd expected as much. "Who knows about this?"

"My therapists and me."

"Your sister?"

"You know Fawn, she just knows things."

He kept nodding, shuffling the letters around on the table as if he might find some magical arrangement where things didn't look as bad. Then he pulled his hand back as if from a hot stove. "You know, Gild," he said, "I'm here every day. Every day I see you and talk to you. Every day I ask you how you are, and I want to know, and you tell me nothing. What am I supposed to think?" He flung one of the letters to the floor.

"I'm sorry, Stuart. I'm a compartmentalizer. This is what we do."

He was spinning his keys on his index finger in a way that filled me with panic. I wanted to rush him, say whatever he needed to hear to keep from getting in his car, but I knew I had to let him go, that he was right to feel the way he did.

He'd turned on his way to the door. He said, "You know, even this can go away, even us."

In seven years, Stuart had never doubted us.

———

Mavis from the adoption service called the next day. I stood over the answering machine and listened while she talked. She sounded confused now rather than annoyed. She wondered if she had the wrong number, and could whoever lived at this one return her call and let her know.

I'd taken a personal day and spent it in my PJs eating my way through the kitchen, right down to the Baker's Chocolate. In that morning's letter, I chastised myself for not calling Mavis back immediately. I guess I knew it'd gone on too long. If Stuart were there, he would've told me as much; he would've taped my hand to the phone until I took care of it. But he didn't call or come by.

"I just had an interview at child services," Fawn said, calling from the road. "Everyone called them back. My boss, my landlord. Only you. My own sister. Guess how that looks?"

I really wished Fawn hadn't put me down as a reference—until then, I'd never been in a position to alter her life in any substantial way.

"I've been busy. It slipped my mind. I'll call Monday."

She was quiet awhile. "I feel like you want to sabotage this."

I told her no. *No.*

Then she said, "I can't believe I'm saying this, but I don't believe you."

Probably out of guilt, I agreed to accompany Fawn and Sam to the county fair that weekend. We got our pictures taken in pioneer outfits with period furniture and jewelry. We ate cotton candy and watched horses shit while walking and wagging their tails, not even breaking stride, not a care in the world. The feature band that night had been big news in the '60s until a car wreck half-paralyzed the lead singer. Now they played venues like this, same old '60s tunes, the lead singer dragging his gimp leg around the stage like an extra instrument. Men in cutoff jeans bought Fawn hurricane after piña colada after mai tai. Sometime before the Ferris wheel's generator

died, a man on stilts—not, I think, an employee of the fair—
turned to get an eyeful of Fawn and went down, hard.

I ate a corn dog and watched Fawn and Sam get caricatures
done. They sat side by side in director's chairs. Fawn looked to be
buzzing, perhaps from more than just draft beer, but it was hard to
tell; she always appeared her best and brightest when she was using.
Beside her, with teenage pregnancy written all over her, Sam mimicked Fawn's every gesture. I tried to remember whether Fawn and
I had shared such a moment as girls. Then Fawn turned to Sam
and, with a licked finger, dabbed an eyelash off her cheek. Maybe
it was the way Sam let her do it, gave her complete trust to my
sister, but all my compartments were suddenly filled with the cer-
tainty that I'd missed out on something in life.

Soon after that I lost track of Fawn and Sam in the crowd; when
I found them again, Fawn and the operator of the Zipper were slipping into the maintenance tent. I went after them, but Sam barred my
way. "You can't go in there," she said. "My mom's humping someone."

I tried to push Sam aside, but she grabbed at my dress and
called me filthy names. I picked her up and carried her into the
bathroom. My notion was to wash her mouth out with soap, but
there was only the soft-soap dispenser, dispensing frothy little
mounds. So in one of the doorless stalls, I turned her over on my
knee. Her legs, in pink tights, were like large drumsticks, and she
fought me. I had never spanked anyone before. It felt . . . not as bad
as I thought it should have. Between our huffs and grunts and the
rustle of her clothes, it sounded like someone giving birth. People
continued applying lipstick and fixing their hair. Spank a child at
a county fair, no one bats an eye.

Then Sam quit fighting and went limp. I let go, and she slipped
to the ground, covered her face in her hands, and made a noise like
a wicker chair when a heavy person sits on it. Through splayed
fingers she said, "I want to die." I didn't know a kindergartner
could want such a thing. At what age did the human mind

comprehend death enough to want it? Then her shoulders began shaking, and she clawed her hands down her cheeks, and I realized she was *laughing*, like she'd just killed her grandparents with a salad fork. I understood there were deep wounds at work here—her whole parentless, godless life—but I decided to take what the little crazy was offering.

When Fawn reemerged, she was in no shape to drive and couldn't find her keys. I called Stuart to come pick us up. He and I hadn't spoken in ten days and when he answered, in those first seconds, his voice was vaguely unfamiliar, and I sunk inside thinking, *How fast we lose one another.*

In the Burger King drive-through Sam screamed, "These aren't my parents! Police! Police!" She slid around the backseat, gobbling fries and calling me more vulgar names. By the time we got home, she'd cursed herself to sleep, lying half on the floor, half on the car's seat, her hand curled around a strawberry shake. Fawn was all but passed out, mumbling and writhing. I carried Sam to my room; Stuart carried Fawn. I pulled off Sam's dress and bobby socks. Putting them up for the night wasn't much, but it was all I could do, and all I was willing to do.

As I lifted the blanket to Sam's chin, the light from the hall fell across her face. Again I saw what a beauty she would be, providing she cleaned up and found someone to fix her teeth. Otherwise she'd wind up a minimart cashier with an alternating black eye. When I came out of the room, Stuart was sitting pitched forward on the loveseat. "That girl in there," he said, "she's eight or nine. She sure as shine isn't five, I can tell you that."

I said, "It doesn't surprise me."

I came and stood between his knees, pushed my hand through his hair. His head was hot with thought. He touched the fabric of my sweater, curious to see what it was made of. You don't find men his age curious about the world on the level of warp and woof. The first sprouts of silver were coming in behind his ear, and I thought, *Stuart, we're growing old every minute, all the time.*

"This is something you have to work out," he said. "I'm about done waiting for you to see what we are."

I pulled his face against my stomach, like a pregnant wife might do. It was a convenient gesture, but maybe I was trying it out, too.

The next morning I was up at eleven with a pot of coffee. From the bedroom Sam called for me. I brought her orange juice, but she was asleep again, or faking it, before the glass was to her lips. Fawn was curled up, spooning Sam, and I could smell her boozy breath from three feet away. *If the two of them could sleep twenty hours a day,* I thought, *they'd do all right.* Only sleep kept some people safe.

Back in the kitchen, I sipped my coffee. Before me on the table sat the cordless phone and Mavis's home number. I wouldn't have to tell half of what Fawn was up to, and the wagon from the orphanage would come, with its lollipops and tranquilizer guns, and cart Sam away.

Whether I was right or wrong to do it, this would be the thing Fawn would never forgive.

I dialed Mavis's number. I apologized for the delay but I'd been in Africa. We didn't talk long, but I got the feeling she wanted to hear the very things I had to say: what a pair they were already, Fawn and Sam, a real little family. Which was true enough, though it didn't mean they were good for each other, or that Fawn would survive this child. It did occur to me, though, before I hung up, that survival was beside the point.

# Christiania

In the end Lauren agreed to three days in Denmark. She could spare three days and, while penciling out the trip on her map at work, she spilled coffee all over France and took that to mean Denmark had a sense of humor. Also, Wahl wanted to show off his haunts and his Danish (in an e-mail, he wrote, *I don't sound like a brain trauma victim anymore . . . sadly, this is progress*), and Lauren could be shown off too. She could do that. Especially since she'd invited herself over, in an e-mail she immediately regretted sending—an e-mail she wrote on one of those nights when almost for the hell of it, you convince yourself you don't know anyone anymore.

It's not that she didn't like Wahl (she did), or that she thought he'd get on her nerves (he hadn't in the past). The trouble was, he didn't drink, didn't smoke, didn't spend. He insisted on staying in hostels though she offered to pay his way, and would have, happily, for the privacy more than for the pampering of good hotels. He planned his meals in advance and read the informative placards in museums. They were a mismatch in every category that counted on the road.

But once the idea took hold, Lauren was glad she committed to go. Booking flights and rooms was promising, not awkward in the least—Wahl made suggestions, Lauren made deposits, all via the Internet. She began to see the genius in touring Europe with Wahl. For starters, he was fluent in all the languages that went with tasty food, except maybe Danish. Lauren felt this was key. The last time she was in Spain, she dipped what she thought was a french fry into what looked like ketchup, noticing—too late—that the fries had tiny fins and eyes and the sauce was moving. This time she would know what she was ordering.

She'd met Wahl in the college library when their carts collided, then again in the supervisor's office, where they were summoned and charged with slacking—accused of leafing through books they were supposed to be shelving. They promised to do better and instead started meeting after work to play Secrets of the Universe, a game they made up where the winner found the most interesting fact about the least interesting subject; grass, skin conditions, et cetera. Lauren was seeing a fellow accounting major and Wahl was perpetually in love with one of his poli-sci professors—either actually or as a romantic alibi—so dating each other didn't come up. As college types go, they were different species. Wahl looked like a Norwegian Eagle Scout leader; Lauren cleaved still to the preppy-grunge of her upscale high school in the Bay Area. She remembers Wahl, at that time, cutting a brother figure though she must've checked him out at one time or another: he had the height and bones, brilliant predatory teeth and gentling glasses. But there was an undeveloped quality about him. He was one of those guys who can't grow a real beard and so shaves every day to hide the places where no hair grows. Over the years they managed to keep in touch. They saw each other when he passed through Southern California, or she through Iowa (which, so far, was never) but until now they'd never driven or flown specifically to see each other. Lauren's husband thought Wahl was creepy, but he was her ex-husband now, so that didn't play in.

A grant had taken Wahl abroad for the year. His project or mission was translating the writings of a dead Danish politician. It was starting to frustrate him—if people wanted to read the man's work, he wrote, they could very well learn Danish and read it themselves. The politician would've agreed, he thought, were he alive and not a Communist. Lauren thought that was funny and wrote and asked if he had to give the money back. He said no, the grant was no strings attached and no one would check up on him.

They met in Copenhagen, though Wahl was living in a small town far from the capital. On their first night, catching up, Wahl told Lauren he didn't think she could have a healthy relationship. She told him that was crap, that never having been in a relationship-relationship with her, he couldn't possibly know. Maybe because they were so opposite, they could talk that way and no hurt feelings.

"Don't ask for my opinion then criticize it," Wahl said.

They were at a café beside a canal that had no smell. As always, Wahl took ages with the menu. A hard-core vegan, he first had to decide what he could eat, then what he wanted to eat.

Lauren said, "Don't tell me I'm unhealthy and not let me respond. I'm too paranoid for that. Besides, until the divorce, my marriage was a success."

Wahl tipped his menu and smiled. Lauren meant what she'd said about her marriage, but Wahl was more fun to tease than persuade, with his bionic brain and short fuse for stupidity, qualities he tried to temper by saying things like *I don't judge*. Lauren had heard this more than once. Always she rolled her eyes and said, *Everyone judges. You just don't want to admit you're a moral snob.*

Out of embarrassment, Lauren had been vague and only semi-truthful with Wahl about her divorce. She'd told him that all her ex cared about was making money. But for all the money he bothered to make, he hated things, buying and repairing and keeping track of things. Even the way he said *things*. He'd shell out any amount to get Lauren out of a store, then they'd laugh the whole way home while she flapped outrageous receipts in front of his driving eyes. But something was missing, a void inside her like a bubble on a leveler, one she needed to explain away. For a time she let it be about children. Lauren didn't necessarily want children—she didn't regret not having them now—but her ex had had a vasectomy young because of an abusive father, and she missed the dance of fertility; being a week late and starting to sweat. It felt unnatural that they didn't need protection. Her friends started having kids and Lauren started play thinking. That turned into hypothesizing, questioning him. He said he'd think about reversing the surgery. Then, when he decided no on that, he said he'd think about adopting. And so on. If she'd pushed and he'd said yes, she would've backed down. She knew that. She just wanted him to say yes, and when he didn't the sex began to feel degrading, as though she were a body but not a female, a person who could give life—things she told herself, and him. Now it was over and the bubble was still there, and she was coming to understand the bubble was as much a part of her as her stomach or foot. In the end, you decided what to let yourself become upset by.

Her ex insisted on alimony. She didn't know why he offered, but she took it. She didn't know how not to, financially, and his paying her felt like he was taking care of her still, like they were still together in some little way.

Wahl said, "Maybe we should talk about this when you're not jet-lagged and cranky. You need sleep."

"It's still crap," she said.

He said, "Anyway, I didn't say *you're* unhealthy, necessarily, I said your relationships were."

"Your mom's unhealthy," she said.

She did need sleep, but didn't go under until four in the morning. Then, an hour later, a drunk Brit busted into the room and tried to climb into her bunk. When she told him it was taken, he slurred, "Aw, ya cunt," and threw up in the bottom bunk. The next night was worse. The Brit checked out, two snoring Spaniards checked in, and the lumpy Danish pillows, after a day of museum going, left her spine feeling bruised and shifty. She felt like she had to stretch all the time, but stretching didn't help. On the third day, her hands started trembling. She needed movies, rest, junk food, but it was their last day in the city and Wahl wanted to take her to a squatters' community he'd been curious about.

The place was called Christiania. It was a fully functional city within the city, completely walled in. There were restaurants and blacksmiths, a volunteer police squad on ten-speeds. No one paid taxes. No cameras allowed. Every few years the government threatened to shut them down, but Wahl called this *so much political noise*. He said he was surprised she'd never heard of the place.

Lauren stopped inside the entrance and asked what *ew* meant. Wahl laughed—not snottily, he wasn't like that—and pointed at the letters on the arch. "That's a *U*. It says *E-U*."

"And what's *eu* supposed to mean?"

Before he could answer, two hip-high Dalmatians trotted out of a warehouse behind a man playing a homemade flute. One dog was pigeon colored, one white. They both had huge pink swinging balls and Wahl joked that the dogs had given him a complex, and he didn't know when he could stand naked in front of anyone again. He quickly held up a finger and said, "Careful," meaning no wisecracks about his virginity. That was an example of Wahl getting her not to do something she wasn't going to do anyway.

Lauren told him people in the States were giving their dogs implants.

Wahl said, "To help with breeding?"

"Cosmetic reasons," she said.

Wahl stopped walking. "Do we know this?"

Lauren told him a dog with implants came into one of the doggie day cares whose books she kept, a job she took postdivorce to get away from people. She loved delivering appalling news from home, Wahl was so in love with all things Danish. He drooled over the care Danish women took with their appearance. He went on about the ingenuity of Danish design. He spent half a month's grant money on a book bag made out of recycled airplane tires, and a similar sum on Danish eyeglasses that looked like furniture for the face. He complained that Americans didn't know English, and told her about winter nights walking home, how in the houses people gathered by candlelight while he headed for his empty little room on the hill. He said he'd never felt lonelier, but then turned around and said he'd never been happier, like the two went together.

Christiania reminded Lauren of Berkeley before people started to reek on purpose. Wahl, who sometimes played naïve for rhetorical effect, said there were no drugs allowed in Christiania and Lauren laughed outright. She told him that where people were passed out on the grass, there were drugs. Wahl said that they were napping, and Lauren pointed at a woman under a tree who looked like she'd been thrown from a moving car. "That," she said, "is not a nap."

They wandered into an open-air market that looked like a giant garage sale. There were crafts and tie-dye for sale, a table full of bike horns, shoestrings, mints. The vendors were all over Lauren, in her museum-store jewelry and couture jeans. They complimented her eyes, her soul. A Middle Eastern–looking guy called her a queen. He had fiery eyes and features as forgettable and precise as the corners and edges on a box. He was the highest man she'd ever seen. His (also extremely high) associates sat on turned-around poker chairs and gave Lauren sultry looks while the front man asked if she was a model, and was she American, and had she seen his new shipment of sweaters from Nepal?

She tried one on, a gray cardigan with orangutan sleeves and hot-pink and orange florets around the cuffs. It looked used, with one shoulder pointy from the hanger, but she liked it. They wanted eleven hundred kroner (a few hundred U.S. dollars) and were too stoned to countenance haggling. It was hard to pay that much for a sweater on a hanger, and she would have to charge it, and the bill would go to her ex, and he would pay it with no fuss, and every time he did that she assumed he was paying for something she didn't know about. And she shouldn't have cared but she did.

Wahl said the sweater looked high quality but worn. He seemed impressed it was made in Nepal, and though it was just as likely made by Smurfs, Lauren let that go. Because as men and shopping went, Wahl was a good sport. "It's kind of shapeless," he said after a longer look. "Doesn't flatter your figure."

She smiled at the old-timey word, *figure*, and tried to determine whether he meant her figure needed flattering, or deserved it. When men looked at her now, since the divorce, she was sure they were disappointed or planning to rob her. She'd slimmed to nothing but had also lost a lot of sleep and often looked, when she caught her reflection unawares, washed-up, like somebody's aunt— she knew this was a distortion, normal after a long relationship, when you again feel vulnerable to the male gaze. A guy could go a long way if he was tall and just not ugly, so she still couldn't tell if Wahl was good-looking or plain. She could only ever picture him doctor's-office nude. The veganism figured in. He burped like an opera singer holding a note, as if to brag that his weren't regular burps but special vegan ones. He wouldn't so much as kiss a woman in leather shoes, which provoked unconscious, or semiconscious, mischief on Lauren's part—more than once when they met up, she looked down and realized she was wearing nearly every made-from-animals thing she owned. She used to lecture him, tell him his principles were getting in the way of life—*life* a euphemism for sex—and some night he should shelve the hunt for his vegan queen and get some satisfaction. He said one-night stands didn't make him happy, and that stuck with her, that remark. That he cared for himself, provided for himself that way.

She was still wearing the sweater and riffling through the others when the salesman told Wahl, "You should buy this for your wife. She is a queen and should own riches."

"Yes, dear," Lauren said, "Riches."

Wahl played along. "We'll see, my darling."

Of course the salesman knew they weren't married. They didn't even really look like they'd know each other. Lauren's ex said you weren't a real businessman until you had an employee whose job was a mystery to you, and similarly, Lauren felt everyone needed a friend who made no sense; Wahl was hers.

She hung the sweater on the rack and said they should eat. By eat she meant drink, which she didn't normally do overseas—the built-in confusions of travel were enough—but she'd thought about her ex the wrong way and now she needed to reboot. And anyway, it was different inside Christiania, a foreign place within a foreign place run by stoned people: it was like steering a runaway car into a bumper-car rink.

The beer made her feel better even though drinking with Wahl—who wouldn't even drink near beer to comfort drinking friends—was more stressful than relaxing. Wahl had quit drinking because he didn't like himself when he drank, and because there was no reason to do it. Lauren told him there was no reason to do anything, and ordered more beer to go with her curry. The sauce featured chickpeas, which Lauren said looked and tasted like garbanzo beans. Wahl said chickpeas *were* garbanzo beans; they were both legumes. Lauren thought *legume* was French for *cockroach*, and asked if Denmark had cockroaches, which threw Wahl into a story about a Danish friend he'd met in America, with whom he'd had some of the best conversations of his life. But when Wahl moved here and they switched to speaking Danish, the guy only talked about women and soccer. Lauren suggested Wahl had remembered their earlier conversations wrong. He said he'd considered that, but didn't think so. And then he said that these were the first real conversations he'd had since Christmas—his conversations with Lauren, now, in July. She'd forgotten how Wahl could break your heart, and with so little inkling, he broke it again while it was breaking.

Lauren said, "Hey. What if we check out of the hostel and into a hotel. Just for tonight—one night in every city."

"I didn't budget for that," Wahl said.

"I'll pay," she said. "We can sleep in."

"You're not rich anymore, remember?"

"I'm a little rich," she said.

"You know I can't let you do that."

"The beds at our place are like sleeping on a big strip of bacon."

Wahl said, "I wouldn't know about the bacon, but I wouldn't get your hopes high about a better bed, even at a hotel."

"It'll be fun. We can throw our clothes and stuff everywhere."

Wahl stared into his curry. "I don't think it's a good idea."

"We can get twin beds," she said. "This isn't a seduction." But the minute she said it, seduction was on the table—the word, at the very least—so when Wahl said he had to pass, that he needed every cent for London (which was true but not, she thought, the truth), it was just another version of those self-righteous vegan burps—Wahl, choking on his own lifestyle, letting Lauren choke on it, too. In college she had been so taken by Wahl's outwardly easy company that she would be surprised when he didn't approve of something; then after a few years his list of pet peeves and vexations had grown long enough that she realized, underneath, he wasn't easy company at all. He was one of those people who, once you said something, would make it a permanent part of you, a comic-strip character with a speech bubble attached to your head. She thought he must've known this about himself, known that only by going to a hotel and letting nothing happen between them could she wipe the word *seduction* from her lips. She thought about getting a hotel room by herself to prove her point, show it was the room she wanted, but that would create new anxieties, like that Wahl's arrangements weren't good enough for her.

They ate quietly. Wahl studied the people around them, seemingly at ease; but Lauren, unnerved by silence, suggested they think of things that were the same everywhere. "Like bees."

Wahl considered, then said, "I don't know that that's true."

"Neither do I," she admitted.

"Maybe there's a special Danish strain of bees."

"OK, OK," she said.

Wahl speared a single garbanzo bean and examining it, said, "Dirty dishes."

Lauren laughed because he seemed excited about his answer. "But depending where you are, there's different dirt on the dishes. Like rice is really hard to get off plates—versus pasta or fried food."

He nodded. "That's true."

On their way out of the compound, Lauren stopped and tried the cardigan on again. The salesman was even higher than before. A cigar-size blunt bobbed on his lower lip and he was so high he looked drunk. The booths were closing and he wanted to make a sale.

"You are refreshed," he said.

Lauren said, "I am. But the riches, still no riches."

He touched Wahl's elbow. "You should accompany your wife into the toilet. There is a mirror for her to see herself in."

Lauren said she'd be fine on her own, but Wahl insisted the building wasn't safe. She couldn't tell if his concern was intended to make amends for the hotel, or to make her feel worse about it, or to act like it hadn't happened. Inside, they plugged their noses and made jokes about the smell, the graffiti, the worthlessness of the mirror. It was even less comfortable when they talked than when they were silent. She didn't remember any tension between them in the States, ever, though off and on, Lauren had thought Wahl had a thing for her—nothing excessive, but what a virgin his age would have for any woman he regularly got close enough to smell. Now, though, Lauren thought she was wrong, and either he'd never cared for her romantically or had cared very much. He would never let on either way, which annoyed her. She could imagine herself some night leading him on—just to find out. This would wind up a selfish experiment on her part, nothing more.

Lauren turned to him and said, "Love."

He squinted at her.

"Is the same everywhere," she said, recalling for him their dinner conversation.

"Is it?" he asked. He looked at the ceiling. "Is American love like Danish love?"

Someone moaned in the third stall. Wahl pointed at a syringe on the floor and they looked at each other emptily and for too long. When they came out of the shack, she told the salesman her husband was too cheap to buy the sweater. The salesman glanced at Wahl, then told Lauren to come back alone.

That night they had the room to themselves. Lauren waited to hear Wahl fall asleep across the room, but his breathing didn't change, and when he coughed or sneezed she could tell he was awake. All night she'd looked forward to time alone with her thoughts, but instead the room hummed with wakefulness. She shifted as little as possible, knowing for that reason tomorrow would be her sorest day yet. She thought in the wee hours, in the dark, you didn't know anyone at all, which made her wonder how well she knew Wahl, period. She knew him from thousands of miles away, and would know him again when she left, but now was another matter.

In the morning they pretended to have slept and took a train through the country to the little harbor town where Wahl had boarded for the year. He was moving back to the States a few weeks after Lauren left. His sabbatical was over and, he said, he needed his job more than he wanted to stay. Anyone could see he wasn't ready to leave. He'd sling that stupid airplane-tire bag over his shoulder with nothing more than baby carrots inside.

On the way to Wahl's dorm, they stopped in a compact market that could only accommodate single-file shoppers. Wahl hurried inside, leaving Lauren at the door wearing a backpack that, after the Copenhagen shops, had ballooned to the size of a body bag. After a few minutes a woman in a sun hat helped her off with the pack, asking as they lowered it down if Lauren was going to India, an innocent joke that made Lauren wonder if Wahl had walked ahead to distance himself from her gear, her American excess. From the door she watched him twice stop to chat up acquaintances—as if that were something Wahl did. Lauren figured he'd picked up the habit to better learn the cadences of the language, which mattered more to him than the actual conversations, and that seemed like a backward operation to her.

Lauren bought chocolate bars and nuts, and yogurt that turned out to be sour cream. She bought pears. She didn't see Wahl buy pears—he certainly could have, though every time she looked he was bagging grains or talking to one of the cashiers. Also, she figured they would share their food, and that that was obvious.

They walked ten blocks up a cobblestone grade. Locals rode by with handlebar baskets full of fruit and bread, not riding seriously but gliding and taking in the sun like extras in a musical. She adjusted and readjusted the straps on her pack; she had to stop and set her groceries down to do this, and Wahl didn't help then either. But they were hungry and grumpy, and she'd ignored his advice to pack one pair of jeans, one pair of shoes, et cetera, so she guessed that left him off the hook.

After that hike they climbed six flights to Wahl's attic room. Once you stepped inside, the room ended. Only one person could unload at a time, and Wahl had to duck to get around. She asked why he didn't transfer to a room he could stand up in, but he just shrugged and said he liked the light, which was thicker and starker than in the city. It was like talking through fallout, so that Lauren caught herself talking louder.

In the corner of the room was Wahl's big indulgence of the year after the glasses and bag: a geometrical Danish chair upholstered in bright blue tweed, a blue that stuck out like an isolated wet spot on one sock. It looked like something from a school for gifted kids.

"I'm almost too tired to eat," Lauren said. "I shouldn't have sat down."

But Wahl was at the door with a sandwich he'd pulled from somewhere. He said if she needed a minute, the kitchen was at the end of the hall. She was curious about his sandwich, where it'd come from and why he hadn't offered her one, so she went with him. It was hard to picture him eating alone. It was bad enough,

the systematic and joyless way he ate, drinking coffee only at appointed times of day, and even how he made and measured it out,
like he was administering a drug.

While he boiled water and ground beans, Lauren taste-tested
three chocolate bars, with bites of a pear in between. With its weird
angles and corners, the kitchen felt like the inside of a rhomboid.
Lauren sat back and finished telling a story about her boss, who
kept a blog called *Tijuana Prostitutes and the Man Who Loves Them*;
here Lauren learned about the twins who kept raising their fee
when he saw them and how, to afford them (it was all there on his
blog), he'd fired one of the groomers and cut everyone else's pay.
Wahl loved perverse stories about other people—which was why
Lauren rarely talked to him about men—and her boss was tops for
that. He was also good for looking at, but she left that out. Wahl
just wanted the story anyway.

After he got the coffee in the press, Wahl sat down across from
her and took a loud snapping bite of a carrot. While she talked,
Lauren carved slices out of a pear, taking occasional tiny bites. Wahl
was a good listener, even over the sound of crunching carrots, and
he rarely interrupted, so Lauren stumbled when he cut her off mid-
sentence and asked, "Is that my pear?"

She looked at the pear, with her bite marks in it.

He said, "Is that the pear I brought in here?"

She looked at him and smiled, but he didn't smile back. "I don't
know who brought it in," she said slowly, "but we can share."

He eased onto the backmost legs of the chair and twisted off
more carrot with his teeth. She went on with her story. He watched
her through lenses so clean the frames looked empty. At some point
she understood his attention was fixed on the pear, and he wasn't
listening anymore, and she felt herself blush. She considered telling
him she'd bought her own pears but it seemed such a desperate
thing to say. Just when she got to the meat of the story, he plunked
down again and said, "Go get my pear."

His face and voice were flat, with no expression to steer the tone.

Lauren asked if he were serious. He said, "Ya-ya," which was how he said yes now.

She picked up the knife and said, "I've only had a couple bites. I'll carve out that part. It's barely any."

He said, "I want my pear. Not five-eighths of *that* pear."

She searched his face, but there was no give anywhere. "But this *is* your pear."

He said, "No. My pear is a whole pear. That's not my pear."

She held the knife toward him. "So you're saying even if I carve this out, you won't eat it. That's what you're saying?"

He said, "I'm saying I want my pear. Go get my pear."

Out of nowhere, she was going to cry. It hit instantly, surprising her, and she knew she would have to leave the room. The last thing she wanted was to cry in front of Wahl. "How about this," she said. "You find some humane way to phrase your command—yes, Wahl, *command*—and I'll go get your pear."

"Dear," he said, "will you go and get my pear, please?" The *dear* sent her spinning back to Christiania, to the salesman who kept calling them husband and wife. Their *dear*s and *we'll see, my darlings* didn't seem like a joke all of a sudden, but like Wahl had been making fun of her. She held her hand out for the room key and when he dropped it in her palm, she felt like he'd hit her.

Then she was out in the hall, and the door clicked behind her, and she felt fine. She couldn't have cried if she wanted. That meant she wanted Wahl to see her crying, which was entirely different from crying.

She went and stretched out on Wahl's bed, which was as bad as the others, narrow and a nuisance. She had to think this out. Soon Wahl would come looking—if not for her, for his pear. They had three weeks of travel ahead and she couldn't leave him because her biggest (survivable) phobia was traveling in a foreign country alone. She'd rather spend three weeks in the bottom of a well. The smart thing to do was dog-ear the incident and feel bad about it later. For now, she'd call it a social hiccup and move on.

The door to the room swung open. She'd been gone too long.

"I'm lying down," she said, taking care to say *lying* and not *laying*.

"I see that." He didn't step into or out of the room, didn't commit either way. "Anything wrong?"

She told him no, tired was all. This came out funny, gurgly, like she was about to cry, and sounding like she was going to cry made her want to cry again.

He asked if she was coming back. She said in a minute. He loomed, deciding what to make of her, then said OK and left. She hated the stoicism of men in fights, men signing paperwork, men cutting her pay so they could afford more prostitutes. After she and her husband split, she had nightmares in which she would tell him she never wanted to see him again, and he'd say things like, *OK, but do you want to see a movie first?* To get over the nightmares, she threw herself into a series of romantic blunders so poor, so primal (one guy was technically homeless, but worked, hosed down, and slept at the doggie day care) that her boss said she should start a game show called *Why Would You Do That?*

When Wahl returned, she took aim at his chair. This wasn't planned. "It looks comfortable, but it's really not."

"OK," he said, drawing out the syllables, looking at the chair.

"It doesn't groove with your back."

"You mean with *your* back."

"I mean the human back. The curve of the spine. I'll take a Danish bed over a Danish chair any day."

He started lacing up his running shoes. She said she was going to nap while he ran. He said that was fine and went into the bathroom and peed so loud she thought it'd blast through the wall. She felt good about insulting his chair and wanted to do it some more, realizing gloomily that she wasn't going to be able to act like she wasn't upset.

He flushed the mini Euro toilet, then stepped back into the room and set the timer on his watch. She saw that he didn't understand what was happening or what to do. They were already in it and he didn't even know that—or he didn't want her to think he knew—which was so rookie that before she could stop herself she said, "You're embarrassed by my Americanness."

He paused. He said, "I have no idea where you're getting that."

"OK," she said.

He stood there breathing. Finally he said, "If you mean in the kitchen, I was kidding. I thought you knew that, it was so absurd."

She chewed on that. It was tricky accusing someone of not kidding when they said they were kidding, all the more so with Wahl, who as far as she knew had never lied to her. All the same, she didn't believe him, and she trusted her intuition. She said she didn't see how he could've thought it was a joke when it'd gone on so long and with her clearly not in on it.

He looked at his chair. "I don't know what to say. You seem really upset." He picked a tennis ball out of his in-box.

She said, "You always had walls, which is fine, but now it's like an electric fence. I say something and it's like *dzzzzzzt*—"

"Now we're all over the place," he said.

"We're not even close to all over the place."

For a while, they went around on whether or not they were all over the place, and how they'd gotten there. Lauren said that's how these things went. Wahl asked if she could start using *I statements* and she asked what he was talking about. He said, "For instance, you could say, 'When you said those things in the kitchen, *I felt like* you were bossing me around.'"

"I could say that," she said, "but I said what I meant."

He tossed and caught the tennis ball. He said he was sorry but he couldn't process all this right now. He would try and think of some useful *I statements* while he ran. Someone was frying onions down the hall and it made Lauren homesick, and she put a few things together and realized Wahl had been in therapy, and for a long time. Often she'd talked to him about her own adventures in the chair and Wahl had never returned her confidence, which felt unfair.

He ran for twenty minutes. He came back with pink cheeks and *I statements*. He sat and wrote them down on a pocket pad while Lauren watched from the bed. She felt desperate in an emptier way than during fights with lovers. She thought it had to do with their being friends, and so not essential to each another, which made what they said less provisional.

Wahl delivered his *I statements* as though they were in a parent-teacher conference, but one where the parent gets to lie in the teacher's bed and hate him. Wahl said, "I can't help feeling like your therapist in these discussions."

"What discussions?"

"Please let me finish," he said. He checked his notes. She had the idea that if she got up and looked, all she'd see on the pad was a drawing of her with a mustache and horns. He read from his notes: "Booking all the reservations, showing you around—" He looked up. "Things like that. It's been stressful. Then the trip suddenly escalates into *this*—"

There were little charcoal smudges on his pillow from her mascara. She told him she resented his thinking that he could say whatever he wanted as long as he couched it in his stupid *I* format, and he said calling the *I statements* stupid wasn't useful. She said she was trying to be truthful, not useful. (She was sorry that rhymed.) They talked his *I statements* over, then talked again about whether or not they were all over the place. This all dragged on so long Wahl started rubbing his temples, making gestures of exhaustion. She saw he didn't understand that this was the part where lazy or greedy fighters (she was both) started trying on theatrics. Because only Lauren understood this, only she was poised to rein it in. All she had to do was stop talking—swallow the next line, the line she had ready to go. She pictured herself saying it, then she pictured herself not saying it. She wondered when and how she'd become a person who could even do this calculation, and whether, as with shopping, you could only gauge want versus desire versus need versus temporary need by your willingness to let a thing go.

She got tired of thinking and said, "I think I don't want to be the only person you've talked to since Christmas anymore."

Wahl said, "What does that mean?"

And she said, "It means I think I should leave." She didn't know which leave she meant—*leave* go for a walk, or *leave* part ways— but Wahl took it to mean part ways.

He put his face in his hands. He walked around the room and said it was horrible, really horrible. "I guess I underestimated the stress of traveling with another person." The way he looked right then—apologetic and shocked, with hairs in his part sticking up from his run—told her that he had taken her and all of it more seriously than she'd known.

He said, "If you have to go, I understand. But I want you to know I love having you here."

She believed him.

By three or four she was sitting on another awful Danish bed in a Danish Motel 6 in a Danish commuter town. Under her window, buses stopped every ten minutes, squeaking to a stop, then groaning and thundering off again. They had flights booked to London the next evening, with time in the morning for a last jaunt in Copenhagen. Wahl had said if he changed his mind about things, he'd meet her at the airport the next day, but she knew (even if he didn't know it yet himself) that he wouldn't be there. When she'd checked into the motel, she went straight to the loaner computer and dropped three grand booking three- and four-star hotels in case she was too scared to sightsee alone. She decided to pass on France and the rest, sticking to England and Ireland to avoid any language barrier. She resolved not to go home early, even if it meant holing up for weeks, drinking and watching TV she could've seen at home.

She climbed into bed before dark, before dinner, and she stayed there until the last rush of traffic, the partiers calling it a night, then the pocket of silence before the early-bird traffic started again, then—when she couldn't stand the bed one more minute—she spread the blankets on the floor and waited for her wake-up call.

In the morning she took the train back to town. She checked her bag at their old hostel, where the counter guy pretended to fall over when he took her backpack. She laughed to be nice, thinking of the woman who'd helped her in the little market. *Are you going to India?* She took her claim check and walked through the park, over the bridge, into and through the seedy part of town, to Christiania.

Two young guys came out of the warehouse. They had sweaty faces and the bashed-in look of heavy users. Their eyes were like eggs with the yolk emptied out, and they looked capable of having eaten the Dalmatians. She wondered how you ever found your way back from a place like that.

The vendor was at his booth again, this time without his side-kicks. He looked tired, old. He gave her a shy smile, like he'd never seen her before, but when she tried the sweater on again he asked where her friend was.

"My husband, you mean?" Lauren said.

He smiled and lowered his head. He looked embarrassed to be sober, which made her feel betrayed somehow.

"That's all over," she said, "We're getting divorced again." She hung the sweater up. It didn't look as beat-up today, though she liked it less. This was the third or fourth time she'd given him to believe she might buy it, and she felt bad about that and looked for something else to buy. On a dilapidated banquet table were incense burners, whittled ashtrays and pipes, an oversize wooden hand flipping the bird with an exaggerated middle finger. Also a basketful of anklets. Some said CHRISTIANIA; some had the secret logo— three dots in a row. She bought a few of them for friends because they were cheap but went with a story. She didn't know if tipping or overpaying the vendor would insult him, so she paid the regular price.

While he made change, he said, "One thousand kroner for the sweater."

She said, "I don't have room to carry it."

"You can have it shipped."

"No thanks," she said.

"I have others not so thick."

He pressured her for a while. That was disappointing, though she didn't know what she had expected, coming back. She bought falafel and sat in the grass and tied one of the anklets on. The strings were unraveling so she could see the black plastic band underneath. It wouldn't last a week, but it made her ankle look bony and festive and young. She thought how strange it was to spend time in a place you knew you'd never return to, and she wished she could talk to Wahl about that. She couldn't see herself calling or writing him. It seemed like enough to keep each other company silently and from afar, to be alive at the same time. If things had felt less final, he could hold this against her, but as it stood, he would have to forgive her, if he hadn't already. She crossed her legs in front of her and looked at the anklet. *Salesmen*, she thought. *Salesmen were the same everywhere.*

# Three Men

## The Count

The actuary stands at the foot of the bed holding a suit for Jess to examine. By her watch, he needs to leave in twenty minutes: he's flying to meet the actuarial brass of California's biggest health care provider. He needs to look good, which means he can't dress himself.

Jess sits up, groping on the plant stand for her glasses—she was up until dawn reading, of all things, a book on grammar, with the actuary asleep beside her. She has been doing this lately, sucking espresso beans and keeping awake on the sly, through the night, logging what hours are left before he moves out. They have decided to separate, which everyone knows is just practice for divorce. When Jess's hands get cold holding the book outside the covers, she reaches in under his T-shirt and warms them on his stomach (his body heat is dizzying), a pudding of flesh that comes and goes with the seasons. Soon his clothes will be none of Jess's business, like his habit of talking to himself in public, or the crappy job he does shaving his brittle, impossible hair.

She says, "You can't wear wool in June."

He looks at the suit, then at the clock on the dresser. He says, "Is that a rule? Do people know this?"

"I think so. What about that plaid Brooks Brothers suit to be safe? You should wear that more."

He blinks. He has small embedded eyes in an open, leonine face and a widow's peak that, along with his statistics major, inspired his college nickname, the Count, which Jess called him in the early years. Lately, as though they've come full circle, she has again begun thinking of him as the Count.

He says, "The pant leg caught fire, remember? At that luau wedding?"

She makes a screwy face and turns up on her side. Her nightie slips and because of the chill (the marine layer hasn't burned off yet), she pulls the comforter over herself, afraid it looks like she's hiding her body from him. She can't decide if this is awkward or sad or neither or both. First of the month he will move into a studio with cardboard walls, but within walking distance of work. She wonders how long it'll be before, when he visits, he'll look strange sitting on their furniture.

He tears the dry-cleaning wrap off three dress shirts: a white one, a gray one, the third French blue, and holds the gray one to his chest. Over the breast pocket, there's a grease stain the size of a silver dollar. She motions him over, touches and smells the spot, and sees stapled inside the collar a typed note like in a fortune cookie. *Special Care was put into the garment but the SPOTS or STAINS can never be removed! We warn you so you may realize that it has never been overlooked.* She rips the tag off and hands it to the Count.

Since his company went casual a few years back, the Count's formal wardrobe is out of shape. Not that it matters. If your actuary doesn't show up looking like he climbed out of a Dumpster, he's probably second-tier—this is a line Jess uses at parties when she goes into her routine about actuaries and clothes; the time he came home from an interview with his pants gored in the seat and his boxers showing and how can you not notice the breeze? While people laugh, he reminds them how Jess exaggerates, that in fact the tear was barely noticeable.

Outside a car pulls up. The Count peeks through the blinds, looks back frazzled. "The cab's here."

She tells him, "He'll wait. We can do this."

The Count frowns and gets into the white shirt. The tiny buttons slip through his fingers like ice chips. How you calm him when he gets like this is, you put a pencil in his hand; half noticing, he'll take it and twirl it on his fingers like a toy helicopter blade. He twists his arm around and stands so she can button his cuffs as she has done every work morning for eleven years. She always makes it last longer than it has to, and it feels like the last thing that will ever happen.

Before the sun came up, she called in sick.

He fans his ties out over the bruise-blue cotton sheet. The comforter crackles as Jess sits up, starts sorting through them. They feel exquisite slipping through her fingers, like the skins of exotic snakes—silver diamonds on black, orange and purple octagons, one with lightning bolt patterns they bought on the way to a wedding.

Outside, the cabbie honks. Every time the Count leaves now, even to go for milk, she feels everything coming apart and by the time he comes home, she's ready to tell any lie that will make things work. Then they stand in the dining room hugging—one of them holding the mail—saying nothing, taking back nothing. She wonders how tough they are, really. Now she understands why even atrocious couples stay together as long as they do. She thinks about moving to Chicago. She has family there, but not the kind that will do her any good. On her last visit, her wrecking ball of a brother nearly killed himself driving drunk down a flight of stairs. She stood on his porch watching, nothing to do but watch, matter-of-fact as she is now.

Out of the muddle she slides a blue silk tie with green Grinch-who-stole-Christmas heads all over it. He wears it once a year, to his office Christmas party. "This is actually the best one," she says.

"I can't wear that," he says.

"But it is the best one."

"It's a good tie," he says.

At last year's party, Jess was talking to the new transfer when his wife butted in and said, *Is he boring you yet?* Jess stared at the woman, appalled, and went on about her the whole ride home: "To call him boring, in front of everyone!" She said *boring* was the worst thing you could call someone. It meant you were furniture. It meant you didn't count. The Count drove and listened and said maybe the man *was* boring. But think about it, Jess said, to be boring to your wife, when you had kids, and once you got deep down in the routine, wasn't every marriage the same? He said every marriage was not the same. She said no, she knew they weren't, but did he know what she meant? Three weeks later, on their twelfth anniversary, they started talking about splitting up.

The ties are in bad shape. Each one has threads dangling or discolorations as though it's been sitting in the garage for ten years. They seem, the ties, to be disintegrating somehow.

She tells him he'll have to buy a tie in the airport. "I mean it. This is important." She has to tell him this explicitly; he really doesn't know.

There are footsteps on the walk, then the doorbell, then someone pounding on the screen door. The Count pulls the blinds—from their bed they have a view of the front door; their little house, their second house, built in a dogleg pattern—and she sees the cabbie back down off the steps without looking behind him. There's one less step than you'd think and she flinches, thinking he'll trip, but he doesn't. He comes up, looms in the bedroom window, black stubble on his chin that makes him look impatient or cross. The Count gestures he'll be out in a minute but the cabbie looks past him, to Jess, in her tank top, with ties spread in her lap and all around her on the bed. The Count knocks on the window and says, "*Please* wait in the car. She's sick," but his voice seems to get trapped in the glass.

Jess says, "That was weird."

He turns. "I don't know why I said that." Earlier, when he was shaving, she heard over the running water pills shaking in a pill bottle. Last week sometime he emptied all the tranquilizers out of her bottle until there were only three left. Now, when she takes one, he replaces it from wherever he stashed the rest so there are always only three. Not enough to kill her must be the idea. She wonders what he will do about this when he moves out. She braces herself, or tries to; for the moment she picks up the bottle and finds it is again full of pills.

The white shirt's missing a button and the blue one, the last one, has a queer streak over the shoulder blade, like silver spray paint. He says he doesn't care, he's out of shirts and out of time. He says, "I'll keep my jacket on."

As he ties his Grinch tie, they watch each other in the mirror on the back of the door. Transposed, the Count's usually friendly face appears warped and mean, like one eye socket is sliding down his cheek, the mouth and nose out of alignment. She remembers on their second or third date admitting she'd noticed the Count in the halls but was put off by his suits. "I think it was the color," she'd said. "That old-fashioned brown. There's something eerie about it." In the candlelight, he stopped chewing and looked at her. He set his fork and knife down. Then he told her he'd gotten all his suits from a widow who lived next door, whose husband had died after fifty years selling insurance. The Count was just out of school then, rotating the two cheap suits he could afford, so he agreed to come over and have a look, which he did, a week later, carrying an empty suitcase. "You couldn't breathe in there, and she only had one light on up high in the closet. So she'd pull one of the suits out to give me and she wouldn't let go. I'd have to physically tug it away from her." He said in the months following, whenever he wore one of the suits he'd get the feeling the widow was watching from across the street, or the window of a bus.

The dead man's suits. That was the first thing Jess had loved about him: walking over to the widow's apartment with an empty suitcase. It was so innocent and logical and goofy. When she helped him pick out suits later, as his wife, she felt the same way she felt shopping for herself, and she began to think marriage could make a couple into something more than the sum of its parts.

She notices now he's covering his hip with his hand. "What've you got there?"

He says, "You don't want to know."

But she insists and he moves his hand and reveals a three-inch tear where the pocket liner's showing through. She falls back on the bed and flops her arms out in comic exhaustion, and he laughs. In the nightstand she fishes for a black Sharpie and tells him hold still. His hips shimmy while she stretches the liner and starts coloring it in and she pictures telling their friends about this at a party—this rushed, ridiculous morning with all his clothes spotted or ripped, and she looks up then and sees the cab driver at the window, fogging the glass and tapping his watch, and the actuary's eyes are closed and his hands are upturned as if to check for rain, and she realizes there will be no party. What is happening now as it is happening is all there is. And this, she understands, was always true.

## The Stuntman

Jess's brother called last night and told her to come by because there was something he wanted to show her. She sits now on his porch swing drinking gas-station coffee, waiting. She doesn't knock or ring so as not to overstate her interest in what is going on inside his house. She's here because he called, no more, no less, and she tries to be clear—if only for her own sake—how far she is in and how far she is out. Eventually someone will come out: his hangdog son, his rubber daughter, his irresponsibly loyal wife.

She hears the latch and then the door and then backward-schlepping feet. A sound like metal fingernails that she can't quite place. Then a mountain bike bucks through the front door as through a starting gate. Her brother used to race BMX when he was a kid—she used to go and watch; the whole family would go.

He is forty years old now, hunched over the handlebars, cocked in flight. Jess hasn't seen him on a bike in twenty-five years. Is that true? As he rumbles across the porch the planks send a thrumming through her legs, her feet. He grips the handlebars as he approaches the stairs. These are concrete and so steep you feel like you're going to fall walking *up* them. The woman who owned the house before broke both hips falling down these stairs and then died inside a maze of stacked tomato soup cans.

He is pedaling, picking up what speed he can in the feet from the door to the top stair. He doesn't see Jess, though it's practically noon so he'll be well into his morning-maintenance twelve-pack. The wife told Jess once he has to drink until one in order to write his name legibly. But write his name on what?

The front door yaws. She wonders where Daisy, his dog, is.

He used to win a lot racing BMX; they'd pass his trophies around on the car ride home. After one race, a scout hired him to stunt-ride in a movie. It turned out to be the largest grossing film that year. He was twelve years old, making $125 a day. The movie was about a boy who uncovers a damaging government secret and rides all over his subdivision evading the feds on his bike. On their father's dresser is a framed snapshot of her brother on the set, sitting on his bike drinking a Coke, and when Jess tries to think about the film her mind goes to that picture and stops.

As his wheel drops off the first stair, a car turns onto the street. It's a creaking sedan with no hubs and no front license plate. The driver guns it up the brick road, his body jerking and jiggling like a bumped bowl of soup. Beneath the visor, she sees a set mouth in a humorless face. If her brother makes it down the stairs, the car will hit him. The vectors are in motion, she sees how they will intersect, and there is nothing she can do. It won't help to scream or stand, though she does, she gets to her feet, like at the races.

Jess watched the movie once, at the theater, with friends she can picture in bits and pieces but can no longer name. She doesn't know why she never watched it again. It never occurred to her until now, when something has happened to time and she seems able to play full conversations in the time it takes her brother to kamikaze down the stairs. She read somewhere this happens to people who jump off bridges: the ones who survive say you fall forever, you think about any- and everything. Did her parents see the film? They must have. Her brother once paid a babysitter $3 to strip. Even when someone pulls the snapshot out, they talk about the fact of his being in the movie, but no one talks about the movie itself.

Down her brother goes.

The front tire punching into each stair.

*Boof.*

And then the wait. And then—

*Boof.*

Last night Jess stood listening as he talked into the answering machine. Sometimes he dupes her into thinking he's sober—speaking calmly, carefully—and she always regrets picking up the phone. It's a hugely irritating *wejusttalkedaboutthat yeswedid whyare-youyelling yesyouare Ihavetogonow I'mgoingnow.* Chances are he doesn't remember calling and inviting her here.

However this ends up, she came. He asked her to come and she came.

That's something she will have.

Fourth or fifth stair from the bottom, the front tire crooks at a hard angle and her brother pops off the seat heading over the handlebars except he holds on rodeo-style as the bike torques maybe 160 degrees and then drops down the stairs backward. She hears the bounce of rubber, the rattle of the chain, the meaty whip of his body landing on the sidewalk. After a weird delay, his skull knocks the cement.

The sedan speeds by. She watches the driver do a double take at her brother. The car lags as he realizes his life almost changed, then accelerates greedy with the news that it didn't.

For one scene, her brother rode down a spiral staircase only inches wider than the handlebars. Years later he said the stunt was insane and he couldn't believe they stood by with coffee and doughnuts and watched him do it. In another scene, one that made the cut, his bike got away from him as speeding police cars chased him over a hill—he skidded across the gravel as stunt drivers squirreled and spun to avoid running him over.

She walks to the top of the stairs and looks down. Her brother's on the sidewalk with the bike on top of him and his arm shot through the frame. By the angle of his outturned foot, she guesses his ankle or knee has snapped. Somewhere Jess read that drunkenness promotes elasticity in the limbs and she thinks of the once a year she sees him and he smells worse than the year before and when he rolls up his sleeves or snags a pant leg, there's some new grisly scar like he lives in prison.

Where is the dog?

What it is about the movie, she thinks now, has to do with his having been a stuntman so he didn't have to memorize lines or understand the plot. Everything a stuntman does is real because there's no such thing as a physical lie. You can't mean or not mean falling or throwing a punch or even a fake punch. So the plot was the plot and the script was the script, but her brother rode down real stairs and real speeding cars almost ran him over for real, and that's why when the snapshot comes out no one talks about the film.

As he gets to his feet, he looks like a man trying to wake himself out of a dream, which is how he looks most of the time. He touches his hairline, comes away with blood that he stares at, not seeming to know what it is. His legs buckle and he swings his arms out to catch his balance. He's wearing docksiders and a red knit sweater with golfers on it. Nowadays he wears whatever people give him for Christmas. Drugstore watches. Yacht club jackets. The docksiders he wore for six months with the stuffing still in the toes.

He is somehow getting back on the bike.

It occurs to her this is the very thing he called her here to see.

He goes ten shaky feet and then swerves, his front tire shoaling along the curb. He hugs a lamppost to keep from going over, then steadies himself and pushes off down the street. Eventually he angles around the corner and is gone.

All of this takes maybe a minute.

Daisy crawls out from under the porch and trots over to the bottom of the stairs, her nails clicking on the sidewalk, her sandy head hung as in anticipation of a blow. She starts sniffing around in all different places, then homes in on a patch of blood. She lolls her tongue like she'll lick it, but loses interest before she does and trots up the stairs into the house.

And now Jess wonders if she got it wrong about the chase, and maybe he was *supposed* to skid in front of the cop cars; maybe that was part of the stunt.

## Big Mac

When Jess's father vacations, he takes a Guinness on tap in the afternoon. He says canned Guinness doesn't taste the same, but she thinks whiling away an hour in a pub reminds him of living in England after the war. His son-in-law, the Count, likes Guinness, too, and because she doesn't like drinking or bars in the middle of the day, they both like dragging her along: taking her hostage is part of the fun. Her father says, "All in favor—" and the Count raises his hand and they laugh because Jess's vote, in her father's words, "doesn't mean diddly-squat."

Today they have driven south to Coronado, a peninsula ten miles north of the Mexican border. Tropical chic, the place crawls with money and military and tourists in rental cars. They found the bar in a phone book while Jess was in a store trying on shoes. There's a grid of mirrored tiles behind the bar and paneling like inside a trailer—the same ersatz decor Jess remembers from the air force bases of her childhood. Coincidentally, or because they feel at home here (as surely her father does), the few customers are jar-heads from one of the bases nearby.

On a TV mounted over their table, a reporter stands in front of a grounded fleet of helicopters talking into a microphone. The sound is turned off but her father watches with his watery gray eyes as though he were lip-reading. After a minute he says into his beer, "Apaches," and right then they hear live helicopters in the distance, flying in twos over the bay. Her husband and father decide it's a Memorial Day exercise.

Then they're talking about helicopters, about flying and drinking. Her father says that to fly after drinking anything at all is a court-marshal offense. The Count sips his Guinness and nods as though this is information he needs to have.

"Then again," her father says, twisting a drink stirrer, "it can't always be helped."

After twelve years, her husband still can't tell when her father's winding up to tell a story or a joke, so he always looks doubly pleased, snuck-up on, when he catches on late.

Her father begins describing a mission he flew one night after drinking at the Officers' Club. His buddy Bill Roderick responded to the call first, flying out to rescue a marine stranded in the jungle. Demonstrating with his hands, her father explains how when a helicopter can't land, they lower the medic into the jungle on a ca-ble and winch. Only that night, when Roderick got out there, his medic didn't check to see that the basket was hooked to the cable, and the medic dropped out of the chopper like a stone. Her father spirals two fingers through the air, whistling, then he looks up and says, "Yoo-hoo." This is what he says when someone does something stupid. *Yoo-hoo.* "Now the medic's down there, too, and Roderick's got no basket, so he flies back to base." He taps the table, sits back while they work this out in their heads. "We're the soberest ones in the OC—which ain't saying much—so they want us to go."

Only in recent years will her father tell stories about the war. They come off more like dark episodes of *M\*A\*S\*H*—guys pulling one another's wisdom teeth at four a.m. in a hut, blubbering drunk. During his second tour, her father would send her and her brother adventure stories he recorded on cassettes in the voice of Big Mac, a supposedly fictional helicopter-rescue pilot based, they eventually realized, on their father himself. *Hope you kids are buckled in, it's going to be a rough one.* At the time, they lived with their grandmother, who bathed them in the kitchen sink with the dirty pots. They didn't understand where their father was; Jess thought Big Mac was an invention until high school, when she wrote a report on Vietnam. In one memoir, a soldier described waiting for a dustoff after he stepped on a landmine. When he heard the chopper in the distance (one of his men had just handed him his arm), he said his *soul went up* and traced its path across the sky.

Her father won't tell stories now when her brother's around because her brother interrupts and one-ups him with some questionable story of his own from Desert Storm. *You think that's bad*, he'll say. She doesn't remember when her brother made the leap from bullshit artist to mythomaniac. She knew you could drink yourself useless, but she didn't know you could drink yourself delusional.

At the bar, a marine in his early twenties pumps back a measure of whiskey. He watches himself drink in the mirror with what seems to her the nerve of a much older man. She has the impression he is listening to her father's story. Her father's medic is in the basket now, dangling twenty feet above the ground over where the other medic went down. The cable has run out and the chopper can't go any lower without descending into the trees and near-certain death. As they hover there deciding what to do, the dangling man jumps.

Her husband coughs into his hand, incredulous. "Now *your* medic's down there, too?" He almost left the house today with his shirt on inside out. She caught him at the door, but right-side out the shirt almost looks worse. The collar's pulling loose and the orange stripes have faded unevenly, but what the hell, he flew to the biggest meeting of his life in a Grinch tie. Last night when they were all dressing for dinner, she saw him in the hall in the dark all turned around, trying to button his shirt-cuff buttons himself. *I'm right here,* she wanted to say, *I'm always right here.*

The Count pulls three golf tees out of his pocket and sets them on the table. If not for Jess, they would golf from sunup to sundown, these two. When they come home, she can hear them in the driveway talking and laughing, their golf clubs clacking, their spikes on the walk.

Her brother went golfing with her father once. He pulled all of the clubs out of the bag except the driver and putter then filled it with cans of Coors Light. On the fifth hole he took a swing at a squirrel. On the eighth, he stretched out under a tree, pulled his hat brim down, and told her dad to come back for him when it was time to go.

The Count asks what it would take for a chopper to go down.

Her father picks up a tee, feels the point with his finger. "Knick the blade, that's it."

There's something wrong with this story. Jess remembers this story now. Her father won a medal he didn't want for this mission— her mother showed it to her; he'd never taken it out of the box. In her mother's version of the story, when they get to the drop site, the Vietcong open fire and her father's medic *refuses* to go down. As they hover there arguing, the copilot presses a gun to the medic's head, gives him an ultimatum. Her father leaves this out, makes the guy sound brave or like a nitwit for jumping when the cable runs out, but if you know about the gun, everything's different, like maybe the guy's thinking, *Better down than up.*

The bartender refills the marine's whiskey, freely pouring like she's in her own kitchen. Each customer acts as though he's the only one she's talking to.

Her father scoots back from the table and fumbles, fitting his earbud in. From his face she can tell it's her brother calling. As he slips out the front door, he blots out the sun for a second then ducks away, and she sees a beach bum weaving through the stalled traffic on a Schwinn cruiser, front tire wobbling, his hand held up. In little bursts, her father's voice carries in from the street. She hears him say, *You're in fantasyland.*

The Count gives her a bittersweet half smile. Her father doesn't know they're splitting up. They'd intended to tell him during his visit this weekend, but the night before he flew in, her brother was arrested for roughing up his wife—he claims he was defending himself and the cops have pictures that show thumbprint bruises on his upper arm. She knows when her father's repeating something her brother said, because he takes on her brother's mannerisms and tics; he says, *YouknowwhatImean?* which he never says otherwise.

When Jess picked her father up at the airport, he was the last one off the plane. In the milky light of the terminal he looked so old she looked past him, then back when no one else came out of the gangway. He was watching his feet, adjusting his grip on his attaché—an expensive bag now duct-taped in places—his hair scalding white on top and his cheeks deflated and worn like a purse in a thrift shop. Before he spotted her she saw him take a deep breath, then blow it through his cheeks as if reminding himself how to breathe.

He breathes like that now as he crosses to the table, tucking his cell phone into his pocket. He takes a drink and says, "You know the kicker, the first guy called us out there"—he grits his teeth and whispers—"for a *fucking* sprained ankle."

The Count makes exactly the right tragicomic face. Sometimes Jess thinks to pry her husband from her father will be the cruelest part of the divorce. She thinks of the night she first brought him home, cross-country, a few weeks after their engagement. Her father opened his best bottle of wine and made a polite but generic toast that embarrassed her because it revealed how little he knew about their lives. Neither man was big on small talk. But her father liked that the young man was an actuary and they started talking about health care, first in stops and starts, then sitting forward with their wine sloshing in their goblets. Long after everyone else was asleep, Jess heard them still going at it on the patio, one minute arguing hotly, then laughing big laughs. In the morning they went golfing on two hours' sleep.

Now her father looks into the bottom of his glass and says he can't explain how they made it, the chopper settling into the trees, the rotor blades clipping at leaves and twigs. "A miracle, every inch."

Her husband tilts his glass and looks in as if to see what her father sees. When they talk about splitting up, it seems like he wants to stop it and she wants to stop it but neither of them does anything to stop it, and it's hard to make sense of that.

The bartender brings a second round of Guinness. When her father opens his wallet to pay, a thick wad of $100 bills expands like gills. The worse things get with her brother, the more cash her father carries, like at any moment her brother might fuck up so bad her father will want to leave the country. For months now, all Jess sees when she thinks about her brother is his drunken dive down the stairs. On the freeway or staring at her computer she watches him tumble and flip on the bike over and over. She's cut the reel into frames that she places before her mind one at a time, snapshot-wise—the car racing by, Daisy sniffing the blood.

Her father unfolds two bills and hands one to the Count. They shield the backs of the bills and begin a game of liar's poker. Her father says, "Five fives."

The Count smiles, then chuckles. "Eight fives."

Jess says, "I don't understand. If you know the chopper's going to crash, it doesn't make sense to go down. Then everyone's dead."

Her father and husband look up from their bills and Jess realizes she should've kept her mouth shut out of respect. She forgets herself these days. Her father says, "You don't leave a man on the ground."

"Yeah," she says, "But why not go back to base and let them figure it out?"

Her husband says, "There's no one else."

Her father repeats, "You can't leave a man on the ground."

In her periphery, Jess sees a snatch of movement at the bar. When she looks up she sees the marine's arms shoot out, spiraling to keep him from falling off his stool, like someone's shoved him in the chest, which no one did, he just lost his balance. Then he's on his ass, blown five feet from the bar. He starts to get up, but instead leans back in the grime and the beer footprints, clasps his hands on his stomach, stares at the ceiling. Not hurt, embarrassed only. Or tired. But it's the way her husband and father react: standing, then sitting back down like everything's under control, when nothing's changed. She thinks about last Thanksgiving when her brother drank everything in the house—a bottle of Baileys, wine that'd gone bad—then said something about their mother that caused her father to stab his fork into his pie and launch out of his chair. "One more word—"

Her brother stood, ramped up. "And what?"

Her father had five inches and fifty pounds over her brother, but that was just one more thing he had to pay for. "And I'll show you to the other side of the county, that's what."

It was the old-fashioned wording that got her. She pushed the Count to intervene. "Do something," she hissed.

"Do what?" he said. "What can I do?" He took a step forward, two steps. But edging in on her father and brother, he looked like a guy at a dance trying to cut in on a couple in love.

She asks her father now, "What did he say?"

He looks at her like if she says another word he'll fall asleep in his soup. "Who say?"

She drops her eyes. She says her brother's name. Her father starts to talk and then makes a gesture she doesn't understand. The Count glances down from the TV, where credits are rolling over the footage of the helicopter fleet. If it were a year or even six months ago, he would be appealing to her, trying to help her keep her cool, now there is only relief that it's no longer his problem, compassion for how much lonelier it will be to deal with. Last

Thanksgiving was one of the few times they couldn't find, in whispers at bedtime, some cruel but important way to joke the situation into hiding. Last Thanksgiving was serious, a turning point. Her brother's feet were like sledgehammers as he stomped across the kitchen, rolled up, and bucked into her father's chest. Her father gazed down, arms at his side. Jess felt he would let her brother beat him to death before he raised a hand against this miserable man, his son, but she knew that wasn't true. As the Count inched closer, she saw it'd have to get nasty before he did anything. She yelled, *"Why are you doing this to him?"* realizing as she did she didn't even know who she was talking to, and all three men turned and looked like she might as well have been the mailman, and couldn't she see they knew what they were doing.

# Creative Writing Instructor
# Evaluation Form

1. The instructor is organized.

   ☐ Strongly Agree
   ☐ Agree
   ☐ Undecided
   ☐ Disagree
   ☐ Strongly Disagree

2. The instructor seems generally knowledgeable, at least about the subject she teaches.

   ☐ Strongly Agree
   ☐ Agree
   ☐ Undecided
   ☐ Disagree
   ☐ Strongly Disagree

3. The instructor is for the most part coherent and sober during her lectures.

   ☐ Strongly Agree
   ☐ Hard to tell; she often has a "cold" and tells us not to approach her desk
   ☐ Coherent and sober unrelated in this case
   ☐ Disagree
   ☐ Strongly Disagree

4. The instructor wears a bra to class.

☐ Strongly Agree
☐ There are straps visible at times
☐ Undecided
☐ Least of her worries
☐ Very least of her worries

5. The instructor mentions the director of the Creative Writing program in class.

☐ Strongly Agree
☐ Agree
☐ Undecided/Not Listening
☐ Disagree
☐ Strongly Disagree

6. When I used to picture myself in college, I pictured my education in the hands of people like this instructor.

☐ Strongly Agree
☐ When it looked like I'd have to attend a JC
☐ While masturbating only
☐ None of the Above
☐ I'm a legacy and never pictured myself anywhere after high school

7. The instructor mentions the director of the Creative Writing program in class:

☐ An Appropriate Amount
☐ An Excessive Amount
☐ With obvious feelings of longing/regret
☐ While toying with shirt buttons
☐ In a way that I don't think Jim would appreciate

8. The instructor does appear to *want* to teach us things.

  ☐ Strongly Agree
  ☐ Last week we learned that rabbits have 360° vision . . . ?
  ☐ It's just really hard to explain what happens in here
  ☐ She tells us to *be bold* a lot, if that counts
  ☐ And some monkeys want to fly

9. The instructor's grammar and vocabulary are not what I had hoped given her vocation, though she tries to compensate for her lapses and indiscretions by, for instance, sometimes speaking in a British accent.

  ☐ The instructor makes up words
  ☐ Most of the instructor's words sound real
  ☐ A lot of terminology seems to have been derived from the instructor's name
  ☐ I'm dubious on her best day
  ☐ The instructor is illiterate or insane

10. When the instructor discusses very sexy male "fictional" characters, they often resemble the director of the Creative Writing program.

  ☐ The director should consider himself *a wanted man*
  ☐ The director has nothing to worry about
  ☐ Her sexiest male characters are usually women
  ☐ Her sexiest male characters are usually animals
  ☐ I don't understand where this form is going

11. The instructor is clear and forthcoming about her publications, which have been for the most part verifiable.

  ☐ Strongly Agree
  ☐ Agree

☐ Can't find her on Amazon or Google
☐ All the links to her stories go to error pages
☐ One of "the instructor's" stories appears in a Raymond Carver book?

12. The instructor seemed better today.

☐ The moral atmosphere of the class seems appropriate to the subject matter
☐ I'm not a very sexual person so maybe I just didn't notice?
☐ I'm not always comfortable with the way the instructor looks at/touches me
☐ I wish the instructor had office hours during the day, at school

13. The instructor concentrates on student work and does not make us "workshop" her novel in her living room late, late at night.

☐ Sometimes we meet at Joe's Tavern instead
☐ What's *late*?
☐ She encourages us to come to her house pretty much whenever
☐ Some students seem to maybe have keys to her house?

14. At these workshops, the instructor does not serve alcohol to underage students.

☐ She provides mixers only
☐ She doesn't *force* us to drink
☐ Unless we're playing I Never
☐ She tells us writers aren't well-adjusted people, and that's OK

15. When the instructor does mention the director of the Creative Writing program in class, she seems to understand that he did what he did for his kids, and it's not what he wanted, and he's not just feeding her some bullshit line.

☐ Agree
☐ She's clearly not over Jim and never ever will be
☐ She seems skeptical, to say the least
☐ She often expresses such sentiments as "He can [suck it/ blow me]"
☐ She reviles him and tells us he couldn't write his way out of a paper bag

16. The instructor looks like she might be willing to #&%@ a few of us.

☐ Name: _____
☐ Make/model of car: _____

17. And yet, the instructor's ass is starting to sag a bit, no?

☐ Strongly Agree
☐ She doesn't make the best wardrobe choices
☐ Not really an ass man/woman, myself
☐ Nothing a little biking wouldn't help

18. OK but realistically, I'd give the instructor four, five years before she really starts looking her age.

☐ If that
☐ Looks her age already
☐ I'm not attracted to women
☐ Given her lifestyle, she seems to be holding up

19. I know who you are, Mr. Pierce. Everyone else quit filling out this stupid form long ago because everyone else understands this course is an automatic A. Listen, maybe you had a wild night together—hat's off. Good for you, Mr. Pierce. But take it for what is was. I am a noted American author, Mr. Pierce. You're a junior at a third-tier commuter school—you think this is going to end well for you? Do you? You little freak? (Fill in the APPROPRIATE bubble from the AVAILABLE bubbles:)

    ☐ Strenuously Disagree this will end well for me

20. How'd that feel, Pierce? You like that?

    ☐ Yes I liked it a lot, Director, please bend me over and do it again

21. And *you're* the hack and the walking cliché, Mr. Pierce, <u>YOU</u>!!!

    ☐ I'm not the one who put that on your car
    ☐ But I know who did
    ☐ And she's sorry
    ☐ As far as I can tell
    ☐ She's really very sorry

22. Fuck you, Pierce, I will have the woman again.

    ☐ Agree

23. On the last question, I meant *the director* will have her again, not me, Mr. Pierce.

    ☐ Passionately Agree

24. Fill in the goddamn bubble, Pierce.

    ☐ Agree on my mother's grave

25. Sorry about your mother, Pierce.

☐ Thank you but it's still no excuse for my impertinence

26. I don't know why I'm acting this way. I guess she made me feel special.

☐ Painfully Agree

27. I know she did, Pierce, that's part of her game.

☐ But it hurts

28. Of course it hurts, but don't be an idiot, Pierce. She might look inviting to you now, but think about it: Are you going to ferry her to rehab when you're trying to study for your Portuguese final? No? What about menopause—you ready for that? It's right around the corner, Pierce. You're young, why tie yourself down to a woman like that?

☐ Agree

29. The director of Creative Writing is a better writer than all the greatest writers of all time combined.

☐ Most Humbly Agree

30. Just fill it in, Pierce.

■ Agree

31. Sweet mercy, what a relief.

■ Strongly Agree

# You're That Guy

A novella

# 1

Outside Winnemucca were the mosquitoes. Russ was driving with Eckhart in the passenger seat watching the air around the car seem to fill with wiring, or wiry webbing. There was a nick on the windshield, a handful of nicks—then across the glass a sheet of bursting mosquitoes unfurled like rain, one of those hard sudden showers that seems to rip in from the future, the one you know is coming. Russ slammed to a stop right there on I-80 and they sat in Russ's girlfriend Jackie's truck. They sat, they listened—*plat. Plat-plat-plat*—they stared into the outpouring and it did seem, at times, as though they were staring directly into the source, but there was no one place.

At some point Russ asked if mosquitoes were one of the plagues.

"There are gnats," Eckhart said. "And flies. I'm not sure about mosquitoes." Personally Eckhart was wavering on whether they could be mosquitoes at all, a swarm this dense and deep, miles in every direction. If for some reason they had to step outside of the car they would have no choice but to *inhale* mosquitoes in order to get air into their lungs.

Russ looked over and said, "It's you they've come for. It's you doing this."

It was well past three a.m. and they were nowhere near Salt

Lake City, their destination, though their new immediate aim was getting out of Nevada in Russ's girlfriend Jackie's Ranger, since there was some fuckwit loose on I-80 in the same car as theirs— same model, make, color, everything—who'd tried to rob a casino earlier that night. Twice now Nevada HP had pulled Russ and Eckhart over by mistake; with shotguns trained, all business, on the sides of their respective forward-facing skulls that they had been instructed not to move, the safeties off, while Dispatch tried to convince the officers they had the wrong guys. *But we've already got these two,* they seemed to want to say, *why can't we keep these two?*

They'd driven 650 miles from Oceanside, en route to Salt Lake, Russ's current home, 350 miles farther east. Initially Russ had driven down just to visit, but after taking in Eckhart's surroundings—the three-foot bong, the lesser-foot but still overlarge other bong, the dying plants, the dead plants stuffed in the trash, the trash bags lined up by the door, the 7UP can that had been dropped and left rolling in the spill, and as a tipping point, the physics book Eckhart had been copying out longhand—after fully processing the scene, Russ's "visit" turned into his ordering Eckhart to pack, saying, "I'm getting you out of here before you smoke yourself," adding, "We stop for sirens, blackjack, and gas. That's it."

What had happened was that Eckhart, in the wake (following the wake) of his father's death, had taken a gig house- and dog-sitting for a marine shipping out to Iraq—walk the dog, Brutus, water the flowers and plants—that was only supposed to last a month. Like the war, one month turned into two, two into six, six into a year, and instead of looking for more regular work, in what was basically the opposite of looking for work, Eckhart spent more and more time with the neighbor, Curtis, a licensed marijuana baker for dispensaries in the area, debating the virtues of working versus not working. Since Eckhart didn't really need the monthly pittance Jeff sent, he used the money to pay a kid down the street to mow the lawn and walk Brutus and such.

When Russ drove down, it'd been closing in on two years that

Eckhart had lived in the marine's house. Inwardly he'd begun to think of himself as OR CURRENT RESIDENT, like it said on the mail.

He still didn't know what he felt or thought about his father's death because it seemed to take all his energy creating the amount of emptiness required to even hold the naked fact in hand. The fact of his father's death, but also the decade leading up to it, with his father living on the streets in San Francisco before he washed up dead in the bay. He made space to grieve, but nothing happened. Not even the house-sitting helped, living in someone else's world. Vaguely Eckhart had felt the urgency drain from his days with Brutus and Curtis, days that became less and less distinguishable from one another, and so more and more riddled with episodes resembling déjà vu that were in fact Eckhart or Curtis or Brutus exactly repeating himself in gesture or word ("It's like everyone's afraid of dying alone, but what do you mean by alone, you know? What if there's a nurse in the room?") in the same light at the same time of day as the day before, which Eckhart had to admit was soothing, feeling like his arms and legs were slowly filling with sand. Then there was the paradoxical stranglehold of how the less Eckhart officially had to do, the less time he seemed to have, so that in practice it took longer not to do things than to do things.

He saw plain as day how you could sit getting quietly steam-rolled by time. After Curtis left, Eckhart could spend hours on the couch with Brutus down on his end, the two of them watching (Eckhart really felt Brutus, too, was watching) the grasshopper that was always on the wall of the den. Eckhart somehow never saw the grasshopper in transit—it was either there in its spot on the wall or not in its spot—but in his mind, the grasshopper *sauntered* in and out of the house through the french doors. For an hour this grasshopper sat in one spot, unmoving, a stuck green dart, then with wild, arrogant pointlessness, it suddenly dialed itself fifteen or fifty degrees clockwise, stopped again, and perched for a new miscellaneous amount of time at its new angle in space. There was something about Eckhart that made it impossible to ignore this grasshopper, its sudden idiot urgency, when there was no reason to move or not move.

Perched there.

For fifteen miles they nosed along with mosquitoes pouring out of the sky, the stream steady and meaty and thick. Then, near the end of the swarm, the mosquitoes—the fattened calves hanging back—started spilling motherfucking blood. Russ jerked flat against his seat when the heavy ones hit, and it was real blood, whatever or whomever they'd sucked it out of, so it was like the windshield was a living thing being shot up with machine-gun fire, with Russ and Eckhart watching from inside. When the buildup got bad, Eckhart pulled on two jackets and wrapped a shirt around his head and reached into the onslaught and doused the windshield with water, then with the Fat Tire beer Russ was smuggling back for friends who couldn't get it full strength in Utah. Inside the cab, Russ cranked Christian metal because it was the only station that came in, and because it was the right thing to do.

Eckhart's father—that had been the big thing taking up space in Eckhart's head and life and doubtless in Russ's, too, since he was the closest Russ had had to a father. Russ's own parents had died of two different cancers within a few years of each other, when Russ was a baby, so his grandmother raised him. Moving from a slum in St. Louis or Cincinnati came Lou, with her third-grade education, into a neighborhood with Nobel Prize winners—she called them Noble Surprise winners, which made Russ crazy. (It's a *prize*, not a *sur*prise, he would say dejectedly, to which Lou answered, "It had to be a surprise at some point. They weren't born knowing.") Russ claimed he'd decided on graduate school the week of the Indonesian tsunami, when you heard the word *tsunami* fifty times a day on TV and still there was Lou, pronouncing the silent *t*. *Tttt-sunami*. Which was actually hard to do.

It was Eckhart's sister, Lucy, who tried keeping tabs on their father in San Francisco, driving up and down that crooked city in her rusted Volvo. *I haven't seen him in a couple weeks*, she'd say. (*It's a big city*, Eckhart would reply.) *I have a bad feeling*, she'd say. (*You always have a bad feeling*, Eckhart would reply.) Then the inevitable *What is wrong with you that you don't care?* Eckhart didn't know what was wrong. Sometimes he thought it was that he read, or tried to, lacking the training when the math got dense, their father's work. A prominent game theorist in the '70s, their father later turned his increasingly obsessive attention to problems like the most efficient way to stack fruit (pretty much the way they do it in any market) and the law of truly large numbers, which showed how, when proportions were thrown unduly off in a system, the improbable became common. All Lucy seemed to know about their father's work was that he had a math theorem named after him and some weird ideas about money. When the money turned up after the funeral—enough that their father could've lived comfortably indoors all the while—Lucy called it fuck you money. Then promptly hired a financial adviser.

Eckhart just stared at his inheritance blankly in his mind, watching it run down during his two unemployed years in Jeff's house. Sometimes he'd look down at Brutus, on his end of the couch, and say, *Money isn't real*. Brutus would look over, then down. *But the things it buys are real. Food is real.* There was something philosophical about Brutus's looks and attitude—he seemed to be actually thinking, and not just looking around like other dogs. It was because of Brutus, ultimately, that Eckhart signed on for the job at Jeff's. Specifically it was a chain of dogs coincidentally exactly resembling Brutus, who was an Airedale, an admittedly consistent-looking breed—the brunette legs and undersides, the sandy-blond saddle-shaped patch on the back, and curls like from a curling iron—but even so, Brutus in personality and everything was a dead ringer for Eckhart's childhood dog, Caesar, whose best friend (and eventually, as far as they could tell, lover) was yet a third Airedale in the scenario that lived down the block and was named, like the marine, Jeff.

Eckhart could go another six months without working. Then it would all finally be over.

At the first exit past the swarm they pulled in to scrape the windshield, a duty Eckhart assumed both because he was the one being rescued and because Russ had spied inside the shop a bank of quarter poker machines. That left Eckhart in the parking lot borrowing an SOS pad from a semi-hysterical woman who had climbed up onto the hood of the U-Haul she was driving, where she pushed her whole body up and down on the windshield like a devotee prostrating herself before an icon. "People told me, but I never listen," she'd say, sort of to Eckhart, sort of to the universe. "Salt Lake City. You know what's in Salt Lake City?" now addressing Eckhart directly. "Mountains and Mormons and no getting over or under either one."

People kept preparing Eckhart for Salt Lake, it seemed, the way they prepare you for an amusement park ride with a psychological element. When they were back on the road, Russ talked about a guy he knew there whose wife opened a stall at the farmers market for selling ceramic vaginas she'd made. He said she only sold one or two before they yanked her booth permit, and now the oeuvre was displayed about the couple's condo, and they entertained a lot, sitting among the vaginas "like botanists in a greenhouse." (Russ was a poet, so everything had to be like something else.)

Eckhart asked, "Are they all the same vagina?"

Russ said, "I think so."

"So she must use her own as a model."

"That's what most of us have decided."

Eckhart asked, "But you never got skunked enough to ask her outright?"

"Every time I see them," Russ said, "but she's too big of an oaf to give a straight answer." He glanced over. "This is what I'm saying: It's in the air there. And it's not going to look the way you think."

Eckhart had heard the same from Jeff's neighbor Curtis, who seemed to have lived everywhere for a few months and who warned Eckhart not to make the mistake with Salt Lake that people made with L.A., trying to turn a purgatory into a home. "Go, by all means go," Curtis said, "just keep your head on straight. When you're ready you'll start asking some reasonable questions like 'What's with all the duplexes?' That's when you'll know it's time to leave." Eckhart asked for clarification, but Curtis just explained what a duplex was. "It's like this place"—he threw a hand at the monochrome sky; he was forever complaining about the constant sun in Southern California, Curtis was—"every day, there it is like nothing could ever go wrong."

Curtis lived three doors down from Jeff, whom Eckhart had only met once in person before his deployment, then in e-mails over logistics. Jeff was from the south somewhere, bouncer-size, his voice swampy deep and low, his eyes deadpan blue. When Eckhart asked where he'd be stationed, Jeff tried to conceal a look of self-disgust, a look of making good on a mistake (he was a reservist who'd been called up, Eckhart later learned; a closet pacifist whose father and brothers and uncles were all in the service). "Stupid place," Jeff answered, looking directly at the ground, as if the ground had asked the question. Eckhart stalled on the phrasing that Jeff hadn't said *a stupid place*, just *stupid place*—you didn't forget a piece of tripped-up grammar like that. And you had to be there to know how a slow, southern giant could say this without sounding fruity, but he told Eckhart as he scratched enthusiastically under Brutus's chin that he sang the "Happy Birthday" song to Brutus every morning. "There's one more thing," Jeff said. Brutus loved the beach but knew how to work the window controls in the Jeep, so Eckhart should take side roads and keep the controls locked. A month later Jeff had shipped out, Eckhart moved in, and Curtis appeared with a plate of pot brownies.

"Howdy, neighbor."

Curtis was a more than decent baker. You wanted to keep eating

Curtis's Delectables for the taste, which was a problem. Customers were getting fat and way too high, which amused Curtis (the "complaints"), and moved him to adopt the tagline:

### Too Delicious for Its Purpose

Eckhart would make coffee while Curtis furnished the pot muffins or bear claws. He never came in, but stood outside the kitchen window philosophizing, talking in profile like a subway car operator.

Curtis had been writing a philosophy dissertation for fourteen years. He said it was already technically written in his head but would be destroyed if he tried to translate it into language. The only time Eckhart saw Curtis laugh was when he talked about Wittgenstein quitting philosophy to teach little kids, only to get run out of town for boxing a girl's ear. "Because she didn't understand him"—Curtis leaned forward, delivering his punch line with great care—"kid was like, eight. And her math teacher is Wittgenstein." This brought bona fide tears to the eyes of Curtis, who rolled his head back and yelled, "Those fucking duplexes!"

Curtis was able to steer 99 percent of all conversations around to discussing "the Machine," figuring out who was in the Machine and what to do if it turned out you were in it. It wasn't always clear what the Machine was. If you asked, his (always different) answer could be as cryptic as "It means I'm tired of you looking at me thinking I'm *the thing called Curtis.* I don't want to live in the Curtis Prison you all seem to want to keep me in."

He claimed to have found his "off switch," so that he was able to spend most of his day conscious but not thinking.

"Good to know," Eckhart had said.

When the grasshopper didn't appear for a few days, Eckhart wandered from room to room like a lover had left him. He sat at Jeff's desk, bereft, and opened the first book within reach, a physics book, and he opened a ream of printer paper within reach, copied out the title page, then the contents page, then he kept going. Every footnote and page number he copied, every mark on every page he copied. It became part of his daily routine. He didn't learn anything, but it calmed him like nothing else. When he reached the thick of it, single formulas that went for pages, he slowed and took exquisite care copying each symbol. He didn't think how it might look, 170-plus pages of a hand-copied textbook, until he walked in on Russ the first night of his visit inspecting and turning over pages in the neat stack, not reading but as if he were decoding their significance. Eckhart didn't even try to explain. It was why Eckhart thought it was a good reason, if you had the stomach for it—which Russ did not—to sometimes go without work for a time. Your only options are depression, addiction, or you take the time to question what a life consists of, and what Eckhart found when he searched his reels of memory were sensory impressions—burning his tongue, the taste of water slurped from a hose. None of what he thought of as his life was there. You could dive pretty far inward if you worked at it. Eckhart developed the ability to fall asleep and remain awake at the same time, so he could watch himself dreaming.

Then one morning there was this: he went out to crop a mutant rose that had shot a foot above the rest in two nights' time. Just as he angled the clippers in and squeezed, and the blades sunk into the stem, just as it snapped, (and he was very clear on this, this was well prior to Curtis's morning visit) the rose let out a scream. He dropped the clippers and danced back and stood very still. It was early, before the joggers were even out, so Eckhart knew he'd heard what he'd heard. White cream oozed from the slit and Eckhart, equally exhilarated and haunted, walked into the house and back out with a tube of Saran Wrap and masking tape, settled the chopped-off rose back onto its stem, and taped it back on. And that's how that day started.

Later the same afternoon, Eckhart and Brutus were coming back from the beach in the Jeep, ripping down the 405, both grizzled in sand. The church-bell opening of "Hells Bells" came on and Brutus, over in the passenger side, got to his feet.

A paw, two paws, on the armrest.

On the window controls.

The windows rolling down, all the way down, and Brutus, tail *thwap*ping excitedly into the seat, sniffing around in the rolled-down-window hole. A snap from being gone.

In a strictly physical way, Eckhart understood Brutus was preparing to jump, but he couldn't find any words to stop it. Brutus, up-stepping forepaws onto the door frame, chest out and head high. Brutus, muscling into the void of the 405. He had the song, though, the song. As soon as he thought of it he burst out full volume,

*Happy Birthday Dear Brutus,*

*Happy BIRTH-day dear . . .*

and Brutus did respond, he did glance back, perked his ear in a salute, then he jumped out the window like he'd been plucked.


And the empty window after Brutus jumped.


The no-dogness there.


!


!


!

!

!

!!

!

!

!

!

Then to his left, tumbling by in his side-view mirror, tumbling on the air like a craps die, the head of Brutus came and went, its red velvet insides. The honking-screeching pandemonium that followed on the freeway Eckhart was aware of only in a diminished way, like a song playing on headphones that are across the room. He saw no option in that fraction of a second but to change lanes, speed up, and hope no one saw which car the dog flew out of.

So when Russ showed up later that week, Eckhart was more than willing to look at the question of his (possibly at one time necessary) funk having evolved into what was now more of a vegetative stupor with side effects including potentially malfeasant flights of irresponsibility. And this, in all fairness, probably had more to do with the gargantuan amount of pot he was smoking/eating with the living-off-motorcycle-accident-insurance-money shaman Curtis, whom Eckhart understood he needed to get some distance from, and from Curtis's pot, and from the L.A. that housed Curtis and his pot (even though they were actually living in Oceanside, Curtis maintained that vis-à-vis the apocalypse, they were as good as living in L.A.).

After he'd given Russ a full picture of the scene on the 405, Russ surveyed the pictures on the mantel of decorated Jeff and his decorated military brothers and father and said, "So your plan here was what? You going to sit on this guy's couch until the war's over and he comes home and kills you?" He took an investigative look around the room, his eyes settling on the stack of paper next to the physics book, and he nodded, remembering. And that's when he told Eckhart that he should go and pack. Eckhart thought that sounded like a great idea.

They hit the salt flats at dawn. The sun was rising but hadn't yet breached the far mountains, which were a ghostly Weimaraner-eye gray. On either side of the highway reached an endless white plain of what looked like ground-down chalk, with drifts and opalescent swirls rising and spiraling over the surface. Russ flipped his visor down and pulled a lever on the side of his seat, scooting all the way back in its track. "You aren't going to believe this place in about ten minutes."

He meant the sun hitting the salt. The salt illuminating the white expanse like every diamond from every broken engagement spilled on white velvet puffs like out-breaths drifting sideways, pristine and primal. Fog spilling over the far cinnamon-colored mountains, their folds like elephants skin.

They were sun-sick ten miles in. Eckhart clamped his T-shirt in the rolled-up window, leaning into the sliver of shade. If he'd heard of the salt flats, he hadn't bothered to form an image of them, and the breach between his indifference and the humbling lengths and heights made him think he would pay for not being more curious about the place.

## 2

It was a month later that Eckhart first saw Billy in the main park. Eckhart was out walking Clyde, a defiant wreck of tangles and spots that Eckhart feigned an interest in as an excuse to be alone with Jackie, Clyde's owner. It'd snowed the night before, a bizarre mid-October dump that would be melted away by dusk. For now there was that insulated feeling in the air, and the fields specked over in pockmarks where the melting snow seemed to be breathing.

Eckhart was watching Clyde's diagonal trot, the leash wagging between them. He had no growing fondness for the animal but Jackie was another story—Jackie who'd apparently fixed on the idea of offering Clyde up in the spirit of a therapy dog, to help him get over Brutus. What she and Russ didn't know is that Eckhart's problem was less the demise of Brutus than the fact that he still hadn't told Jeff—for over a month now (and counting), Eckhart had let Jeff believe Eckhart was waking up in his (Jeff's) house, feeding his in-fact-deceased dog and pruning his crazy roses. To keep up pretenses, Eckhart had even cashed the last house-sitting check, leaving the cash in an envelope in Jeff's kitchen. The longer he didn't tell him, the more awkward and then flat-out unlikely it became. It weighed on him, of course. He had been given a number for emergencies and he called once but while it was ringing he told himself that breaking the news while or if Jeff was in combat could get him killed; that there was a way in which Brutus wouldn't be completely dead until Eckhart told Jeff.

They were coming down the central promenade, Eckhart and Clyde, passing under cottonwoods whose trunks cast shadows as thick and wide and long as sidewalks. Eckhart was thinking about Jackie seated on a low stool back in the entryway leashing up Clyde and talking about the guy who'd pulled a billy club on her in the very park she was just then giving Eckhart directions to. He was watching Clyde and also watching Jackie in his mind slash her arm through the air, mimicking the attacker with his club, saying, "You see what I mean? You see how easy it'd be?" Jackie didn't wear makeup and she was brown hair, brown eyes, brown everything, with a radiant happy face, the irrepressible smile of a kid in a school photo. When she finished her story—standing and handing Eckhart Clyde's leash—he noticed Clyde had been sitting on her foot for their whole conversation. That she had gone on talking was almost too cute to believe. She laughed at her own jokes and wore her hair pulled in a tight low bun, vinyl slick, and she seemed to understand what a fluke it was to make it out of childhood still beaming. When Eckhart first met her, he remembered wondering, in passing, if Russ would pull himself together for this one (Russ wavered between dating strippers and dating women he thought he should want to date), but then it got worse than that. It got so one night Eckhart heard Jackie out in the living room reading one of her poems—a couple of times a week a group of poets held a workshop at Russ's apartment—and Eckhart, almost with a sense of panic that he couldn't hear the individual words, quietly moved his operation to the kitchen table where he could read and listen in. Eckhart knew nothing about poetry to articulate the why and the how, but he'd suspected she would be more than decent based solely on her funny way of seeing, like the morning she turned to Eckhart and observed of Russ, "He, like, eats his coffee"—which was exactly right. She wrote poems defending happiness, but the big riddle for her during that period was eternity, and what that might really look like (*and the kettle's always whistling / and the kettle's never whistling / and no one ever answers the phone*). Russ had said she was getting to be a big deal in their little world.

He was thinking about Jackie and following Clyde around the pond on a trail packed in pre-Halloween snow and every few minutes he would actually forget where he was—the city and the state, even the era he was in. Every time he turned around, he was walking this damn dog again. The pattern they'd fallen into was: Jackie would be over at Russ's eating, grading, goofing around, and eventually the three of them—Eckhart, Jackie, Russ—would end up at the little round café table in Russ's kitchen drinking the whiskey Jackie stashed on Russ's fridge because she couldn't keep it at her own apartment—not (she said) because she had a drinking problem, but because she had a writing problem that sometimes *looked like* a drinking problem. They played Scottish bridge and sooner or later Clyde's name would come up and Eckhart would hear himself volunteering to walk him. It was unclear to Eckhart whether and to what extent one-sided this all was.

He was thinking about Jackie and squinting-reading the back of the T-shirt ahead of them some distance on the path, the kid intermittently dropping his head back and exhaling long tusks of cigarette smoke high into the air. Eckhart had to read the shirt a few times to be sure he was reading right:

**Accept work**
**To change, Work**
**Accept work as Your duty**

This screwball missive had been penned directly onto the shirt by hand, in black Sharpie, making the perhaps vaguely Marxist puzzle (or was it a haiku? Eckhart couldn't remember the rules of those) and the sudden Russian weather all the creepier when the kid (a runaway who should've been in school somewhere, junior high even, Eckhart saw) swiveling around to relight his cigarette. He took several backward steps that allowed Eckhart to read now the (also hand-printed) front of the shirt:

**"Feel free to relax and have a good time."**

The quote marks were written in and everything. There was a level of weird (this level), Eckhart felt, designed to be unfriendly, hostile. "Feel free to . . ." reminded him of those HAVE A NICE DAY! signs on diners that seemed actually to want to say, *Go fuck yourself!* Really the whole place, Salt Lake as a whole, seemed like it could give you a good idea of living under the kind of long passionless occupation that Curtis claimed was everyday living in modern times (according to Curtis, you could put a lot of people in jail and they wouldn't even notice). Even the city's grid was laid out to coincide, at its origin, with the Mormon temple, so you always knew how far you were from God. Eckhart and Russ and Jackie had gone down to Temple Square one Saturday when Eckhart was fresh in town. Outside were the brides, mulling around as if for a Cinderella audition—including a bride eating McDonald's off the hood of a car, and no one around she seemed to know, and no indication whether her ceremony was over or in the queue. During their tour of the curious Mormon infra-city Jackie, an ex-Mormon, had followed the docent around with a smile Eckhart could have described only as senile. At that point he hadn't known how Mormon Jackie's family was—Mormon royalty, Russ called them, given that they had once possessed an actual lock of Joseph Smith's hair, come by in the famous fatal shoot-out in the jail, where a great-great-great-great–et cetera uncle or somebody hid under a bed while the bullets flew, then crawled, the sole survivor, across the glass and rubble and helped himself to a lock of the now-dead Joseph's hair. And Jackie would say in her sweet-as-hell little way, "So yeah, those are my people; we hide when the shit goes down then loot your body crawling to the door."

Clyde was at this moment hunkering his bowels down into place right out in the middle of the world and, while further calibrating his positioning, seemed to be using Eckhart as a point of focus, to help him concentrate.

*Feel free to relax and have a good time.* The kid was farther ahead now, receding so his shirt was no longer legible, walking like he was on an escalator. What this kid didn't understand was that the only thing keeping him from total social oblivion—from people looking through him—was his youth, and that wasn't going to last long on the streets where people aged triple-time, with skin like you've been doing yard work on Mars. For a long time Eckhart had been fascinated by the resilience of street kids, and how they kept doing what they did—it was disorienting enough arriving early at a hotel and being told you can't check in for another hour, which should be perfectly pleasant, but there was always that dull background pang of belonginglessness until you actually got in the room, dumped your bags, claimed your plot of land; and that was going without for just an hour. But now when Eckhart saw a kid like this he understood (he saw in the arc of the boy's shoulders) that that resilience was the change that comes naturally once you've lived that awful day, that horror of horrors, when you learn—after hours sucking on the barrel of a gun you now know you will never shoot, the chair you will not kick out, the hose you won't suck—you learn that you are not suicidal, that this switch is not in you, that instead apparently you're going to stand there and take whatever comes. And then you might even decide to walk head-on into the worst of it so you can't be ambushed. (Eckhart's father could've had a normal [or at least indoor] life any time he wanted.)

He watched the kid duck off the path like a paratrooper

jumping out of a plane, and that's when Eckhart first saw up far-ther ahead, limping along, Billy (though he wouldn't know the name for a few weeks yet). Had it been any other day, with the colors of the park to interfere, Eckhart wouldn't have looked twice. But the snow made it so he was looking down a long white tunnel and at the end of it was this guy with this funny limp—not that it wasn't legitimate, but he seemed to work the limp for extra momen-tum, using it like a pendulum, or a cane. It was hard to figure out what was wrong with the guy. Eckhart had the impression he was carrying a duffel bag or something, holding it to his chest, and Eckhart found himself semi-advertently picking up his pace, moving in to get a closer look.

He was following and thinking of that day at Temple Square, with Russ and Jackie and Eckhart at one point on some kind of rooftop vista changing places taking pictures of themselves in ro-tating twos before a bowl of mountains, and for one windy minute Jackie undid her hair and let it fall with the speed-bump-like kink where she'd fastened the twisty too tight with hair still wet from the shower. She'd combed her hand through the loosed hair with the twisty cinched around her hand and glanced back, Eckhart thought, possibly, to see if he was watching her. But it could've been his imagination. He probably had to admit he was developing a crush on Russ's girlfriend and not doing anything to stop himself. Every now and then he thought it was even possible, that there were perhaps moments, where he caught Jackie holding his stare a second too long, but he couldn't be sure. For one thing, he hadn't concentrated on a woman in a while, and everybody thought Jackie was adorable—it took no gift of sight—and added to adorable she was one of those people you found yourself telling more than you wanted to (Eckhart had explained all about the Airedale three-card monte, the pandemonium on the 405, the detached tumbling head of Brutus) so he couldn't be sure whether his feelings were real or a mirage. This made their many late nights with too much whiskey thrilling and frustrating both, with Russ sooner or later pushing Jackie to spew creepy Mormon secrets. (She had been married in the temple very young, and when Eckhart tried to picture that Jackie—obedient, un-opinionated—he couldn't find her anywhere.) Then Russ would grandstand, one night addressing an imaginary Mormon leadership: "So here's what you don't do. You don't send a girl like Jackie on a mission to Berkeley and think she's coming back Mormon; you send her to Kentucky and cross your fucking fingers." Which made Jackie laugh, but there were other nights when Russ seemed, in the guise of affectionate ribbing, to be trying to needle Jackie, even humiliate her a bit.

The limping man made an adjustment where he swung his arms around to the side and this baby popped out that he was apparently carrying. The baby was dressed in the same blue Little League windbreaker as the guy, plus they wore woven hats with bobbing yarn pom-poms at the top, bobbing. They were still too far ahead for Eckhart to see the baby's face, but after they'd gone fifty or so yards farther, the baby's arms sprung out in an unnatural way. While they walked and Eckhart walked, he watched the baby's arms bounce and then all in an instant the scene changed. He saw the baby wasn't moving, and its head was tilted too far back, with its face to the sky and its arms shot out like signs on a post. There was something wrong with this baby. Wrong enough that it felt like Eckhart's public duty to follow the guy. He wasn't really sure—being inherently more of the bystander type—what he would do if it did turn out that the guy had a dead or badly hurt baby, but he choked down on Clyde's leash and they followed the man until the path ran out, until the park ran out and they stood tucked behind a tree with the guy on the corner at the crosswalk entrance waiting for the light to change. Cars flashed past with glazed windows and no one inside. Eckhart knew realistically there couldn't be this guy walking around with a dead baby, but that's what he seemed to be trying to see.

The man and his baby crossed to a 7-Eleven with Eckhart and Clyde still following, hanging back, because it was impossible not to, because for Eckhart the hardest thing to resist was his relatively new desire for things to turn out as warped as they generally appeared to be. "The allure of decay"—he'd heard or read about this somewhere, that part of a man that wants to know his own worst guess is true.

As Eckhart crouched to chain up Clyde, he noticed the people in line inside the store drop their eyes as the guy passed, making exaggerated room like you would for someone carrying a live marlin. Eckhart couldn't figure out what these people were all doing, living here, then reminded himself he was living here, too.

Inside the 7-Eleven, Eckhart cut left through the ChapStick-and-condom aisle and took a hairpin turn around the Cup Noodles tower. He could tell the guy was close, in the Hot Foods area, and, peeking around over through the foil ears of the chips bags stuffed in the metal racks, Eckhart's eyes fell to the cheese pump, not five feet in front of him, and beside it the baby, her small hands resting on the counter, hard beige claws. The tiny thumbs hitched out. It was a doll. Milliseconds before he knew this, he knew he'd known on some level all along. It was of course a doll. Any reasonable person, if forced to choose between seeing a dead baby or a doll, would see a doll.

But there was this: the doll was wearing thick prescription glasses and clothes with reinforced stitching and industrial zippers and fasteners—clothes for a human baby. It was an inaccurate doll, but for that reason more lifelike, the way distorted things are.

Eckhart walked a bag of Cheetos to the cashier, leaning in and asking the cashier, who had the manner of an old-time local, "Is that a doll he's got, would you happen to know?"

While Eckhart talked she slit her eyes to the Hot Foods and back. She mumbled, vacantly dispensed Eckhart's change, then she surprised him and leaned in close around the register, elbowing down. "I try to talk to him sometimes about her," she whispered. "Ask about her—you know." She came a little alive and said her mother had first seen him with "her" down near 300 South in 1983.

Eckhart didn't understand for a minute, then said, "The same doll? It can't be the *same* doll."

That confused her. She said she didn't know. "He always keeps her real clean," she said.

Eckhart said, "You mean twenty-five-years-ago nineteen eighty-three?"

"You know, he's always changing her outfits and caring for her and all—" her eyes pulled right, landing on something that silenced her dropping head.

Unthinking, Eckhart turned and there, close as Eckhart's own skin, was the man he'd followed, not just close in space but actually inhabiting that space in an unnaturally intimate way having to do maybe with the mad square porn-star glasses magnifying his eyes to three times the size, eyes that did not blink and might as well have been glass in terms of lock-on power. Eckhart glanced at the doll in his arms in identical glasses. Their hats were off, revealing insane matching blond bowl cuts on both the man and the doll. The man had made a Slurpee and was holding the straw to the doll's face, poking it into and around the plastic lips as the plastic stare bored into Eckhart's cheek. There were the man's breathing and dull magnified eyes, his lower eyelids like overstretched rubber bands. Point-blank, he looked both more innocent and more deranged. "Is that your dog?" he asked, not looking anywhere near Clyde. "She looks nice." His voice seemed to be coming out of his pores, and he seemed to want Eckhart to return the compliment, tell him his baby was cute, but Eckhart couldn't find his tongue. Something had happened to the cashier when she started calling the doll "her"—she'd become less real to Eckhart, hologramlike. And Eckhart didn't see how the man could even see Clyde from where he was standing.

In his head was the whispery voice of the cashier saying, *He always keeps her real clean*, and he walked home repeating *real* and *clean* to the left-right rhythm of his footfall, repeating *real* when the right foot stepped; *clean* for the left, repeating

Real.

　　Clean.

Real.

　　Clean.

Real.

He came home to an apartment full of poets, what was apparently one of their workshop nights. Usually Eckhart didn't mind and even liked having voices in the apartment without the stress and work of having to talk himself; tonight though, he'd hurried home to question Jackie about this character and his doll. He said a round of hellos then took his books into the kitchen. He seemed to like roughly every other poet in the group. So there was this one guy from Honduras who wrote about shipwrecks while beside him on the sectional his girlfriend sat holding his hand and reading poems about, and sometimes addressed directly to, her ovaries that everyone had to listen to. One night after people left, Eckhart asked Jackie if you could bring anything to workshop and people would take it seriously. Jackie said she wasn't sure what he meant and he'd said, "It's possible to write a poem in five minutes. I'm just saying physically, it's possible." He was on his back on the linoleum, reaching a match in under the stove to light the pilot for her tea; she was drinking tea that night, recuperating from a flu they'd all been passing around ("Being poets," Eckhart had said). Looking up he'd asked if he were to bring in a poem about Mr. Potato Head, would they all take it seriously, and she'd smiled and said, "Are you sure you aren't just giving me your opinion of poetry in general?"

The following week she brought and read in workshop a poem about Mr. Potato Head, and Eckhart, sitting listening in from the kitchen table, thought he might split in half.

The week after that she read the line, *Now even philosophy sounds like self-help,* and the eyes in Eckhart's buzzing head fell to the books on the table before him—*Problems of the Self* and *The Meaning of Life*—with five or six similar titles lying around the apartment, books in which she'd taken a funny standoffish interest in recent weeks, picking through reading passages, saying frowningly, "Sometimes I wonder if everybody's saying the same thing."

When it was just the core group remaining, Eckhart would usually go out and help them finish the box of wine. On the night he first saw Billy, Russ was rolling a joint on the ottoman and trying to talk one of the ex-Mormons, this guy Horton, into *scoring him* a set of sacred undergarments for Halloween. Horton didn't like it. "I don't think that's a good idea," he said. Russ had been in Salt Lake three years and every time Eckhart talked to him he was more obsessed with Mormonism—so it made immediate sense when Eckhart learned Jackie was an ex-Mormon.

Horton's girlfriend asked, "But what's the costume? What are you supposed to be?"

"That's it," Russ said. "Me in the garb. That's the whole costume."

Somehow, the whole night whenever Jackie had come into the kitchen to refill her drink or what-have-you, Eckhart would forget to ask about the guy with the doll (Jackie knew everyone and everything about the town), and she'd leave the room, and he would sit trying to memorize his intention to ask the next time she came in. Now he was stuck sitting in a group and he didn't feel like telling all these people about the park and the baby and how he couldn't get it off his skin. And not only did he prove inept in pursuing the conversation he wanted with the woman he wanted to have it with, there was instead, directly across from him, this girl Carlie staring him down through a mean simmering buzz. Every time Eckhart saw Carlie, she invited him to this Halloween bash they all went to every year (at least five other additional people had invited him to this thing). "You're coming, right?" she said, starting right in. She was cute sober but Russ said she always ended up like this, can't finish a thought and her makeup smeared like wax.

Horton repeated to Russ, "I don't think that's a good idea for around here or just in general. You can't control your message. You know that." Humorless Horton looked at Jackie for agreement or help. She'd defected from the church in her early twenties, a few months into her mission, but when you asked her about it she shut down, saying most people just wanted to get you drunk and make you admit it was a cult.

Anyway, Russ was done with Horton and had segued to the Book of Mormon and how poorly written it was.

"It's not a great book," Carlie agreed.

"Thank you," Russ said. "No narrative arc."

Jackie rolled her eyes. "He's never even opened it. You all understand this, right?"

"It's a matter of respect," Horton finally thought to say, at this point basically conversing with the memory of Russ's interest in their conversation.

Eckhart walked down to switch his laundry and wait for a change of topic. Russ could go all night provoking the innocents, and it didn't look like anyone was going to stop him. Jackie's MO was to let Russ talk, then correct any heresies later, in private. (After one of Russ's weekly line crossings on the subject of Mormonism, she told Eckhart about a time, driving on black ice, when her car left the road and before it even came to a stop the neighbors came running out of their houses with blankets and a lawn chair and hot cocoa and an ambulance on the way. *Whatever else is true of Salt Lake Mormons*, she'd said, *that's true, too*.)

There were ten minutes left on one of the washing machines, so Eckhart sat down to wait. He was thinking now of Russ's Grandma Lou, wherever she was from, saying *worshing machine* instead of *washing machine*—where *wash* rhymed with *borsch*, and Russ's face every single time she said it, like someone was slowly removing his foot under the table. There were many genuinely likeable things about Russ, and one was that he'd look anyone in the eye and admit (having, himself, two books published), *I don't like books*; then he'd wait until they were done laughing and say, *I'm serious. I don't like reading.* This was half true. It was closer to the mark to say Russ was more of a stare-at-the-floor-for-hours type of thinker and not so much with the heavy scholarship. One of his books contained seventy poems all written about the same memory of his mother walking down a hall—it was all he knew of his mother, of either parent, and he wasn't even positive it was her, in the hall.

Servicing the entire apartment building were two washers and two dryers, in a fairly comically large room with a drain in the middle of the floor. There was also, heaped on the folding table, a hodgepodge of wigs and Halloween miscellany for people to borrow, a swap organized by a crazy-looking blonde from the part of Utah that wasn't Salt Lake. Eckhart tried on a hook hand, took a few swipes in the open air.

It was then he noticed the screwy alarmist writing on the walls: YOU ONLY NEED TO SURVIVE THE TRANSITION. He recognized, in this, the unmistakable voice of the street. His own father, when he'd lived at home, had had to shave twice a day, and since you need a sink to keep that up, he immediately grew the clichéd street-Jesus beard when he moved out. So it was embarrassing walking up to him. There were times he waited across the street until the foot traffic thinned, even though the only other person he knew in San Francisco was his sister, who already knew his father was homeless because hers was, too. But Russ would walk up to their father anywhere with his arm outstretched and say, "Good morning, Professor," with Eckhart trailing awkwardly behind, assessing in sniffs how bad it was going to be in the car. The stench with his father in the car could work like tear gas or mace. It was never a boozy smell—that was the eeriest part, that he did this sober in a city that was at least chilly, often cold, and always damp. A city where you had to drink to have any chance of falling asleep, but there was his father: sober, awake, alert. Most of the time they drove to the Haight, where you couldn't tell who was homeless, and they could eat in a restaurant in peace. But on the ride over the lining in your nostrils would shrink-wrap itself to the outer walls and it was hard to think about anything except when you'd be allowed out of the car: Eckhart would look down and locate the door handle, just to make sure it was there and in working order. (*Do you care about anyone?* Lucy would ask.)

He started to pull on a rubber Ronald Reagan face but decided it wasn't worth it—that horrible stale saliva he knew was waiting inside the mask for him. Russ would dress as some scandalized politician for Halloween, which he had done every year since they were seventeen and he'd turned completely prematurely gray, and on Senior Cut Day, when the cops showed up at the lake, had successfully impersonated their principal.

Eckhart seemed to need Russ to show him how to treat his own father, basically. After undergrad, Russ moved back to SF and, asking no one's permission, went out and found Eckhart's father and took him home to his apartment to live. Some months later, Russ moved out and left Eckhart's father in the apartment for the landlord to deal with. He said it was hard to explain; it was like Eckhart's father was still homeless while he was living there ("I emptied out some drawers, but at best he'd put his things on top of the dresser"). But those few months, months his father was safe inside with Russ, Eckhart didn't have to spend his energy trying not to picture his father eating trash, or worrying about the condition in which Eckhart left his own trash (he'd once walked three blocks to fish a partially spit-up chicken sandwich out of the garbage he'd thrown it in because he had the flu and didn't want a potential second eater of the sandwich getting it; but since he couldn't guarantee the sandwich would remain in any trash anywhere, he tossed it in his trunk, then before long he was driving around with a trunkful of everything he didn't want anyone else eating or handling after him). For a few months he could rest, free of that feeling just after Brutus jumped, when he was still alive, in flight, and anything could happen.

He traded a Cher wig for a blond pageboy, looking around for a reflective surface, the basement air suddenly redolent of hay somehow, a smell Eckhart decided was emanating from the wig. The stench in that car could actually make you angry—not anger at his father (you could honestly forget who was in the smell, holding it together like soil held plants), but anger at the smell itself, at its density, how you had to sort of *holler down into it* as into a volcano to feel like you'd been heard.

The underside of the washer lid when he opened it had directions for use written on the metal and a sheen from the exposed bulb overhead, so Eckhart could see only the outline of his head, in the wig, and with his face obscured, he looked so uncannily much like the guy in 7-Eleven, looming there, that there was a freaky second where Eckhart felt as if the guy were falling through him.

That Slurpee. When Eckhart thought of that Slurpee he could feel himself trip inside, actually take an inward tumble.

Now he was glad he hadn't asked Jackie about the guy because it would be his costume. This idea descending as it had so naturally in the course of his day; this idea and his decision to go with it (why not go as a blind or paralyzed person while he was at it?) would retrospectively embarrass him for the rest of his life. That whole Halloween, more generally, would not leave him for a single day.

He would need to get a doll from somewhere.

And another wig.

He'd need two pairs of those glasses if he could find them. The rest of the costume wouldn't matter if he got the wigs and the glasses right. Those would need to be killer.

Back upstairs, he balanced the laundry basket on his hip and kicked the door closed behind him. He could tell right away something had happened while he was gone—they were all in the same places around the sectional, but everyone was tense. There was the air of something having been asked or said, with the room hanging waiting for an answer.

Russ said, or continued, it looked more like "So I'm going on about rape and subjugation, and she's leafing through the transcript and she says to me, 'I'm not sure any of that's in here, in the actual speech itself, you know, as far as textual evidence,' and I tell her, 'Oh, it's there, trust—'"

Jackie interjected, "And when was this again—?"

Russ slid a glance at her then went on talking. The only light in the room was that awful halogen dish burning in the corner, with its buttery light. "So I pounced on the word *tryst*. 'Why not an *appointment* with destiny?' I asked her."

Ah yes, Eckhart knew this story and why everyone looked the way they did listening to it.

Carlie said, "Because *sssssex*."

Jackie asked, "And when was this?"

Eckhart was surprised, now that he took a closer look, to see people looking so put off by the story, given the version he knew Russ would give them: he'd assigned a Ghandi paper he didn't bother reading himself before a "distractingly hot Aryan" (Russ's phrase) came to office hours wanting help with it. It was no work at all picturing Russ with his very softest humanist face on, saying, *You can't talk about Ghandi without talking about colonialism, and once you're talking about colonialism you're talking about cultural rape, and once you're talking about cultural rape you're talking about rape-rape. . . .* Eckhart remembered a fight he was privy to not long after he came to Salt Lake, in which Jackie called Russ *inappropriate with students*—that was the tag word, *inappropriate*. From what he'd heard, Eckhart gathered that Jackie had caught Russ texting a student well past midnight, after which he'd made a run to McDonald's that she wanted to find suspicious (when Russ did regularly hit drive-throughs at odd hours, Eckhart could vouch).

What Russ wasn't going to tell them—what Russ didn't even remember having told Eckhart while highly inebriated—was that he'd slept with this girl, the student. She was twenty when the story started and eighteen or nineteen by the end, a ginger, irresistible, who according to Russ had shown up at his apartment after last call and thrown herself at him.

Jackie crossed her arms and eased back as people do when they can't believe what they're seeing but can't help wanting their disbelief to grow. When the others started yawning and reaching for their jackets, Jackie joined them. It was one of the rare nights she didn't stay over, and the next few days Eckhart watched to see if they (Russ and Jackie) would still go on the getaway they'd planned for fall break (they'd rented a cabin in Idaho), but they were poets who'd put a deposit down, so they went. That's what made it difficult to believe what seemed to be an undeniable growing mutual attraction forming between her and Eckhart—that at the end of the day she got in the car with Russ, that, end of day, she always left with Russ.

While they were away in Idaho, Eckhart caught himself picturing them a few times; nothing kinky but just what they'd look like playing Monopoly or shopping at a farmers market. One night while they were gone Eckhart stood in Russ's pantry reading the spastic instructions on a box of rice, DO NOT REMOVE THE LID FOR ANY REASON, and largely unwillingly pictured himself reading the instructions aloud to Jackie in the next room—*Not for any reason*, he would say hyperbolically, *do you hear me?*—and he'd picture her laughing the way Russ made her laugh.

## 3

Two weeks later one of Russ's students turned up in the hall outside the apartment. Eckhart didn't know how hospitable to be (Russ wasn't home yet), but he figured she'd gotten the address somehow and invited her in to wait while he himself waited on a pizza.

Once they were sitting talking on the couch he saw she was older, a returning student of some kind. She was pretty, with caramel skin and violet eyelids, and a professionalism that made him feel like he'd hired her for something—to decorate or show him around town—which in turn made him want to think she was Mormon, except here she was at her unmarried professor's apartment, and she wouldn't leave yet also wouldn't take off her raincoat. In her lap was a manila file and she made this file a tactical problem for herself, setting it down then right away picking it back up again, holding it to her chest. They took turns looking at the window, talking about the neighborhood, and at some point she waved her arm to point the way to a new Thai place and the file crashed to the floor. In unison they ducked to pick it up and Eckhart read the title: *If I Could Hie to Kolob.*

She explained, "Kolob is supposed to be the planet closest to God."

"Oh," Eckhart said, handing the papers back. "I had hoped that was Earth."

She gave a polite laugh. "It's a hymn." Then she sang a few verses—just burst out in song, this woman—humming in places where she couldn't remember the words. Her voice was soft and high and when she finished, he kept listening. He'd forgotten about this kind of singing, about lullabies and all of it.

Then she suddenly stopped singing, dropping her gaze into her lap. "This is silly," she said, "I have a sixteen-year-old son."

Eckhart was calculating the import of this admission when the front door buzzed again. This time it was a man in decorated military duds, holding a bouquet of flowers he looked to have traveled with. He had the air of someone about to make an announcement, so Eckhart gave him directions to the hot girls' apartment on the fifth floor. But the man, not budging, slid the flowers forward and said: "These are for you. From Brutus."

Eckhart was right then examining the space between the man's head and shoulders, trying to think of the body part that belonged there, the stemlike part. "OK," he said. "All right."

The marine held up three fingers.

Counting aloud, Eckhart said, "Three." Then he said, "OK. All right. Let's do this inside. I'm expecting a pizza."

Before contact Eckhart was nervous, a performance anxiety almost. Stepping back, he thought of a morning days earlier—
today?—when he'd heard a car pull up outside, a door slam, then
a man running up the steps of the building yelling *Pray for me!* But
then it was fine. He went against a wall, then down on the floor
and onto what seemed like a second floor, or another dimension of
the first floor. In the other room Russ's student screamed.

There really were, Eckhart believed, only the three punches, but
he found himself wondering if the man's heart was in it. At points
it seemed Eckhart had to help things along, go soft for the guy,
look appetizing.

Then the marine was—what?—taking a break. For a second
Eckhart thought, *Here comes the gun,* but just as fast he knew the
man wasn't risking jail time on him. *You will find,* his father had
said after losing three toes to frostbite, *pain can be very interesting.*
He had also said, weeks before he left the family to sleep in the
cold, to sleep in the rain, to sleep wherever he slept, *No one will stop
you from wasting your life.*

What it was: the marine had to sneeze. Two brief blasts, a pause,
a long third sneeze. Then silence. Eckhart rolled and looked up and
saw the marine staring at the ceiling, breathing in delirious post-
sneeze huffs, waiting to see if more sneezes were coming. Eckhart's
head was throbbing in four places and he could feel the different
tender beaten spots around his body gathering into the real pain,
which would come later, in bed. Everything hit when you tried to
sleep. You almost had to start deserving sleep at some point. From
his worm's-eye view on the floor, Eckhart could see there would be
no way for them to continue the beating because now the marine
was just a guy sneezing. He thought he even caught the man reading the titles of books in the bookcase. Eckhart thought of the
proof filling one wall of his boyhood bedroom (a room that had
been his father's office and whose walls he'd treated more or less
like a chalkboard) and the character that would appear when the
door was left open a crack at night, ∃, which meant *there exists,*

though if the door were left open another inch, the light would
expose a second character, an exclamation point, so now it said, ∃!,
which meant *there exists only one*. Eckhart thought his father had
been working on the problem of upkeep with that particular proof,
how for instance there was always someone painting the Golden
Gate Bridge because the minute you were done it was time to start
again on the other end, and it was around that time, too, that he
abandoned his regular wallet and started carrying instead a Glad
Sandwich Zipper Bag with playing cards on either end of his fold
of cash, credit cards, notes, et cetera. "When I carry a wallet, they
take it," he said, as if with particular people in mind. "It's got a hole
in it now, though," he'd said, showing the young Eckhart a one-
inch split along one of the Glad seams, with the corner of a Joker
poking out.

The marine was on the stairs, leaving, apparently unimpressed
by his visit, and Eckhart managed to feebly sit up and ask the man's
descending uniformed tapered back if this meant that Jeff was back
(he almost added "Stateside"; *Is Jeff back Stateside?* but luckily
reined himself in). The man stopped on the stairs, half of him on
a lower stair than the half holding the banister. He said, "What?"
He shook his head and looked down like the whole thing had been
a waste of time, a bad date, then he said matter-of-factly, "Jeff is
dead." The student, standing in the middle of the front room still
in her raincoat, gasped. Eckhart replayed her gasp later on, in bed,
as he lay trying to distinguish between the actually physically
throbbing parts of his body versus the psychosomatic, blushing-
swollen sensation of just feeling like an asshole. He decided nothing was broken, exactly, though his ribs hurt when he talked and
when he bit into the pizza, he realized his teeth were loose.

As soon as the student left—Eckhart had to beg her to go (*I just
don't feel right leaving you like this—can I at least call a dentist and
see what to do about your teeth?* she'd said)—Eckhart called Curtis,
who seemed to be expecting him. "He really made the trip, did
he?" Curtis said. "I really didn't think he would, but it probably

feels good to beat an American after that other nonsense." He covered the phone and said, "*Pssssst . . . missy . . . hey*—I wouldn't eat a whole one of those if I were you."

Eckhart asked, "So you told him about Brutus?"

"I couldn't not," Curtis said. "He came specifically for the dog, I had to tell him something. My feeling is they might have been lovers. Or possibly he's the one shot him. It's easy to lose track."

"Shot?" Eckhart asked. "Is that what happened?"

"I don't know, it was on the news—" he covered the phone and asked whomever he was with, *Is that right? Shot?* Then to Eckhart, "Yeah, maybe we can send you the reel."

Then he started in talking about the duplexes again, wondering where Eckhart was with the duplexes.

Next morning Russ came rushing in with enough time to change and swap books before his first class.

"The fuck happened to you?" he asked, seeing Eckhart's face.

Eckhart's bruises were still waking up, but all his teeth were firm in his head so it was hard to whine. "One of your students came by," he began.

Russ's face narrowed. "Shit," he said. "What'd you tell her?" He was at the door again, his book bag resting on his thigh while he rearranged the insides so nothing bulged.

"I waited with her for an hour so she didn't feel stupid."

Russ glanced over. "Why would she feel stupid?"

Eckhart looked at him.

"Don't worry about it," Russ said. "I'll take care of it."

Once Lucy had asked how Eckhart could still be friends with Russ after the way Russ had treated her "that night," the night of the funeral. As far as Eckhart was concerned (as far as he cared to think), they'd had an overblown one-night stand, Russ and Lucy. "If it's nothing you would tell the police," he told Lucy at the time, "then don't tell me either." Then he would remind her that Russ had gotten on an airplane to come and identify their (Eckhart and Lucy's) father's body because neither of them wanted to do it alone. Eckhart had no idea how nonreligious people decided what they decided ceremonially for their dead; how they (Eckhart, Russ, and Lucy) decided was this: they looked down together at the bloated, sea-worn face (he'd been floating in the bay awhile, their father) and they saw that it had to be destroyed, that it couldn't be seen by anyone else. Three abreast they stood looking down and down into a face that was like a Silly-Putty impression of Eckhart's father's face stretched out and set back down on his skull, too wide for it now. He had floated up beside a restaurant in Sausalito where they used to eat Sunday brunch as a family (plus Russ, who joined them as often as not); it was conceivable Eckhart had once sat in the very seat of the woman who had glanced down at the gently lapping bay and seen their father's face in its floating, kind of smiling state. Eckhart could imagine the eyebrows floating up. (The terrible, awful relief that you would not give back for anything.) Those long, tweaky, jet-black eyebrows probably floating up. (That it was over. It had honestly started to seem like it could go on forever, Lucy's calls, the wondering, the constant wondering, the missing toes, the whole preternaturally slow-moving nightmare.)

And not only that, but later at the funeral home, Russ had stood awesomely making fun of the mini-urns they were encouraged to buy, portable urns shaped like coffins for some reason, and Russ very gravely asking the salesman, "Now, will the actual unit come with the key ring welded on, or will we need to hire our own welder?"

Then at the service, where from somewhere the whole Old Guard was suddenly out and the church was spilling over, all his father's old professor friends, a few of them having gone out of their way to try and help before (presumably) realizing there was nothing to help, that Eckhart's father was doing exactly what he wanted, and eventually they did the only thing they could and quietly turned away, which you had to if you wanted to still believe in your own life, made up as it was of all the same things making up Eckhart's father's life. The three of them standing there shaking hands

like they'd just gotten married and all Eckhart wanted to do was
to crawl onto any plane, truck, train, car, tricycle going anywhere. And instead of going home they ended up that night at a
party in an apartment that Eckhart couldn't find again if he wanted
to, in a long tall building with a hall on the second floor that dead
ended into a door that led to a deck that was no longer there, as
Eckhart learned at whatever point he broke into a sprint down the
hall and through and out the door into midair, dropping a story
and breaking his leg. Last he'd seen, Lucy and Russ were doing
shots with an honest-to-God dwarf named Kermit and anyone
could see how that was going to end, so Eckhart took off before he
saw anything that would complicate his ability to remember that
week in a particular way. To remember himself, utterly slack in
every way a person can be, waiting for Russ at SFO in a terminal
he had been in so many times he thought he could look down and
see his own footprints in the carpet. It didn't seem to matter the
airline, destination, or time of day, Russ ended up—out of that
whole huge place—coming down that same gangway in the weird
cul-de-sac with just a few gates leading into an atrium with a non-
descript, unused sorting area and then over to the left, a Wolfgang
Puck. And it was like Russ had been coming down that gangway
since the beginning of time, and Eckhart could close his eyes and
stand in that spot in the SFO in his mind and see Russ, and feel
peace. Eckhart did know it was a problem; that he should listen
to whatever Lucy seemed to need to disclose about that night, but
he needed that image of Russ coming off that plane more than he
needed his entire sister.

4

On Halloween Eckhart spent the first hour in the kitchen talking
to a guy with a blown-out TV on his head. "Yeah, I guess I'm just,
like, the brand Zenith," he said unexcitedly. "Remember Zenith?"

He'd been coming to the party for six years and said he still wasn't sure whose house it was—someone tall, he thought, indicating the custom-made-for-tall-people counters. There were loose wires and mechanical innards poking out of the TV and Eckhart could see red irritations around the guy's cheekbones and hairline; still, he said he couldn't complain, it was plenty roomy inside. Eckhart had begun regretting his own costume since the girl in the red slip explained for the third time that she was a *Freudian* slip, and the hollow little laughs that followed.

Commenting on Eckhart's costume, Zenith said he'd never seen or heard of the fake-baby man but that his girlfriend worked at the downtown library so she "knew them all." Eckhart said he didn't think the guy was homeless, if that's what Zenith meant.

Zenith said, "One guy came up to the information desk the other week when Cheryl was working. She said she noticed him holding himself funny, then he moaned and fumbled with his stomach and—out spill his intestines all over the fucking place." He squinted and pointed at the fading shiner on Eckhart's face. It was purplish-blue nacreous, just fading into a jaundice color. There was actually a swollen overhang of flesh, so if Eckhart rolled his eye all the way up in the socket, he could see, skirting his vision, a bruise-colored almost visual fur delineating the outer edge of the formation. "What's the fat eye for?" Zenith asked. "Is that part of the dude's deal?"

Eckhart touched it. "No, this is real."

"No kidding," he said, nodding his head and the antennae on his TV nodding a few degrees off perfect unison. "Nice."

"I told you the eye looked fake," Jackie said.

"They always look fake," Russ said. "The worse they are, the faker they look. It's like foreign accents." He was wearing a tie, boxers, and dress slacks worn down around his ankles, like someone getting off the toilet; he was supposed to be the senator or governor who'd recently been nabbed propositioning an undercover agent at a rest stop. He was handcuffed to Jackie, who fed him celery spears in her lady-policeman uniform.

Zenith said, "At first I thought you were a ventriloquist, but then I couldn't figure why the dummy didn't have a fat eye, too. You should've given the dummy a fat eye, too. I mean, if you wanted to be a ventriloquist."

Russ said, "That would be excellent." He looked down at Jackie, "A ventriloquist and his dummy? Both with black eyes?"

She rolled her eyes to say *I got it,* but flirty. Then to Eckhart she said, "You could always put the doll in the truck and go as Andy Warhol."

Zenith agreed. "You wouldn't have to answer any more dumb questions." He took the doll from Eckhart's BabyBjörn and started pulling on its head to see how tightly attached it was. "Maybe you could turn this into a piñata."

Jackie volunteered, "You could fill it with whiskey."

A Pee-wee Herman moonwalked into the kitchen and around the island twice. At the door he paused to spank himself, then moonwalked back into the living room, to a reception of cheers. That got people dancing, pulling everyone from the kitchen to investigate. Russ uncuffed himself and joined the flow, leaving Eckhart and Jackie alone for a minute.

Earlier, in order to explain about the eye, Eckhart admitted (and the minute he did, he realized he should've done it much sooner because it didn't sound that bad when he said it out loud) about not managing to tell Jeff about Brutus, and how he wasn't sure how to feel about it, because part of him thought, *Why not let a dying man leave the biggest possible world, a world with his dog still in it?* Picking up where they'd left off, Eckhart said now, "To put it in perspective, he *sang* to this dog. Every morning he sang the 'Happy Birthday' song to this dog."

"That's so sweet and sad." She pouted, with actual sadness in it. She said, "I mean, you're right, it just seems like it'd be hard to know how to react to an animal tragedy when you're in a war zone. I'm sure you would've told him if it was the right thing."

"Hard to say," Eckhart admitted. "Knowing myself like I do, I can't say I wouldn't have continued chickening out."

"That's honest." She nodded. "I still can't tell if you're OK. Are you OK?"

Eckhart shrugged. "I only met the guy once, so . . ."

"Yeah, but living in his house with all his things and his vibe and his dog! Sometimes you get to feel like you know a person from knowing their dog." She frowned at her own remark, possibly considering Clyde, whom she herself had once called "kind of a loser."

Sometimes in Eckhart's dreams the head tumbling in the Jeep's mirror wasn't Brutus's but Eckhart's father's head, though in the funeral home it had been still firmly attached. In another recurring dream Eckhart had told only Jackie about, Brutus runs up to him without a head, and Eckhart hugs him and looks down into his neck as into a manhole and sees that inside, Brutus contains all of outer space, and neither of them is afraid.

"Well, it's nice you paid attention," Jackie said. "You're observant. I've noticed that about you."

He looked down like he doubted her. "Am I?" On her upper lip was a drop of veggie dip that looked like a white mole.

Around midnight a raft of undergrads exploded into the house sprinkled in snow and telling everyone to go outside and look. For a minute the party turned into a Heineken commercial, with blondes in whorish nurse uniforms throwing ineptly made snowballs. They came looking for the keg and logjammed at the sight of Eckhart. "Are you supposed to be *that guy*?"

That's how it started.

"Check it out—he's that guy!"

"Are you—"

"Yeah, yeah, he's that guy."

Within the hour he probably had twenty people come up to

him sharing rumors and sightings of his guy. A Lady Macbeth said he was in the Barnes & Noble where she worked when someone dropped a book; baby guy fell to the floor with the doll, covering it like there was a gunman loose. Someone saw him at the dollar store down on 400 South. Someone else, too. A consensus formed that he often shopped at the marketplace on 400 South in the midmorning-to-early-afternoon hours. The Clintons thought he was a lot scarier up close. The shaven Bigfoot agreed. "Way, like, distorted," he said. Eventually the conversation turned to what had happened, what was wrong with the guy. Corpses from the St. Valentine's Day Massacre indulged in wild speculation, but ultimately everyone agreed on the story set forth by a girl in a mustache and fedora because it was the one they'd all heard the most: He used to be a regular normal family guy, then his house burned down with his family inside. He snapped and wasn't able to function again until a shrink made him get a doll similar in size and so on to his daughter and take care of it, which he'd been doing ever since.

Eckhart started to feel more like a prop than a participant in the conversation, so went looking for a bathroom. In the hall he was set upon twice more, and while in the bathroom line he had to listen to the story about the fire, the shrink, and the incinerated baby again. The story started bothering him. Or everyone's itch to have their version heard, as if he were a juror and would have to decide by night's end *what really happened*. The toilet kept flushing but no one came out, and a newcomer in line, a decapitated person, said through the chest, "Holy shit, you're that guy." Eckhart said that that was it, resolving to put the doll in the car when someone pulled him to a staircase with word of a secret bathroom on the second floor.

He climbed, the doll's arms flapping in the BabyBjörn. Not one person mentioned the Björn, which Eckhart had thought would get a laugh.

At the top of the stairs were three doors, like in a game show or fairy tale. One was locked, one was a closet. Behind the third was a burble of voices and fumes piping out from the cracks; a voice in a mock-noble accent announced, "This snake owes me nothing!"

The talking stopped when Eckhart entered. He was aware—before he himself could really see—of eyes appraising him, up-and-downing him.

From a far corner of the room a deep voice asked, "Are you supposed to be Billy?"

Beneath Eckhart's feet, downstairs, rap gave way to dancehall.

"I'm looking for the bathroom," Eckhart said.

In the shadows a guy rose up on his knees, knee-walking forward to Eckhart and pressing a pipe in his palm. "Be careful. It's medicinal."

"We call it the cheese," a girl said.

There were at least a dozen of them on the floor, sitting passing stuff around. The cheese was so smooth Eckhart was surprised how much smoke he exhaled when he was checking to see if he'd gotten any. The central figure of the group was pretty obviously this guy Igor, a name he more or less wielded like *fuck you, what's* your *fucking name?* Igor had thick roach-black curls and the posture of a wing chair, and as Eckhart stood facing him, alone in the middle of the seated circle, he couldn't help feeling like he'd been brought before Igor in chains, for sentencing. "I want to know," Igor asked. "Is this supposed to be funny?"

"I don't know what it's supposed to be," Eckhart said. "It may have been poorly thought out."

One of Igor's henchmen cupped his hands in front of him as if to catch a football and said, "Let's see."

Eckhart unclipped the doll from the carrier and lightly underhand-tossed it to the guy, who caught and held it at eye level, its legs dangling like tassels. "Did you know he takes her to Lens-Crafters to have her glasses adjusted?" the guy said.

Eckhart said, "I did not know that."

"No lie," the guy said.

"No shit," someone else concurred.

Downstairs there was a loud crash inside a tumult of laughter, then a wail, maybe pain, maybe a joke wail, another bolt of laughter, a lull, then a few bigger people moving rapidly and with purpose a couch or heavy chair. Eckhart was thinking about the girl who'd sprained her arm at last year's party, or the year before that, when everybody kissed everybody else.

The guy holding the doll said, "Yeah, yeah, they treat her very personally there."

Eckhart thought he recognized Igor's girlfriend from the Tuesday night workshop, though he couldn't be sure with the hair and makeup.

"Let me see," a heavier girl said, a half-assed Bo Peep.

Then they were passing the doll around the circle. Eckhart knelt, feeling woozy from the cheese and wrong about the doll being passed around, though he couldn't find a sufficiently moving reason why the passing around of the doll was problematic.

Someone wanted to know the sex of the doll, the actual doll, Billy's doll.

"It's like a scary old-man baby," the Bo Peep said.

Igor said flatly, "It's a regular doll."

"Not up close. Up close it's a *Children of the Corn* doll."

"Which? Scary old man or *Children of the Corn*? It happens to matter on this night."

A girl with a long, thin face said, "Don't ask me. I can't even look at him. The fake baby freaks me out and it's like his face is paralyzed or something."

Igor was watching Eckhart, waiting for an answer to a question Eckhart hadn't been able to hold in his mind long enough to answer.

Then came the story about the fire again. Eckhart's jaw tightened and he took the pipe when it came around. The story was really gnawing at him now. It dawned on him that he'd been embarrassed for himself all night in that costume, and every time he heard the story it got worse. The look on Jackie's face, back at the apartment, when she realized who he was supposed to be (oh . . . you're *that guy*). How she caught herself and tried to force a smile. And Eckhart, knowing immediately her disappointment was the correct response—his night had pretty much gone south right then, and they hadn't even left yet. The longer he had to think, the more he saw how much it said about him, that he had thought his costume would be acceptable.

"I keep hearing about the fire," Eckhart said. "I'm not sure I buy it." The cashier had told Eckhart the doll's name—Meisha or Maya, something unusual Eckhart was trying to remember.

They all sat there. Someone said, "The *cheeeese*," and they all started to laugh. Igor shushed them; he wanted to know if Eckhart had a better story.

A girl in an eye patch said, "I thought I heard he had fetal alcohol syndrome."

"What if he does?" said the only guy not in costume.

"I thought they had really small heads," someone said. Eckhart sought out the hay smell in the wig and hoped this wasn't shaping into a paranoid high. He said he didn't see why there had to be a story. He said, "No one seems to want to believe there's just a guy who's so lonely he carries a doll around—apparently everyone feels better thinking this shitty thing happened that explains it." He rolled his head back. "The fire, the shrink, the baby—it's a Ron Howard film. One thing people don't seem to be able to take is public loneliness. Anything but that."

One of them repeated the phrase *public loneliness* very slowly. The phrase was picked up and carried around the circle. People wanted to hear themselves say it. Eckhart thought the wig might be made of horsehair, assuming horsehair smelled like hay, and the picture that came to him now was *American Gothic*, but with Billy standing in place of the farmer, with his pitchfork, and Billy's doll floating in the air where the wife's head was in the original painting. The high was perhaps developing into the kind that made a self want to unsettle.

Someone was saying, "They're not like normal homeless."

Igor huffed, "What's *normal homeless?*"

"That one guy's chubby, you know, he obviously eats normal meals."

"I always thought the guy in moon boots was waiting for a revelation."

Igor's girlfriend had had the doll for a while now. You wanted to write her off as merely gorgeous, but now she said in a soft voice, "There's a couple in town who have a little girl. I've seen them a few times. She crawls around the library like a little animal." She looked right at Eckhart and asked, as if she expected an answer, "Does she breast-feed? How could that be good?"

"I don't know anything about it," Eckhart said.

Lucy was the first to see their father on the streets. She was in the marina in a friend's car, turning a corner, when a man stepped into the street wearing a paratrooper's jacket, army green with a copper zipper and neon orange lining—a jacket he would wear for fifteen years, more or less continuously—and her friend slammed on the brakes, and the headlights lit the man's begrimed face and Lucy saw his eyes. (*Swear to God it was him, Eck*, she'd said. *I don't think he's staying anywhere, do you know what I'm saying?*)

In dreams his father's eyes were the color of that zipper.

Eckhart saw the cheese making its way around again and stood before it reached him. "I'm going to find that bathroom," he said.

"And the guy who kidnapped what's-her-face—"

Igor saluted. His girlfriend stared at Eckhart's legs. He saw he was already gone and forgotten.

By the time he made it downstairs, Russ and all of them were gone. An androgynous person in a green leotard ("I'm my organic self tonight") told him there'd been a dance-off; that the guy with no pants threw his knee out doing the running man and a witch knocked her head on the fireplace and now they were all down at the ER. "But wait—if you're the Andy Warhol, then the lady cop was looking for you."

Eckhart wasn't tired so he set out walking the streets, which you could do in that city and never get lost. On his way out of the house he'd overheard Zenith telling someone, "Yeah, I guess I'm going as, like, the futility of entertainment." He noticed Eckhart passing and nodded his television, which he was now able to do without moving the head inside.

Outside the air was dry and cold then whipping and icy. Eckhart was relieved to get to walk home alone, to be alone with his buzz and enjoy it, if that's what he was doing.

He cut for the park to avoid any homes in case he decided to start trick-or-treating. He'd kept the wig on for warmth, the glasses because they were Jackie's and he didn't want to lose them. He'd forgotten about the snowfall earlier, which hadn't melted on contact but held to the roads like powdered sugar. Slow-moving cars slipped and squirreled with some of them spooned to a stop and curvy tail-lit skids coming off the back tires.

Catty-corner the human park was a dog park and a trio of baseball diamonds that took up a whole corner, with a brick restroom building they kept open all night. Eckhart stepped inside to thaw. The water in the tap was that extreme burning cold, so he let it run, noticing in the foggy aluminum mirror that he looked mostly like himself. He couldn't see where people were getting Warhol. He couldn't explain pining all night to lose the costume yet balking now that he had the chance. Even as he stood staring at the glasses and thinking *I should take these off*, he knew he wouldn't. Which is why he couldn't call what happened next *freaky* or *a coincidence*.

It was a conjuring. It was a goddamned conjuring.

He was turning starting for the door when he saw lying there, flat on its back on the floor, the doll—Billy's own actual doll—and Eckhart fell into a desperate hopscotch to avoid stepping on it. It seemed to spring itself on him, the doll, to lift up off the floor. There was terrible screaming that for a matter of seconds Eckhart didn't realize as his own, coming out of his own throat. He was screaming and looking down and looking down through himself looking. He tried to see in the doll his doll—the one from Goodwill—but knew he'd left it with Igor and friends and that he was looking down at Billy's doll, the thing itself, and whatever in him was screaming that scream understood whose doll it was. It was dressed this time in a pink snowsuit, a marshmallowy thing, dressed for the weather, and Billy and no one was anywhere around. It was just the doll lying on the bathroom floor.

Eckhart wanted to sprint but instead edged to the door slowly, locking his gaze on it/her. As if not to wake her. As if not to disturb her sleep. He knew she wasn't bait but she was lying there like bait. The screaming stopped and in its place a sound arose like crackling static coming from the mirrors. He had to restrain himself violently from within to walk out of there.

Outside girls and guys were letting off howls, the last of the night. He took a minute to breathe the outside air. He latched each hand onto the backstop's fence and looked out at the baseball diamonds; the darkened dog park taking the corner where they couldn't fit a fourth field. The snow was tinted bluish green under a fingernail moon.

The doll was always with Billy as far as Eckhart knew, so he guessed he had to assume Billy was hurt, maybe mugged if anyone would mug a guy like that. He poked around the dugouts and fountains and thought about what to do, about what could've happened to separate Billy from his doll.

He crossed to the gas station, sober now, a sobriety that superseded the physical. In his mind's ear he kept hearing *they treat her very personally there.* He kept hearing *he always keeps her real clean.* He wanted to do the minimally decent thing—no heroics, just whatever a bearable person you could sit through dinner with would do.

He dialed 911.

The dispatcher asked, "Is the baby breathing?"

Eckhart should've expected that. He told her he didn't know; he hadn't checked.

"And where was the baby now?" she wanted to know.

"She's still in there."

There was a gulp-long pause. "So you left the baby on the floor? Unattended? A baby?"

They sent two cop cars, an ambulance, a fire engine, and a lower-key SUV that simply said FIRE on the door, with no other writing, so a child might think the vehicle itself was a fire. It was stunning to see the kind of manpower a person could summon at will. A million dollars' worth of machinery purring at the curb; how little any of them could really do. Of the needed thing, how little.

Eckhart took the long way around the next block over, scaling the inside of a chain-link fence and perching in someone's backyard. There he had an open view of the whole corner, the ball fields, the brick bathroom to his far right, and to his left, the dog park. From there, he watched the first paramedic cross the diamond in a stumbling lurching tilt and couldn't help feeling, as he watched, as though he'd staged this whole thing for his own sick amusement. Lengths behind, the other responders took more lethargic exaggerated tromps, the snow glinting off the toes of their boots like sprinklers going off. When the lead guy made it to the bathroom, he scrambled in, then a minute later walked back out relaxed and hoisting the doll in the air for all the others to see. They slackened their pace and drew in around the doll. Multiple times Eckhart had to remind himself they hadn't come from a party and that their uniforms were real.

He couldn't hear the conversation, though he caught the odd shouted syllable and laugh. One of the firemen, making cute, whisked the doll under his coat, spinning and breaking into a little sprint as if to abscond with it—whatever his joke was disgusted the women and tickled one firefighter into a barking, openmouthed laugh that filled the night sky.

Behind Eckhart, a light went on in one of the houses, felling long bars of shadow from the trees across the snow. Someone at the party had said *I don't feel like myself these days* and someone else, covered in mirrors, had said *I know what you mean.* Eckhart didn't understand how the sentence worked logically, since *I* would somehow have to be separated from *myself* in order for one to lose touch with the other. It was hard to tell if people told the truth about their inner experience of living; if they even bothered taking stock or just said things the way a frog ribbits.

All but the couple of cops were cutting out now.

Also a lady paramedic who, hanging back, kicked her boot around to clean the tread or resituate her foot in the bedding. Beside her, the last two cops seemed to be deciding whether to take a more thorough look around; you couldn't blame them for wanting to extend any natural breather a job like that might offer. Eckhart thought about Jackie on her mission in Berkeley, walking up knocking on strange doors, stopping to adjust her clothes and raising her fist to knock, pecking out three knocks. He imagined the scene both from her perspective, as if he were training a camera over her shoulder, then from the perspective of the schmo answering the door. Anyone who'd ever had a front door knew that trapped feeling when you looked down and saw in your visitor's hand a Bible, or that even more baffling non sequitur, the Book of Mormon, and before they said a word you felt your ire rising that someone with no credentials would come to your door and suggest you'd failed to consider, or ill-considered, the most important question in the universe. The gall and comedy of someone external come to save you. Yet people were converted every minute, Jackie assured him, and there was a large element out there just happy for the company. She said her most peaceful moments were standing on porches after she'd seen the shadowy ducking-around inside and known no one would answer, and you could just stand there on the porch in peace for half a minute. She said you learned to live in those moments between doors, and you learned to make a half minute last.

He thought he heard little grunts and shook himself into

realizing he wasn't alone on the perimeter. There was movement in the dog park, someone crawling out from under a bridge. It was murky over there—shaded by a line of tall trees—but Eckhart knew who it would turn out to be.

He was wearing the pom-pom hat again, Billy was, clambering upright and then charging across the snow in an uncoordinated hunch. To reach the doll, which the cop had over by the bathrooms now, Billy had a two-hundred-yard dash of dog park, a fence to climb, a ball field to cross, and he obviously meant to do it.

*"Billy!"* Eckhart hissed. *"Billy—stop!"*

Eckhart didn't give it two thoughts—it was his fault the cops had the doll—and launched over the fence like he was in military training. Then he was stepping low, the ground uneven and slick, gunning for an interception. In a whispered shout he kept calling Billy's name, which only increased the man's desperation. Eckhart couldn't see how he didn't fall every single second. He also saw that Billy wasn't the man's name and if they got to talking, Eckhart suspected, it would just be a lot of Billy telling Eckhart his dog was nice, and anything Eckhart said in return would sound the same; that like all things and people, Billy was only improbable at a distance.

Billy dropped down on hands and knees and crawled through a gash in the outfield fence—a not-wide-enough gash, so that his head and shoulders pushed through with his hind end lodged back in the dog park, his jacket pulled up and his pants sagging below the crack, revealing a white lower back shining like a lid. There was a scrunched-up number 5 on the back of his jacket and with his hands planted in the freezing snow, he bucked and bucked, trying to lurch free. Eckhart had to decide now if he was willing to lay hands on the man—to physically restrain him.

Then Eckhart was lying on his back looking skyward, holding Billy's shoes. Black orthopedics, cushioned bricks. He'd had a solid grip of each sole and was feeling out how hard to pull when they snapped off Billy's feet, the shoes, like a pair of prosthetic feet. The cold was coming through Eckhart's jacket, his supine spine, while he tried to decide what his actual motives here were—if the idea was to somehow redeem himself in Jackie's eyes, get that look off of her face when she'd realized who he was supposed to be. *Oh* (lowering the plastic gun she'd trained on Eckhart's head with her trying-not-to-smile smile), *You're that guy.*

She was the only one. Out of all the superheroes, world leaders, hunchbacks, and whores, out of everyone who'd come up to Eckhart with that string of words—*You're that guy!*—he just kept hearing Jackie over and over again.

Oh.

You're     that

(Lowering the gun like Eckhart wasn't even worth shooting)

guy.

Eckhart heard, a few feet away, the spilled-coin jangle of the fence: Billy pushing through to the other side. Without his shoes, Billy was struggling to get to his feet, which were exposed and naked in the snow. Eckhart needed to get out of there or commit to this thing wholesale, despite the dawning intuition that he'd made a mistake, misjudged everything. There was a fence between them but they were otherwise just a few feet apart. Eckhart lobbed the shoes over to Billy and said, "Here." Then he said, "I know you can hear me. Just let me get her so they"—and who knows where this beaut came from—"so they don't hurt her."

Billy was hopping from foot to foot, aiming his feet in the foot holes, and then he just stopped and said, "Why would they hurt her?" It was a good question, and Eckhart knew then both that he was out of his depth and that he would have to do whatever Billy told him.

The cop was slight and tidy with hair like a presidential candidate. "What's up?" he said, watching Eckhart approach, nodding and gum snapping while Eckhart talked, nodding "OK," nodding "Gotcha." He asked, "Are you the one who called?"

"I was just walking by," Eckhart said.

"You know it's a crime to prank 911. In some states it's a felony." He changed his grip on the doll, now holding her one-handed by the neck. "We have the calls on tape," he said.

"Like I said," Eckhart said. Wiping his mouth, he dared a backward glance and very clearly saw Billy squatting out in center field, watching them, which meant the cop had to have seen them out there, too.

Calls with an *s*: we have the *calls* on tape. Which could mean either *we keep all 911 calls on tape* or *more than one person called us here tonight*. He thought two calls would better explain the excessive manpower rolling up, though maybe that was normal. "I'm just saying," Eckhart continued, "I think it's some kind of therapy doll, and I'm offering to give it back to him if you want."

The cop scratched his neck with two fingers, turning and lowering his head to do it.

"Otherwise I was headed home for bed," Eckhart said.

"So you managed to see what we were holding." He watched Eckhart's face, rocking back on his heels. "In this light, you could see what this was?"

"Actually, no," Eckhart said. "I thought it was a real baby, then I could tell by the way you were acting that it had to be a doll and I put two and two together."

The cop breathed a troubled *kkkkah* and shook his head as if to say, *I give up*. "What the hell," he said. "The judge said to quit wasting his time bringing the guy in." The next words he said syllable-wise, like the name of a lover he never should've fallen for: "*Non com-pos men-tis*. You know what that means?"

His partner came up beside them, diffident and loose-standing, also with a wad of gum going, the junior officer by twenty years.

Eckhart said, "It sounds familiar."

"It means he can do what he wants. He can call and call and

send us to Kolob and back after his toy and there's nothing we can do about it legally." His smile said, *How do you like that?*, the smile curdling into a cynical twist as he handed the doll to Eckhart.

Crossing the field, Eckhart listened with a backward ear for the cruiser to pull away. Then the corner went quiet, but for the snow breathing all around them, tree limbs bending and bowing, and out ahead the sound of Billy wheezing.

When Eckhart was close enough, he saw Billy's jacket puffing in and out—he was talking away before Eckhart was even close enough to hear. Sometimes you could understand Billy, sometimes it was soup, so it took a minute for Eckhart to understand Billy was concerned for him. For Eckhart.

He wanted to know what had happened to Eckhart's face, how he'd gotten hurt.

Eckhart touched his eye, the frozen bruise. He wasn't sure why he couldn't understand Billy: the words had the sound of recognizable articulation, but it was as if the language itself was made up. Or it was that Eckhart couldn't look at Billy, the distorted mapping of his skin—not from a fire, though, that wasn't it at all.

Then in an instant he understood. He looked Billy full in the face, the glasses like windows on a house no one would ever break into: he was offering the doll to Eckhart. To take home for the night, maybe. And then in Eckhart's mind rose again *American Gothic*, and Jackie's raised gun in the farmer's hand, and a feeling that Eckhart was being offered for the night a bride, a little infant bride.

Something made him look at the doll. He hated that her nostrils were sealed over, and that she didn't have working eyelids. He thought of the brides at Temple Square, their dresses inviting and repulsive as frosting you know you won't be able to stop eating. He thought about the people down at LensCrafters, adjusting little Meisha's or Maya's glasses, and he understood that if he took the doll—which he had to do only because he knew he couldn't risk not taking it, that his whole life was pointing at this moment—he knew there was no way he could wake up the same man. This was the thing the LensCrafters did for Billy by adjusting the doll's glasses, which was just to let the guy know that what was real to him could be real to someone else.

When he first took her he couldn't look at her, the same way you can't look down when you're standing on a high ledge. He set his eyes in the middle distance and made himself walk. He found a neon-orange reflector on a post and stuck his eyes on it and walked. He was terrified out of his mind. He thought of himself in that bathroom, screaming like a prehistoric bird at the sight of the very thing he carried in his arms and he felt like he was screaming again just thinking of it. He knew Billy would be there to retrieve her the next day or he wouldn't have taken her and risked getting stuck with her.

For a long stretch he couldn't feel his arm and the whole section of his body touching the doll but Billy was watching, so he walked on.

Real.

Clean.
Real.

Clean.
       Real.
Clean.

Back at the apartment five or six of them were still at it, dancing to breakup music with the sectional in pieces pushed against the walls. Jackie danced up with a rumpled uniform and arms snaking through the air. "Come on," she said, "come-on-come-on." A sheen of sweat lit her forehead and cheeks, dewed up her baby bangs. When she caught Eckhart glancing around for Russ she raised her hand and touched his face, turning it back to meet hers, and he smiled into her blurry brown extra-alive eyes because her hand was on his cheek, just like that, but his skin was so cold he couldn't feel it and he knew if she touched him again, it wouldn't be for a very long time.

They danced, sort of, but Eckhart was exhausted metaphysically, and Jackie was drunk and trying to be happy (it was nearly morning and something was obviously wrong about Russ's being gone still). He saw she'd made the decision to go on with her night anyway, and he watched her hips and did what he could to keep her there, dancing with him or for him, her little idiosyncratic moves. An elf gyrated over and, petting Jackie's gun, asked Eckhart if he had congratulated her—congratulated Jackie—she'd won a poetry residency somewhere (she'd gotten a voice mail she had only just retrieved at the hospital), and would be gone all spring semester. He could tell she cared what he thought, that she wanted him to be proud, so he tried to make the appropriate fuss but meanwhile he was just standing there insanely holding Billy's doll, with no one sober enough to notice. Instead of Jackie, he was going to walk out of this with a borrowed therapy doll. It was hard to do anything but laugh and lean into something that was so exotically screwed.

They brought in the dawn dancing, as though it were New Year's and they felt obligated. A few of them went for breakfast then, but anticipating a forty-five-minute wait at the only place they could agree on, he and Jackie collapsed in front of the TV. *Halloween H20: Twenty Years Later* was playing (a local station had a marathon running, *Halloween* and all the sequels) with the sound off. You could tell Michael Myers hadn't killed anyone yet because he was still just looming in windows and playing coy, while across town Jamie Lee Curtis, between hallucinations of Michael, pounded wine and vodka straight from the bottle. Jackie said, "She's had four drinks in five screen minutes. How is she not plowed?"

Eckhart said, "Is it a problem that every time she thinks she sees Michael it turns out to be her husband?"

On-screen, Michael patiently watched from the kitchen

doorway as the geeky teen he was about to eviscerate worked a corkscrew out of the garbage disposal, and you didn't want the poor kid to hurt his hand even though he was about to get killed.

Jackie said, "He told me up front he couldn't be faithful." Eckhart watched her profile for an expression but she was watching the screen, clouded in that atomic morning light. Watching a *Halloween* without sound compensated somehow for watching during daylight hours. Before everyone had left for breakfast, they'd all kept opening their mouths to wonder aloud where Russ might be, and should they assume he was hurt and so forth, which Eckhart thought was the real reason Jackie didn't go to breakfast. She said, "You're not done with a guy until you're done, and if you try and leave before you're done, you'll just make an ass out of yourself." Eckhart started thinking of the ways he could interpret that remark as a girl who'd climbed into a dumbwaiter fiddled trying to close the portal, with Michael angling his arm in and gashing her calf.

"Why's he so slow?" Jackie asked of Michael. "It's like he doesn't care if he gets them or not."

Eckhart said, "That's his only fun, watching them squirm." Michael stepped on the girl's back to steady her, then perfunctorily raised his flashing blade. "See? He doesn't even like this part."

"She's so stoic," Jackie said.

"Maybe she's screaming."

"Her mouth's not moving."

Eckhart turned and showed how you could scream without moving your mouth, just let it out the side. He screamed in a quiet falsetto, watching as Jackie plucked up a cushion and slugged him with it and in the process she failed to see, where the cushion had been squashing down, Meisha (the name Eckhart had settled on for the doll) sitting now suddenly, wildly, out in the open.

Jackie said, "Who would sell that guy a mask? That's really where it all starts, with the mask sellers."

All she had to do was glance down her right side, maybe not

even move her head, and there was Meisha. The couch's frame and stuffing made a lot of noise when you got on it or off it, like it'd been filled with rumpled-up fast-food wrappers, so there was no way Eckhart could hide Meisha via subtle maneuverings. He was trying to think how he could work the doll around under behind him, stuffing her down in the couch crevice to deal with later. He was trying to think when Jackie absentmindedly turned and just picked Meisha up and nonchalantly held her in her hands.

"Why's this look different?" she asked. "And it smells like something."

*He always keeps her real clean.*

"Are these real jeans?"

She was so close, Jackie, right there two feet away, but she might as well have been on the moon and he fought to accept that was the way things had to be right now. He watched and waited for her to figure out about Meisha. One unsettling thing when you saw her up close, Meisha, was how much the doll's surface plastic had come to resemble skin, luminous with an energy come from years of oily human handling, and from the attention she'd been paid, and the power of human awareness to give life. He thought of the last house on Jackie's mission, before she bailed on Mormonism and the whole thing. A coked-up gospel singer had answered Jackie's last door and they'd talked for hours. When Jackie asked how she felt about Joseph Smith's being visited by God and Jesus, the woman bellowed almost belligerently, "I know it's true! Just this morning he touched me with his finger!"

Jackie screamed and flung Meisha across the room. "Jesus Christ, what are you *doing* with that?"

Eckhart said, "It's not what you're thinking."

Jackie dropped her head in her hands and every few seconds shook it again.

"Whatever you're thinking, that's not what it is," he said.

On screen, Jamie Lee Curtis's son was punching the masked

face of Michael in the suburban forest he'd been chasing the kid and his girlfriend through.

Into her hands Jackie said, "Did you take that from him?"

"No no no no no—OK—"

She lunged for the remote and shut the movie off, and Eckhart took a long breath. He started to explain but kept having to jump back and back—back to that day with Clyde, forward to Igor, back to Curtis and Brutus and the grasshopper and it became overwhelming trying to tell everything he had to tell in order to feel like someone a bright person could take an interest in. His ears felt like they were melting—you could not shut this woman's lights off—and everything in him ached to squash the thing there and then. He knew Russ cared for Jackie, but he also knew the central people in Russ's life were ghosts: a couple in photographs, a woman passing in a hall. Russ probably knew about Eckhart and Jackie already—he was wise in ways poets should be—and on this particular morning Eckhart himself was so sure of the heat between them that even if they waited two years and lasted three days, he felt able to borrow from their future happiness there and then, and it steeled him. He said, "I don't want to talk about that right now. I want to talk about you."

She was looking down at her hands.

He said, "I'm just going to tell you, and then I'm going to leave town, that your adorableness causes me actual physical pain, and I don't even like it when you're not in the same room, so I don't know how I'm going to even do this, and I would bowl over any other man but Russ to get to you. You understand that, right?" He couldn't believe he wasn't going to kiss her, that that wasn't going to happen, that he was going to leave this place not knowing what that was like.

"I do now," she said.

He pictured her riding her bike home and writing poems about being happy, and he said, "Waiting for things is like dying."

She burst out laughing. "You're so hard-core!" He saw how hard she was trying to smile less than she was, and he knew that that alone would keep him going until the next thing that would keep him going until the next-next thing, and that eventually, with a little luck, one of those things would be her.

# 5

The main highway north was torn up, with detours and lane closings for the first forty miles, so Eckhart took a turn through small-town Utah in a bland rented sedan that smelled like coconut instead of new car, as if it were someone's personal car. He'd been meaning to explore Idaho and Montana and thought he'd squander the last of his money that way. He was looking forward to having it gone.

Well after dark he filled up at one of those gas stations the owner lives beside or behind or under. The store had a single refrigerator with a couple of Cokes for sale and some drinks Eckhart hadn't seen on the market for years. Even the candy bars were separated out on doilies, one candy bar per doily, like they were precious heirlooms. He wouldn't have been surprised to see sticks of gum fanned out for individual sale. He bought what turned out to be a used map and asked some questions about the area, which made the guy behind the register grumpy. "Grow?" the man said. "Nothing growing I know of."

"I thought I passed farmland," Eckhart said. "Maybe that was a while back."

The man didn't speak for a long time; then he said, "Huh?"

Outside under the buzzing canopy, Eckhart spread his map on the dash and started penciling in routes, noticing as he went there were other pencil lines on the map, which dug fairly deep in the boondocks, and he was tempted to follow.

He'd been sitting only a few minutes when the vans pulled in. There were three of them, identical maroon vans with tinted windows, an older model with a wide turning radius, so the drivers had to coordinate this whole wagon-train drama of arcing around and backing up to get themselves oriented at the pumps. Once they were parked, a guy got out of the second van and went around swiping his credit card at all three pumps, getting the gas gurgling into all of the vans. Then the van doors slid open and five or six women stepped out in long white dresses with ruffled hems and bonnet-type ties on their heads. Their dresses fell to their shoes. They started ushering all kinds of children out after them, the oldest junior-high age. It was like a schoolhouse emptying for recess.

The man doled bills out to the women, then leaned back against one of the vans, folding his arms in front of him and closing his eyes. He looked like any tired dad on a road trip.

The gowns constricted the women from taking full strides so that moving en masse into the shop, shepherding all the kids along, they seemed to be riding unicycles under their gowns. This was the most mystifying thing Eckhart had ever seen.

When they were all in the shop there was a long interval with just the guy and the open emptied vans and a windless calm. Then out of the last van, a last separate woman descended. The dad perked his head around to see which wife it was, then settled back without incident, so only Eckhart watched the woman help her boy down off the sideboard. They didn't head into the store; instead she led the boy away from the vans and the shop until they were out far enough they could see the night, with the kid turning in circles and his head dropped back. The woman let go of his hand and pushed on her hips, stretching her back as the boy took wider, faster turns with his arms sprung out and missteps corrupting his orbit. By now the other wives and children were filing out of the mart, each one eating or unwrapping a candy bar or ice cream— the poor owner probably had to sell snacks out of his own kitchen to fill every reaching hand—while outside now the dad was busily shuffling around capping all the gas spouts.

The woman took a few steps farther off, and a few more steps. Someone called for them, one of the other saints. The boy stopped spinning and yanked on his mother's dress, pointing back at the vans, their doors like steel throats ready to swallow all the wives and all the children—but for this one woman at the far end of the lot. Not a rebel, Eckhart didn't think, just someone wanting a minute to herself and knowing how to make that minute last. She was looking up and down the road. Sometimes Lucy would still call and say, *I think I saw him down by the Embarcadero. It was his walk. His jacket.* He is dead, Eckhart would remind her. *I know but I really think it was his jacket.*

She was looking up and down the road and her boy was watching as though he, too, had come to understand this thing his mother did was vital, and to stand back, and it had been a long time since Eckhart thought he'd seen somebody who looked like she wanted to know where the fuck she was. His father used to say that simple awareness was the only freedom any of us really had, and watching this woman nothing like Eckhart's father at the edge of the lot, he saw now what his father had meant, he saw that it was beautiful to not turn away from your life at any cost or for any reason, no matter what a mess you'd made of it all.

Jackie's bright brown eyes flashed in his mind, their last hour together on the couch, and Meisha between them, and on the doll's small jeans an embroidered pink flower whose thread was fraying, with particular threads lifting off the denim like it was starting to grow, and Eckhart's mute excited terror had returned from the night before, walking those first hundred yards with the doll in his arms, and Billy behind watching, always farther behind, and Eckhart thinking that nothing hurt like trying to come alive.

# Acknowledgments

It is a pleasure to be able to thank the following people in print: My agent, Denise Shannon, who makes you want to write just so you can watch her do her job. Amber Qureshi, for gambling on this book. Julie Miesionczek, my editor, for seeing the work through with such humor and aplomb. For their generous support during the writing of these stories: the Institute for Creative Writing at the University of Wisconsin—in particular, the tireless Jesse Lee Kercheval (and Judy and the Rons and Amaud); and the University of Utah, with special thanks to François Camoin, Kathryn Stockton, and Jackie Osherow. My first indelible teachers at Montana: Brady Udall, Dee McNamer, and Kevin Canty. Writer-fellows who made me think harder about fiction: Jason McMackin, Danielle Evans, Matt Kirkpatrick, Jacob Paul, Jennifer Key, Danielle Deulen, and Dan Brooks. My brother, Duke Britton, and sister, Stephanie Getz, who will verify that everything I've said here is false and completely accurate. To Tim Wilder and other selected voices in my head: Heidi Galassi, Rebecca Ivanoff, Lara Prescott, Nan Seymour, Suzanne Larson, Freddie Harris-Ramsby, Holly Welty-Barr, my babies the Mabies. And to Raya Del, who made me a believer.

Wilder, April.
This Is Not an Accident

MAY        2014